THROUGH THESE VEINS

A NOVEL

ANNE MARIE RUFF

Please see the glossary on p. 237 for definitions and background about the italicized words in the story.

Open Door Press - First edition
Copyright © 2011 by Anne Marie Ruff Grewal
All Rights Reserved
Front Cover Design: Kris Ruff
Interior Layout: Astrid Chevallier for Purple Red
ISBN: 978-0-9832498-0-1

For Lali

Prologue

Washington, D.C., 2004

The grandfather clock had already struck twelve when Robert slipped into bed next to Sidney. She grumbled in irritation, half-asleep. He said nothing, thankful for her sleep and the darkness. He was unprepared to speak aloud of what he had seen tonight in the lab. If the results of his initial viral screenings were accurate – he had performed the screening twice, disbelieving the initial data – they signalled the discovery of his career. The plant samples that Stefano Geotti had so intriguingly sent Robert from his latest expedition in Ethiopia seemed to harbour something no one else had yet found. In Robert's lab, the compounds from the Ethiopian leaves had battled against one of the modern world's most insidious diseases, HIV, and won.

A drug based on the Ethiopian compounds could mean husbands could stay with their wives, mothers could live to care for their children, babies born with the disease could grow up and grow old before they died. Millions of people would take a step back from the brink of death.

It was too early to say. He knew that. There would be a host of other tests; different viral strains, toxicology tests, animal testing, before the human trials could even begin. There would be articles to publish, papers to defend at conferences, funding to justify. Isolating, synthesizing, testing, standardizing, and transforming the natural compound into a useful drug would take years of work.

But for tonight, he let his thoughts wander through the possibilities, knowing the plant in his lab would be waiting tomorrow, ready to seduce him again with its potential.

Chapter 1

Chochotte, Ethiopia, 2004

"Thank you, sweetie," Ato Worku said, patting Zahara's hand as she offered him honey. He repeated "sweetie" again in English and winked at her. She admonished him to lick the stick clean of the remaining crushed honeycomb.

"Ato Worku, don't waste your energy looking at a woman," she said teasing him. "I am just eighteen and you are much too old for me to marry."

He laughed at her boldness. "My dear, you do make me feel young, but this old man doesn't need a wife. I look at you as if you were a daughter who is caring for me."

Ato Worku had spent two weeks in the village. He had insisted on staying in the same *gojo* with Zahara and her father, Nataniel, instead of with the other sick people in the gojo they had nicknamed 'the clinic.'

Zahara had grown familiar, occasionally even cheeky with Ato Worku, which seemed to please him. With Zahara's father, Nataniel, he was surly and proud, speaking few words. But Zahara saw through the rich man's bravado, saw his weakness, instinctively knew how to care for him, humbling him without humiliating him. She no longer noticed the sound of his labored breathing or the occasional conversations with himself emanating from the other side of the mud wall that divided the circular gojo into two half moons. His noises became just another part of the village, like the shouts of children and the sound of women pounding *teff* for their sour *injeera* pancakes.

During the first week Nataniel had prepared teas and pastes, blood and bone meal to restore Ato Worku's strength. At first, the rich man with a prodigious belly had refused to eat anything and vomited up what Zahara insisted he swallow. So she boiled beetle broth to calm his gut and burned fragrant *oud* to cover the stench of stomach acid that lingered in the dirt floor. By the second week, Ato Worku had been able to keep down a few lentils sopped up with injeera, so Nataniel had given him the red-veined leaf medicine. Today he felt well enough to walk to the stream to wash his own face.

"My shoes, where are my shoes?" he mumbled as he groped around the floor just beyond the shaft of light that came through the door. Zahara saw him fumble with the tassels of his imported leather loafers. He started to brush off the coating of dust that dulled their shiny surface, but gave up with a sigh.

With Zahara's hand under his armpit, he groaned as he stood up in his dusty city shoes, balancing his sizeable body over his thin legs like a bird. They walked out the gojo door and he stopped to look around the village. Children ran up to him, dirty hands outstretched, "One *birr*, one birr!" they shouted in greeting, jumping with excitement. He had no coins for their requests, but he pinched their cheeks with a soft palm and they ran off squealing and laughing. Old women poured sour teff batter over black iron griddles to make injeera. The smell of charcoal and dried straw mingled with the fragrance of oud and roasting coffee beans. Hawks circled far overhead and flies lit and landed endlessly. The men and middle aged women, absent from the village, hidden in the surrounding forests, gathered bright red coffee berries into coarse baskets. Only the reddened eyes of the newly arrived sick, peering out of the clinic gojo, watched Ato Worku as he started to make his slow, unsteady way through the village to the stream.

As he splashed water on his unshaven face, he felt the delicious heat of the sun on the top of his balding head. He whistled a tune and Zahara exclaimed with delight, "My father sings that song when we are walking in the forest. He says it is from Haile Selassie's time."

Worku laughed a bit self consciously, "Yes I suppose it is. For me it is from a time when I had a real sweetie. A beautiful woman she was..." His words trailed off and he seemed to look for his past beyond the surface of the water.

She waited for him to say more, but Worku only sighed. Zahara stepped into the waist-high plants and reeds growing just upstream, respecting his reverie. Deftly, she picked at flowers, turned over leaves, rubbing them and smelling their fragrance on her fingers. She pinched off leaves to pack into the pockets she had twice resewn onto her faded blue dress. She was familiar with the common plants, her father had taught her their names and uses since she was a child, and she imagined them her companions. She could identify plants as easily as she could identify the rigid angular letters of the English alphabet written out on the village school's donated blackboard.

Eventually, Ato Worku clapped his hands, indicating he had completed his morning washing. Zahara returned to him and held his arm as they walked back to the village, her pockets bulging with plants.

The sick people arrived in Chochotte with almost every sunset these days. At first they had come only sporadically. Every couple of months, a ragged shepherd boy or a gaunt woman with her dozens of braids fuzzy from neglect would drift up from the road like a ghost. Each afflicted with some persistent illness that would not release its grip, not allow them to tend their sheep, or their coffee bushes, or their children, some sickness each had watched tighten its fingers around people they knew and loved, carrying them relentlessly, painfully to the grave.

They came because of Zahara's father – a man they knew as the witch doctor of Chochotte village, a man who could cure all ills, a man who gathered wild spirits from the forest and unleashed them on the evil that caused the sickness. They came offering whatever meager surplus they could sacrifice – a stiff goat hide, a handful of roasted wheat grains in a worn basket, an empty plastic food aid sack refashioned into a shoulder satchel. They came on blind faith – a familiar, abiding faith, with which they had long ago submitted themselves to Allah's will – a faith they now, desperately, fearfully, directed to the rumored mercy of the witchdoctor of Chochotte.

When the people with the sickness arrived, Zahara made a place for them, a space to sleep on her own plastic woven mat, in the tidy mud and thatch gojo where she lived with her father and cousins. She brought a bucket of water for washing because they were too exhausted to walk to the stream. She brewed tea with dried flowers to help them sleep. She looked into their eyes, clouded with terror and fatigue, felt the lesions on their skin as they took her hands in theirs, and listened as they whispered, "*Al-hamd'Allah*, thanks to God, bless you sister."

Of course the story was not true. Nataniel was not a witch doctor filled with the power of wild spirits. He was an Ethiopian Orthodox Christian, armed only with a carefully folded paper from Addis Ababa University certifying he had completed his studies in pharmacology in

1974; the same year the ancient imperial line of Abyssinian rulers came to a spectacular end with the overthrow of Emperor Haile Selassie.

In that year the triumphant Socialists had quickly recruited Nataniel to their cause. He had cooperated, enthusiastically dispensing imported Soviet medicines from a tiny state-owned shop to the proud, never-colonized people of Ethiopia. After a few years, when the Socialist Mengistu regime turned to purging the traitors and subversives, when the Red Terror bloodied the streets with mute headless, handless bodies guilty of unspecified crimes, Nataniel averted his eyes, focusing on his well-ordered world of pills and powders, syrups and syringes.

He had tried to ignore the suffering in the city, selling endless bottles of analgesics and sleeping pills. He had sipped coffee in the evenings with friends from the university, avoiding talk of politics with discussions about vaccination programs and antibiotics. One night, while sitting in a café, the strangely beautiful sound of breaking glass had rung up from the street, cutting through their conversation. Nataniel ran down the broad avenue to see a mob of young men dragging the owner of the shop next to the pharmacy out into the street. He heard a scream and then an eerie cheer of rage as the young men moved away, leaving only the shop owner's decapitated body in the street. It was the spring of 1984, when the violence in the capital mirrored the famine and dislocation in Ethiopia's eastern deserts.

The next morning – the streets still blanketed in a thin predawn fog – Nataniel stepped into the pharmacy. He retrieved only a heavy pharmacological reference book, which he tucked under the white cotton *gabbi* wrapped around his upper body, and fled west for Chochotte, his family's ancestral home in the highlands.

More than a decade later, when Nataniel first saw the sick people come to Chochotte – tired and dusty from walking, disheartened from failing to battle their way onto a chaotic public bus – he imagined they also were fleeing a wave of terror. When he learned of their sickness, their exile from frightened families in even poorer villages, he felt relief and anxiety in equal measure.

Nataniel treated them as best he could, giving them traditional medicines rather than imported pharmaceuticals, homemade potions and poultices that had earned him the respect of Chochotte's residents.

Periodically he gave them an intoxicating mixture of *chat* to chew and *taej* to drink, dulling their pain. Then, helplessly, he watched them die.

Nataniel, despairing, retreated for long hours to the forest, seeking refuge from the eyes of those who beseeched his help. The plants and the trees surrounded him, protected him and eventually restored his faith in life, in a God who endowed the world with intricate beauty and order. One day, after watching a woman die, leaving an infant child behind, he brought his rage to the forest. He pounded his fists against the trunk of a massive tree, against the smooth bark, as if it were responsible for the bitterness of his fate, the bitterness of this death – so like the death of his own wife shortly after Zahara's birth.

He shouted up the trunk, willing it to telegraph his message to God. He asked why God had laid this impossible burden before him, why he had been tasked to heal others with so little power to do so. He shouted; asking, imploring, demanding help until his voice grew hoarse. Drained of his anger, he fell forward against the tree in a childlike embrace and sank to the ground.

In the silence that followed, a single leaf, green with red veins, floated down and landed on the ground beside him.

An answer? An omen? A meaningless coincidence?

He looked up and noticed the leaves of the tree, many with red veins, fluttering in a silent breeze he could not feel. In an effort he later recognized as sheer desperation, he gathered up all the leaves he could find with these red veins and stuffed them in his pockets. He ran back to the village and boiled them furiously over a raging fire. He gave the resulting brew to the sickest man in his gojo. Nataniel had no idea what the effect would be. Unlike the other plants he used as medicine, his Aunt Darjena had told him nothing about this tree, nothing of its benefits, its dangers. He did not worry that the brew might be toxic; the man would be dead from the sickness in a few days anyway. Amazingly, a week later, the man rose from his bed, Lazarus like, and returned to his village.

Then the people with the sickness came every week, sometimes every day. And Zahara's life became consumed by her father's urgent work.

Zahara hardly looked up from the wooden mortar where she was grinding an orange fungus with a stone pestle.

"Zahara," her cousin said excitedly, "you must come to see, now." Zahara had no time to protest before the younger girl grabbed her arm and led her toward the road.

A crowd of villagers crushed around a convoy of three vehicles; curious children pushed under legs and arms to get to the front, old men silently observed, women talked hurriedly among themselves. Zahara had seen other four-wheel-drive vehicles before. From them had emerged pale young men and women. These khaki-clad people from somewhere in Europe asked questions, inspected the school and the hand-dug latrines. They spoke of "development" and "self-sufficiency" with great earnestness before they ducked back into their giant vehicles never to be seen in the village again. Zahara noticed this car, unlike the others, was protected by a man, an Amharic man from the city, machine gun in hand. He nudged the children with the butt of his gun every time they pressed too close, trying to peer into the car's dark glass windows. She moved to the edge of the crowd, looking for an emblem, a red cross or initials on the side of the door, something to identify the foreigners inside. The car displayed no markings.

Nataniel joined Zahara, placing a protective hand on his daughter's shoulder. They both turned when they heard Ibrahim cough to clear his throat behind them. They nodded to the village headman, and stepped aside to make way. "Let us see who has come," the old man said calmly, passing through the crush of arms and legs until he stood in front of the armed guard, unspeaking. To Zahara's surprise, the guard opened the door and helped Ibrahim into the vehicle, even handing him his walking stick once he had struggled onto the seat.

She worried, thinking maybe the vehicle had been sent by the government, and would take Ibrahim away. Maybe he would be killed and the village would be renamed in honor of a new regime as Mengistu's government had done in decades past.

But the vehicle did not move. The villagers waited in a moment of hushed silence. When nothing happened, people began talking, shifting from one foot to another in agitation.

Zahara felt the pull of her work: water to be drawn, bandages to be boiled, plants to be collected, but she could not move from the spot where she stood. She waited, barely breathing, until Ibrahim emerged and called out for her and Nataniel. Her heart pounding in her chest, she moved only because of the gentle pressure of her father's hand upon her shoulder. Together they walked to the car, close enough to feel the engine's warmth. The back door opened with a rush of cool air, revealing a man; not a foreigner but an Ethiopian man, crumpled on the seat, dressed in an ill-fitting suit.

Worku Demisse had arrived in Chochotte. Worku Demisse – Ethiopia's biggest coffee baron, the man who single-handedly moved the lion's share of Ethiopia's prized coffee beans out of the country to companies on far-off continents, the man rumoured to own half the buildings in Addis Ababa, the man no one in the village had ever seen but all referred to deferentially as *Ato Worku*, Mr. Worku, this man, one of the most powerful in the whole country – had come to a village with a few dozen gojos and no running water or electricity. He arrived weak and sad, begging mercy from the witch doctor of Chochotte.

Chapter 2

Nataniel followed the stream away from the village and into the coffee forests. Today he would gather leaves and an orange fungus so he could prepare sufficient medicine for Ato Worku. As soon as he was out of sight of the village, he took off his black plastic sandals and tied them to the strap of his shoulder satchel. Although the buckles had fallen off, the sandals themselves had not required any repairs. With these shoes, his button down shirt, and his coat he had attempted to preserve the professional appearance of his past life in Addis. But he loved to feel the earth – its changing temperatures and textures – through the soles of his feet when he walked into the forest to gather plants.

As a scientist, he tried to discern order and reason in the forest, the trees, the underbrush, the fungi, the soil. All living things contained active substances: alkaloids and volatile oils, compounds toxic or anaesthetic, antiseptic or even hallucinogenic. He wanted to know the compounds' secrets, wanted to wield them against the illness around him.

As a Christian, he often fell into meditations on the power of God. He revelled at the pervasive miracles of creation: sparrows in brilliant gold feathers, beetles of royal blue, generously canopied trees that hosted orchids and tree ferns on their outstretched arms. To give voice to these feelings, he occasionally sang the joyful songs he had heard Christian pilgrims sing on return from Ethiopia's holy sites in Axum or Lalibela.

Nataniel liked to bring Zahara with him on these walks. When she was small, he brought his motherless daughter so she would not feel abandoned. As she grew older, he intentionally waited for her to return from school so he could explain the names and uses of the plants, the knowledge he had carefully accumulated to compensate for his helplessness.

When he had first arrived at his maternal aunt's gojo in Chochotte, almost two decades earlier, he had known nothing of tending coffee plants. He had tried to be useful, but he picked the red berries slowly, filling half a basket for every three the other men picked. So he had come to prefer staying with the old women – helping them tend the sick and the dying – to fecklessly picking coffee in the forests with the other adults. Because of his carefully folded paper certificate from Addis Ababa University, many in the village looked to him for cures, answers to their questions about illness and disease. He knew to counsel good hygiene, boiling water, locating latrines far from the stream. But without his foreign medicines he had felt helpless in the face of their questions.

So he asked the old women for advice, asked what plants they used for different purposes, and how they prepared them. Most of the women deferred to his aunt, Darjena, as the most knowledgeable. In the few years he spent with her – before she finally succumbed to recurrent malaria – Aunt Darjena taught him to see plants as healers, to observe their effects in the world for clues about how they would act in the body.

With an exacting handwriting he wrote all she taught him in his big reference book, trying to marry her folk wisdom with the methods he had learned at university. In the margins he drew small pictures, wrote the names and details of plants that served as alternatives to the drugs described in the adjacent text. The plant names he wrote in the jagged angles of Amharic and the rest in English – the language of science. He pressed leaf and flower samples in between the pages, until dried pollen and leaf sap dotted and stained the white background of most pages. Aunt Darjena often spoke wistfully of plants, roots and berries she had used as a young woman, but which she could no longer find nearby – 'they have abandoned us,' she would say. These things he wrote in parenthesis, separating them with curved lines from the things he had seen with his own eyes – the things he knew as real and true. With each plant he learned Nataniel grew to see Chochotte not as a place of temporary exile, but home.

Nataniel hurried through the woods today without Zahara, because he was eager – perhaps overeager – to prepare the second round of medicines Ato Worku would need. If he worked quickly, he could prepare the medicine today and give it to Ato Worku tonight. Then soon enough the man could leave their village, cured, and let them resume their lives. He walked deliberately off the path, searching out the massive trees bearing leaves with the blood-red streaks that marked a disease survived.

Nataniel returned to the village with a satchel full of leaves and fungi. He headed directly to the kitchen gojo, intending to boil water for the medicine. He stopped short, however, seeing all his neighbors gather around a vehicle. In contrast to Ato Worku's well-maintained vehicle, this was dented and dirty, with an insignia – too small to see – in English and Amharic. The pair of outsiders the vehicle had delivered stood at the village gate. Nataniel ducked into the gojo, hung his satchel on a nail next to the door, and trotted back out to join the gathering crowd.

A small Ethiopian man, with an official air, spoke politely with Ibrahim, Chochotte's headman, occasionally making gestures toward the car and his companion. The companion, a white man with a shock of handsomely combed hair, towered over the children, bellowing with laughter as they tried to catch the bright red coffee berries he threw into the air.

"Tadesse," the white man said with a wide smile to his Ethiopian companion, "please ask the headman to excuse me. I always get caught up with the children." In two great strides he stood at Tadesse's side, reaching out his right hand for Ibrahim's. Nataniel watched as the two men greeted each other with traditional Ethiopian embraces – shoulder-to-shoulder gestures that mimicked the back and forth of European cheek-to-cheek kisses.

"Please tell Ato Ibrahim I can say hello in Amharic, but my *Oromo* is a very poor. I am Stefano Geotti, from Italy."

Ibrahim replied in Oromo. Tadesse translated. "He says you are most welcome. We are invited to have dinner at the house of this man."

As the visitors walked toward Ibrahim's gojo, the assembled crowd transformed into a procession – the men leading and the teenagers and children stringing out behind. Ibrahim pointed to rough hewn logs where his guests could sit, while his wife and daughters put out a plate of injeera. Other women quickly checked their own modest stores of food and within five minutes Ibrahim's daughter hospitably assembled a small feast: a heaping pot of lentils, some roasted corn cobs, and even a small dish of lamb wat with an impressive pile of red chilli powder for their unexpected guests.

Nataniel caught Ibrahim's eyes. Ibrahim waved his hand cheerfully at Nataniel. "Sit, sit Nataniel," he called out in his proud gravelly voice, "*Insha'Allah*, God-willing, there will always be a place for you at our home."

Each time foreigners had come in big vehicles, Nataniel had spoken eagerly with them, using the rare opportunity to speak again the English he had used at university. They had offered him slim books, tracts about sanitation or agricultural development, or small readers about birth control or HIV. He had added every piece of literature he had received to the small shelf in his gojo, where he kept his reference book and a small notebook, a kind of altar which he kept protected from dust with a cloth cut from an old gabbi.

Nataniel listened to the cadence of this foreigner's English, recognizing an Italian accent for the first time in decades. He began to follow the sentences after several minutes. "...and the Institute knows you are the guardians of this biodiversity." Stefano looked directly at Ibrahim as he spoke, although the old man understood nothing until Tadesse translated into Oromo. "You are providing very valuable service to Ethiopia and to the whole world. We are here to help for the protecting of that biodiversity..."

Nataniel did not understand the word 'biodiversity'. He wondered if maybe the Italians, Ethiopia's former would-be colonizers had returned to oust Mengistu and the Socialists.

"...so Tadesse and I would please to ask your help," the foreigner concluded with a smile to the whole gathering and a nod to Ibrahim.

The Italian seemed to deflate slightly as Tadesse translated and explained, "You all know Chochotte is the birthplace of coffee, and as coffee was born here, Chochotte is the richest source of biodiversity," Tadesse spoke the word 'biodiversity' in English. "It means that the individual plants have different genes inside, the coffee plants are different from each other, just like your children and your nieces and nephews are different from each other because they have different genes. God blessed Chochotte with this, and Chochotte gave this to Ethiopia and to the world."

Villagers nodded in understanding and pride, men stood a bit straighter in their mended clothes.

"Now the world wants to help pay back Ethiopia, to pay back Chochotte," Tadesse continued. "A scientific institute in Rome asked for us to come and collect this biodiversity. We will collect samples of your different coffee trees around Chochotte and bring them back to our Biodiversity Institute in Addis Ababa for safekeeping. The institute will know what is here, and will come back to set up a living collection of coffee trees. All kinds of different varieties will grow in a protected part of the forest, preserving the history of your coffee for your children and grandchildren."

Tadesse paused, waiting to see whether he would have to struggle to explain these points further.

Ibrahim took a deep breath, "How much money, how many birr will we get?" He swung his walking stick in a great arc, including the whole village. "How do we know the Italians won't just steal our coffees once you bring them to Addis?"

Tadesse, prepared for such questions, patiently detailed a checklist of safeguards he said had been negotiated by international organizations. "The Italian is only here at our invitation to help us collect. All the samples go to the Institute in Addis. None leave the country without written permission from the government. There is an international treaty both countries have signed – if any country wants to use Ethiopia's coffee, or Chochotte's coffee, they have to negotiate an agreement to share the benefits. So there is no birr, no money now, but there could be in the future."

Ibrahim scowled, thoughtfully furrowed his brow as the other men murmured amongst themselves. Stefano tapped Tadesse's thigh in a silent request for translation. They tilted their heads together as Tadesse spoke in low tones.

The foreigner straightened his head, grinned knowingly, "Yes of course," he boomed, "this are very good questions. Even my country had our plants stolen, the Americans once stole seeds for our very best Italian rice. But taking seeds for your crops is now illegal, the whole world would to hate us if we steal your coffee. And I love espresso, but coffee will not grow in Italy." Stefano laughed at his own humor, only Nataniel joined him while the rest of the village waited for translation.

Stefano exhaled, as if exhausted by his attempt at humor, and then reached into the pocket on the side of his khaki pants and pulled out a stack of photographs. "Other farmers have asked the same questions, but the collection and conservation of their crops is for their own benefit, not only the benefit of the whole world." Stefano started to pass the photos out like a dealer at a poker table. He continued, unflustered as the children rushed to him, grabbing at the photos, creasing the corners and smudging the images with dust.

One photo made its way through the group to Nataniel – a picture of Stefano towering over two dozen smiling Congolese pygmies, bowls of seeds in their hands. Other photos showed him in scores of distant locations; in mountains, deserts, forests: here Stefano standing in an apricot orchard with Afghan farmers wearing pie shaped hats, there in a Vietnamese rice field with a little boy in a black tunic perched on his shoulders. In every photo the Italian wore the same posed smile and in every photo people looked as though they had flocked to him, holding his hands and offering him every kind of plant, fruit or seed.

Stefano watched the photos working, just as he had watched them work in other villages, in other countries – as a sort of international letter of introduction. People eagerly inspected the images of their equivalents around the world, comparing the condition of their clothes, their houses, their fields. Potentially hairy questions unravelled in smiles, giggles, and pointing fingers. Ibrahim seemed to concede the photos were a suitable answer to his questions and gestured to the food. Stefano reinflated himself, reached with theatrical gusto, and tore off pieces of injeera to scoop up stew and lentils. Tadesse precisely and politely took his portion, while Ibrahim smiled in approval. Stefano grunted with pleasure at the food, and looked up to the women, "Wonderful, really!"

Nataniel felt the pull of hunger in his own stomach and remembered the work he had to complete before he would eat a small evening meal with Zahara. He stood up, glanced at the darkening sky, estimating he still had enough time to return to the kitchen gojo, to pound tree bark, and boil fungus and leaves for the medicine. After eating they would move Ato Worku to the dark gojo and address a dozen details of his care. As Nataniel reluctantly turned to leave, he was startled to see Stefano stand up, only to stumble and fall. The villagers let out a collective gasp.

Three tall men quickly appeared at Stefano's side and hauled him to his feet, leading him inside Ibrahim's gojo to lie down. Tadesse looked slightly embarrassed, following the cluster of men inside. Nataniel quickly joined them, deciding Ato Worku's medicine would have to wait another day.

Inside Ibrahim's gojo, Nataniel moved a candle near to Stefano's face. He touched the Italian's forehead. Fever. He pulled open Stefano's eyelids. The eyes, still white, indicated the illness was not hepatitis, which frequently afflicted foreigners. "Do you have malaria, sir?" Stefano tried to smile in the direction of the accented English he heard.

"No. Have mefloquine," Stefano said.

"I think it is typhoid," Tadesse said over Nataniel's shoulder. "He has had fever and stomach pain for the last week. But he refuses to return to Addis. He claims elephants, floods and civil wars don't stop him, so what can a tiny demon in his gut do? What could I do?" Tadesse added helplessly.

Stefano heard the rapid fire Amharic as if from another world. He felt his upper body trembling, felt his own skin burning hot. A wool blanket scratched along his neck and he would have relaxed but the voices seemed loud now, as if they were inside his head. He could smell the musty mat beneath him but could not see those around him through his closed eyelids. A hand, he imagined it was his mother's, raised his head and put a pill on his tongue. He struggled to swallow water from a plastic bottle and then his body sagged with exhaustion.

As Nataniel opened the foreigner's first aid box inside his gojo, he felt as if he were welcoming in an old friend. The compact steel case held not only first aid basics: antiseptic towels, loose gauze, and sealed bandages, but also intriguing medicines. He identified malaria tablets, powdered electrolytes for dehydration, snake poison antidotes, even treatments in syringes: immunoglobulin, tetracycline, penicillin. This professionally packed box had even provided a course of treatment for typhoid. He turned over each item in his hands, remembering the feel of the cardboard boxes, smiling at the twinkling sound of foil blister packs.

"It's like an entire hospital," Zahara said admiringly. "They are prepared for anything," she said, pulling a field surgical kit out of the box.

"Who is he?" hissed Ato Worku, reminding the girl and her father of his presence.

"A scientist, an Italian," Nataniel said, adding defensively, "that's all I know," in response to Ato Worku's suspicious expression.

"Do not tell him I'm here. The last thing I need is for him to blab to all the *faranji*, all the Europeans in Addis, that Ato Worku has gone mad, run to the witch doctor of Chochotte because he got sick from the ladies who dance at the Concorde disco." Worku shot a threatening glance at both of them.

Nataniel pretended not to notice, looking directly at him and saying only, "Yes, Ato." His hands, however, trembled ever so slightly as he held a cardboard box of malaria pills. Worku's eyes narrowed with insistence, an expression Nataniel had seen with Mengistu's thugs, who had backed up their words with their fists, or worse, their weapons.

"Good," Worku said as his fist clenched, the flesh of his little finger squeezing around a square gold ring studded with small diamonds.

Nataniel steadied himself, turned to Zahara and pointed out the paper inserts accompanying the mefloquine. Zahara sounded out the headings: 'indications, dosage, warnings.' She tried to imagine a world where so much information about a medicine was available from a single piece of nearly transparent paper, a world where people would not need to consult with a wise elder.

"Sometimes faranji came to my pharmacy for anti-malaria medicine," Nataniel told her. "Most didn't have to worry about malaria in their own countries. I had to warn them that chloroquine would cause them to have strange and vivid dreams. I don't know about this one, this is a new version."

Ato Worku rolled on his side, turning his back to Nataniel and groaning at the hardness of the mat beneath him. The rich man closed his eyes with a disgusted sigh, despairing that fate had delivered him here, into this gojo, where he had absurdly entrusted his life to a man barely fit to sell cough syrup to his servants in Addis.

Chapter 3

While the earth made a full rotation, Stefano hardly moved, except to curl into the fetal position with waves of nausea and intestinal cramping. Rose colored spots that had appeared on his chest had been covered with a brown paste – although he had no memory of being touched.

He could not remember the name of the village, but burned with humiliation remembering his collapse in front of the villagers. He would never tell his mother about this. He would not include among the photographs he sent her every month any photographic evidence of him – her handsome youngest son, the son who had abandoned their farm with his ambitions to attend university, the same son who had travelled to distant corners of the world, winning the attention and adoration of the strange foreign people he met – lying sick in a hut in the highlands of Ethiopia. He drifted into unconsciousness.

His mother appeared as a feverish vision. He saw her kneading bread dough in the kitchen, the waters of the Po River flowing just beyond their fields. She turned to look at him, the ball of dough in her hands. In the place of her usual flowered headscarf, she wore the shaggy white turban of Afghan shepherds. The walls of their centuries-old farm house dripped with rivulets of blood. The motions of her kneading became distorted, her strong arms twisting and pulling, threatening the very life of the wheat, until the dough itself screamed, cried out in agony and fear. He lunged toward her, reaching protectively for the dough. In his hands the dough disintegrated into a pile of wheat seeds, slipping through his fingers and disappearing into a chasm in the floor just beyond his bare feet.

With a jolt Stefano reached his arms out beyond the edge of his mat. His mother disappeared with the broken dream, but the screams continued.

Stefano felt his head lifting from the mat, watched his long limbs gather beneath him as if they did not belong to him. He staggered out into the night, followed a path weakly lit by a waning moon. He heard blood-curdling screams give way to a low wail and childlike weeping. He heard people stirring inside the gojos he passed. Children whimpered, women sighed in frustration, but no one joined him to investigate the source of the screams.

Stefano followed the sound – now a guttural growling, definitely from a man – to the edge of the village. A few towering trees blocked the light of the moon. He could barely see for the shadows, but willed his aching body to reach the screaming man. Stefano did not see the guard, until the cold steal of his gun knocked him to the ground. A gruff voice said simply, "No. Go back!"

Stefano sat for a long minute, feeling air rush into the void in his lungs. He heard a motion coming from a small gojo behind the guard – a muscular man holding an AK-47. The screams continued from inside the gojo. A young woman appeared, only the whites of her eyes visible. She came to him quickly, and reached out her hands. Instinctively, he reached up and felt the smooth skin of her forearms as she helped him to his feet.

"You must go," Zahara whispered over the moaning from behind her. "No thing wrong. Sick man. Bad dreams," she said quickly.

Stefano silently wrinkled his eyebrows in question. She smiled in answer, as if to say 'don't worry' her lips spreading to reveal white teeth that seemed to float in the night. She turned him with a restrained strength, speaking into his back, "Go. Sleep."

Zahara sat with Ato Worku in that cramped little hut for nearly three days, although later he would have almost no memory of it. Within an hour of the first dose of medicine he lost all sense of time and place. He knew only the sensations, the pain chiselling through his body. He grew furious with the pain. He imagined the little bastard witch doctor of Chochotte was trying to kill him. Worku felt it first in his armpits, his throat and groin, just a dull ache at first, then a collapsing pain, as if his flesh meant to rip itself away from his bones. Through the whole ordeal, Zahara sat beside him, sometimes singing, sometimes putting a cool cloth on his forehead.

When the pain reached his gut, he clutched at her.

He meant to threaten her, *call your father to make it stop*, but in his weakness could only grab desperately, like a frightened child. She spoke to him, but he had no idea what she said. He only knew the sound of her voice – like a physical presence – distracted him for split seconds from the disintegration of his body. He tried to focus on the point from which the sound came, the flow of air from her mouth, his sole tether to life.

When the pernicious pain reached his head, the soprano tether of her voice snapped; he lost consciousness.

In the place beyond her voice, he battled for his life with enemies. Visions menacing but ephemeral. The man with the AK-47 blindfolded him. Worku felt the muzzle of the gun in his mouth, bullets burning down his throat. Nataniel, the damned witch doctor, put a cloth over Worku's abdomen concealing his actions – coiling Ato Worku's intestines around a big wooden spool. Then farmers appeared, small as ants, crawling over every inch of his skin, burrowing stores of shining red coffee berries between the fibers of his muscles.

He felt Zahara's shadow behind him, enveloping him, protecting him, shielding him from his attackers.

Then he felt nothing.

Chapter 4

"He will be fine," she assured Nataniel. "He is sleeping now. He struggled so much with the pain, I wasn't sure if he would survive the first night. You gave him so much medicine." They both knew the medicine could kill; Zahara had watched some of the sick slip into death before Nataniel had learned to moderate the leaf medicine with the pulp from an orange fungus.

"He is a big man," Nataniel said, unsure himself whether he spoke of Ato Worku's physical or economic stature; unsure himself whether his motivation to give Ato Worku the extra dose was sound medical judgement or resentment. Nataniel could not look at Ato Worku as just another sick man. Everyone in the village could see who he was – a man who had grown fat and rich because of their coffee beans, at their expense, the man who perpetuated poverty not only in this village, but in thousands of Ethiopian villages. They had all suffered as the prices the traders and middle men would pay for their coffee dropped and dropped until they could no longer afford to buy their children pencils, much less pay the government school fees. Elders ate only once a day, so there would be enough food for their working children and grandchildren. Some in the village considered abandoning coffee altogether for other crops. If the man responsible for their suffering should have died at Nataniel's hand, would it have been a sin?

"Big man," Nataniel whispered to himself.

"He is a big man," Zahara affirmed. "And he has survived," she said definitively. "Maybe now he will be grateful to Chochotte, maybe he will help us."

"We don't need help from Ato Worku," Nataniel said with a clenched jaw, "we only need him to pay us fairly for the coffee we give him. The Italian has been telling everyone our coffee is valuable, even as seeds."

"What has he been saying? Where is the faranji?" Zahara asked, suddenly eager to know the happenings in the village after her three days of isolation with Ato Worku. "I want to see him." She rose quickly to her feet, ignoring her fatigue.

"He went with the government man, Tadesse, to the southern forest," Nataniel pointed in the direction he had seen the visitors walk. "But he is still weak from his illness, he really shouldn't be out."

Under the shade of the forest canopy, Zahara watched the foreigner, the faranji, for a long moment. His fine white shirt stuck to his back where his sweat gathered. A belt around his lean waist swelled with tools: a metal torch, pens, knives, electronic equipment, camera, plastic bags, cotton bags. He glanced at a small screen on an electronic box, jotted something in his notebook and squatted down over a pile of freshly cut twigs.

He paused in his work as she appeared in front of him. He was startled by her height, momentarily speechless at her smile. He ignored the global positioning satellite coordinates on the small screen half transcribed into his notebook as the crescent of her white teeth, vaguely familiar, gave way to her words.

"You are welcome to Chochotte. How do you find our village, our trees?" she said politely in the formal English of missionary textbooks.

"Wonderful. The architecture of nature is always wonderful," he said sweeping his arm to include the whole forest. He stood up and offered his hand to her in greeting. "I am Stefano."

"Yes, I know" she reached for his hand, undaunted by the big English word 'architecture'. "I am called Zahara."

"Like the desert?"

"Yes, like the Zahara desert. Have you seen it?" she asked, still shaking his hand.

"I have been to Mali, but only to the edges of the desert. I am a man for plants, not sands." He returned her direct gaze. "Have you seen it?" he asked her.

She dropped his hand and looked away. "Not yet," Zahara said, and began absent-mindedly stroking the leaves of a plant. "But my father speak the world is big. He want I will leave Chochotte one day to see it. Maybe I will go Addis, Insha'Allah, God-willing, where there is my father's university."

"Yes, of course you will see your desert, Zahara." Stefano, who habitually encouraged others, often disingenuously, found the improbable idea completely plausible.

"What do you to write?" she asked, reaching for his notebook, which he willingly showed her.

He enthusiastically explained the numbers in the notebook as a very specific address others could use to find this part of the forest. He leafed through the pages, showing her his work to document Chochotte's wild and cultivated plants. Zahara inhaled with each of his points. To most foreigners, Ethiopians' quick inhalations gave the impression of perpetual surprise. Stefano, though, had been in the country long enough to know Zahara's inhales signalled affirmation and understanding. Encouraged by her comprehending inhalations, he explained his methods for collecting samples and the value of biodiversity. Words tumbled from Stefano's mouth as if he could only hold her attention with the sound of his voice, as if he paused too long, she might disappear as suddenly as she had appeared – this unusual young woman, as rare and beautiful as the plants he sought.

Stefano rushed to catalog the dozens of piles of coffee samples Tadesse had cut before the sun dipped below the forest canopy and the shadows fell across his notebooks. Through Tadesse, he politely declined Ibrahim's invitation to another evening meal, excusing himself to finish his notes by battery light inside the gojo. His excuse, only a cover for his lingering weakness, allowed him to rest on his mat and let his thoughts return to Zahara.

She was undoubtedly a beautiful girl. Her skin shone bronze – no, copper – as though illuminated from behind, stretched gracefully over her fine features – quintessentially Ethiopian cheekbones and a long straight nose. Her almond shaped eyes – like those that inspired the exaggerated white and black features gazing out from traditional Ethiopian paintings – had looked directly at him. The admiration he felt for her, though, was not sexual, which surprised him, for he was a connoisseur of women. He had spent years sampling women, in almost the same manner he had sampled plant varieties. He had observed silken skin covering impossibly thin women in Thailand and the giant curves of brown flesh flaunted by West African women in cacao plantations. He had felt the passive embraces of South Indian women, and bland moans caught in the throats of East African women whose genitals had been cut by dull knives. Stefano observed and enjoyed these women with his own brand of generous pleasure and reverence, free from the complications of long term romantic entanglements.

Zahara, though, did not inspire his collector's desire. Her form intrigued him as a physical manifestation of the open mind, the spirit he had glimpsed this afternoon. She had laughed with him today in the forest, and then grew serious when they walked past a single towering tree. "This tree we use for the sick people coming to my father. It is powerful medicine for the bad sickness," she had told him. Stefano had questioned her about the bad sickness. He knew the disease she described. He had seen AIDS in huts, in shanties, in haunted eyes around the world. But she did not know its name, or refused to speak it aloud if she did. He admired her compassion, and inwardly disdained the superstition, the desperate hope of impoverished people who would walk for days on the strength of rumours of cures.

When Stefano had walked back into the village with her, he felt the vague bitterness of guilt in his stomach. He watched her sprint back to her father's gojo, to care for the sick whom she had neglected while she had been with him, offering him knowledge about the forest's plants. He was accustomed to extracting knowledge from the farmers and rural people he met, those who always knew more about their plants than he did. He took their knowledge with charm, knew he served his ideals of science and conservation, so felt no qualms about the imbalance of the exchange. Until today. Stefano felt an obligation toward Zahara, as he felt she had given him something inexplicably valuable today.

Tomorrow he would show her his Manual for Field Collection. Then he would take her picture with his digital camera. He would show her what he saw.

Chapter 5

When Zahara entered the clinic gojo, the half dozen people inside stopped their talking, as if expecting something unpleasant. Zahara apologized for being away so long. After she had checked on the woman from the nearby town of Jimma, she noticed that something, someone was missing. The young man from Woliso. Zahara knew he had been strong enough to walk around the village the day before, so she thought he might just have gone for a stroll. Then she noticed his stick, his gabbi, and his worn Koran were gone too.

"Where is he?" Zahara demanded of the others. She surprised even herself at the severity in her voice.

"His wife was pregnant when he came here," the woman from Jimma explained. "The baby will come any day and he wanted to be with her. He is well now. He left this as thanks." The woman extended her thin arm to show Zahara a small plastic pot of honey.

Zahara sank down to the woman's mat. With her head in her hands, she let out a low groan. "He wasn't finished. He hasn't had the final medicine yet. He will be back, if he doesn't die first." She looked up at those remaining in the gojo. "Please stay until my father can be sure you are well. There is no point leaving before then. You will become sick again and will only make your families suffer."

The woman from Jimma glanced nervously at an old shepherd who had traveled three days from Gambela. "Sister, we are afraid of what we heard the last few nights," the man said.

Zahara understood. The first few times her father had used the medicine, after the first survivor, the sick people had stayed in a gojo in the middle of the village. The medicine induced hallucinations and the patients' screaming had practically caused a riot. So Ibrahim had organized a couple of young men to build a special small gojo at the edge of the forest. Zahara had suggested they plaster all the cracks with mud, to keep out all the light, thinking the darkness would render the hallucinations less frightening. The patients still screamed, but had slept more and recovered more quickly. Zahara's neighbors sometimes complained when they had not slept after the nights someone stayed in the dark gojo, but more often they asked about the outcome, genuinely hoping for good news.

"I know, it does sound terrifying," she said in a motherly tone to the old man, "But the illness is strong, it holds on like a lion with his claws in you. So please, stay. The time you are here makes you stronger so you can fight it." She looked directly at each one, willing them to trust her. "The time in the dark gojo is the last battle. No one dies there now."

The old shepherd did not challenge her out of respect, but asked skeptically, "Who was the last man in the dark gojo? Was it Ato Worku? Why doesn't he stay here with us?"

She paused, choosing her words carefully. "Yes, it was him. He is staying with my father and me, because he is rude and demanding. My father knew he would disturb you."

They were silent, they knew she was right. She had seen a few educated Ethiopians, those who had travelled and worked abroad, treat villagers with a shameful arrogance. They put on Western suits and spoke only in English, as if denying they had anything in common with people who smelled like the sheep they tended, people who produced the coffee and animal skins that brought money into Addis.

"What about the faranji, what's he doing here?" asked an Oromo woman with a tired voice.

Zahara turned to her. They were almost the same age, but unlike Zahara, the Oromo woman already looked old from childbearing and sickness. She had left her four children in her mother-in-law's care. Since she had arrived in Chochotte she sang to her children before she slept, hoping her lullabies would travel the distance between them. Always eager for village gossip, anything that might distract her from her absent children, she listened intently to Zahara's description of the faranji.

"He is a scientist," Zahara said proudly. "Italian. He has come for Chochotte's coffee. He has amazing tools, and he has been everywhere." She reported his trip to Mali, described the box that pinpointed his location on the earth, the tools around his belt, retold his story of escaping wild lions and elephants in Zimbabwe. With her voice and her hands, she brought his expansive world into the intimate circle of the gojo. For an hour the visitors with the sickness forgot their coughs, forgot their wasting muscles, forgot their loneliness as Zahara – their healer – also became their window to the world beyond.

"Tadesse, my friend, you have done fantastic job," Stefano boomed, thumping his colleague on the back. "We must to take a photograph."

Tadesse had methodically piled more than a hundred plant samples – a week's worth of collections – in the back of the vehicle, carefully ordering their unwieldy shapes. Stefano glanced once more into the vehicle then turned his attention to assembling the villagers for a triumphant final photo he could send to his mother. He teased the children who had tugged and poked at him for the last ten days, implored his favorite injeera makers to come and pose, clasped the shoulders of the men whose faces he had learned (their names still confounded him), and brought them near the car.

One of the village men, singled out because of his steady hand for the privilege of taking the picture, held the camera awkwardly, looking from his neighbors to their image in the small digital screen and back again. Stefano held two little boys in his arms, and put on his photo face. "Yes, now! Push the button."

For a single moment the crowd paused, quiet enough to hear an electronic whir and then a click. The village photographer looked very pleased, held up the camera like a trophy and cheered.

"Wait, one more!" Stefano tried to shout above the crowd, too late. The boys in his arms squirmed to get down, rushing to see themselves in the camera's little screen. Everyone jostled for a view until the village man ceremoniously returned the camera to Stefano. The towering faranji turned the camera screen out and spun around slowly, so everyone could see. There were hoots, inhales and thumbs up as the village unanimously affirmed the photo's quality.

A moment later everyone dispersed, returning to their individual tasks to prepare the evening's feast in honor of Stefano and Tadesse, who would leave the next morning. Stefano ambled between the gojos, observing the preparations, inspecting with mock scrutiny, patting men's shoulders, nodding at women's efforts: a slaughtered goat stewing in a giant iron pot, the day's injeera sliced and rolled into neat little piles, mounds of vegetables and beans in chipped enamelled tin trays, cut grass and flowers strewn on the ground for the coffee brewing ceremony. Three of Chochotte's lovelier young women – Stefano noticed – roasted and pounded coffee beans for brewing.

Spontaneously, the whole village gathered on little stools, or logs, or squatted around the fire. The coffee was served with much toasting. Stefano gave an impromptu speech about goodwill and the political neutrality of science and conservation. Ibrahim responded with hopes for Allah's blessings and for prosperity. Tadesse grew tired with the translation.

And then the feast. Stefano ate his injeera and goat stew quickly, knowing the others would wait, as hospitality dictated, until he had had his fill. He maintained an expression of pleasure. He had long ago mastered the ability to feign delight at sour milk, gristly meat and dry bread – knowing the subsistence cuisines of most cultures ended a meal with some fruit: a papaya, bananas, dried apricots, dates, some sweetness to genuinely please his palate. Since he had arrived in Chochotte, however, he had sipped sweetened coffee, but he had not tasted a single fruit, which only served to accentuate his perception of their poverty.

After the food had been eaten, Stefano retrieved a cardboard box from the vehicle, as he had done in dozens of villages before. He opened it under the watchful eyes of the dozen children who had followed him, revealing an enormous treasure of Italian hard candies. Plastic and foil wrappers rustled with every hand that reached inside the box. Squeals of delight and laughter soon accompanied a fierce trade in candy wrappers. Little boys traded apple wrappers for orange wrappers, which were traded for strawberry wrappers. Small hands pointed to unknown fruits, small blue or purple berries and what looked like yellow limes. The trading activity soon established that the most coveted wrapper featured a small brown coffee bean next to a green cup with rising steam. "Chochotte candy!" a little girl declared.

The box quickly emptied and Stefano noticed one little girl sitting quietly, examining her hard candy with one hand while she picked at the buckles of new plastic sandals she wore with the other hand. The little girl's mother – also in new sandals – picked up her daughter and Stefano noticed the child had only three fingers on one hand, the kind of physical anomaly he had seen befall countless undernourished children at birth.

Stefano looked more closely at his companions. Every third person seemed to have new sandals, or a clean shirt, or two new pens – the same 'Scripto!' pens children constantly begged from faranji – prominently displayed in a frayed shirt pocket.

Nataniel wore a 'new' second-hand, blue, double-breasted suit coat with three brass buttons still attached. Stefano scanned the crowd, looking to see if Zahara was also wearing new clothes or sandals. But none of the women's faces matched hers. He walked over to where Nataniel stood observing his village with a satisfied expression.

"Your suit looks very smart, Ato Nataniel." Stefano's long arm rested across Nataniel's shoulders.

Inhalation.

"Everyone has new shoes, this is special occasion, yes? Or is there money in the village from the coffee harvest?" Stefano asked.

"No there will be no coffee money for three weeks more. Even then, not much money," Nataniel said shaking his head. "The middlemen all say the international coffee markets fall down, down, down."

"Where did all the new shoes come from? And your fine suit Ato?" Stefano asked with a broad smile and a nudge.

"We had a visitor, a man from Addis came for medicine. He was grateful to the village." Nataniel fingered a bundle of new bank notes in his suit pocket.

The previous morning, before sunrise, Ato Worku had left discreetly, wordlessly handing Nataniel an impressive stack of money and kissing Zahara delicately on her forehead, before he and his armed guard drove away. Nataniel, almost fearful of this sudden wealth, had given most of the money to Ibrahim, who immediately dispatched his wife to town. She returned with sacks of goods on a mule, the results of her shrewd bargaining.

"Medicine for what, Ato Nataniel?" Stefano probed. "He came all the way from Addis?"

"He was very sick, he had heard our forest gives medicine for everything."

"Medicine even for AIDS, for HIV?" Stefano thought back to the first afternoon he had spent with Zahara, her talk of medicine under one of the towering trees. Desperate farmers did not surprise him.

But he was intensely curious about a man from Addis, a man who had money to give.

"I don't know Mr. Stefano. It has been a long time since I was at university. This disease, I don't know its name." Nataniel's reference book in fact spoke nothing of this disease. The pages did include descriptions of and treatments for tuberculosis, pneumonia, skin lesions and dehydration. But this disease could be all of those. Nataniel had collected leaflets from a group of Danish medical volunteers, describing AIDS and he guessed what they warned against was this sickness, but he would not speak the name out loud.

Nor would he speak any more of the man from Addis. Before Ato Worku had walked out of Nataniel's gojo, he had spoken quietly, one last time. "Nataniel, I am grateful. I give thanks to God for your help. But remember, I was never here. I was never sick, and you will never speak my name to anyone."

Stefano was about to counter what he perceived as Nataniel's false modesty. But he turned at the sudden sound of voices, singing. Nataniel quickly excused himself and left Stefano to watch musicians and observers who had assembled in a circle. In the middle, Zahara. She and three other women – dressed in gleaming white cotton tunics with colourful sashes around their waists – danced. Their silver necklaces jingled with each thrust of their shoulders, keeping time to the music, so unfamiliar to his ears. Chesty voices belted out bright and sinewy tunes, coarse stringed instruments carried the beat, punctuated by grunts and exhales – erotic counterpoints to the affirmative inhalations. The music animated the women's fantastic dancing. Stefano watched Zahara, speechless. Her shoulders led her whole body – shaking up and down, forward and backward – her breasts bounced and her head bobbed ecstatically to the rhythm.

Two men carried a big plastic bucket filled with bright yellow taej near the performers. An assembly line formed, as men poured the local alcoholic brew from the bucket into bottles and yet smaller bottles, and eventually into cups, tiny bottles and cans. Hands passed taej to hands and then to mouths. The honey beer looked innocently like orange juice – but the fizzy fermented froth delivered a strong kick.

As the village grew intoxicated, the dance performance transformed into communal ritual. Little girls at the edge of the dancing area mimicked the young women's impossible moves, men called out suggestive new lyrics – goaded on by the singers and dancers.

Ibrahim walked directly from the taej bucket to Stefano, pulling a reluctant Tadesse with him. Ibrahim brought taej glasses, shaped like pregnant science beakers, to offer a toast to his two honored guests. Stefano held the glass by its long thin neck, and took a long draw, Tadesse followed suit.

Irbahim spoke through Tadesse's translation, "My friends, you must to come back to Chochotte. A special protected forest will be good, especially if you bring money from Addis. My village suffers much since the fall of the coffee price."

"Thank you Ato Ibrahim, we will be back to set up the project." Stefano said, adding "Insha'Allah," God willing, as the Muslims said of everything that would happen in the future.

"The project should happen quickly. You see that man?" He pointed to a middle aged man dancing with the women. "That is Esmail. He says we should forget coffee and grow *chat* instead. He says we can get a good price for it, the addicts in the capital and even abroad can't get enough of it. We quarrel often, I tell him we cannot abandon Chochotte's tradition. We have only coffee, it is everything for us. But Esmail wakes early every day, going from gojo to gojo, trying to convince the village that only chat will end our poverty. He is going crazy with his belief in chat."

"Does chat grow here?" Stefano asked.

"Not in the forests, too dark. But Esmail says if we cut the trees, as other villages have done we could give chat the sun it needs."

"I see," Stefano nodded solemnly. "I will do what I can." Stefano reached out to offer his half drunk glass to Ibrahim. "You won't have taej with us?"

Ibrahim smiled and held up a bundle of tender green leaves. "I don't take alcohol, Ato Stefano. I am a good Muslim, al hamd'Allah, thanks to God." He smiled ironically, holding up a bundle of tender green leaves, "I only chew chat."

They all laughed, repeating "al hamd'Allah," thanks to an ancient prophet who had never heard of the narcotic chat, so had never forbid its consumption.

Stefano drained his taej glass and Ibrahim tucked it safely into the folds of his gabbi. The headman stood contented as the big faranji rested his arms on the shoulders of his friends. Men never shied from Stefano's bear-like embraces, never rebuffed him, or misunderstood his physical camaraderie as sexual.

Stefano marvelled at the situation: an Italian man, honored and feted by an Ethiopian village headman. More than a century earlier, similar men would have fought each other to the death. On the whole of the African continent, only the Ethiopians, then known as Abyssinians had successfully resisted colonialism. The Italians enduring legacy here in Ethiopia, Stefano mused, amounted to little more than a tradition of good espresso and pastries in the cities.

He looked up at the night sky and let his arms drop to his sides. He breathed in the fullness of life, the world, the people, the plants he had encountered here. In a moment of frisson, Stefano thanked his god for Chochotte and for his place in the great tapestry of existence. His was a god he looked to only in strength, never in weakness, a god he only paid homage to, never beseeched. Unlike the God of his mother and her beloved Pope in Rome, his was not a god of rules and authority. His mother had once called him godless, shaking a fistful of rosary beads at him, fearing for his soul. He had not bothered to defend himself. How could he explain to her that he knew his god well? Encountered this god in every corner of the world, revered the brilliance of his god in every plant he held, the beauty of his god in every woman he touched, the joy of his god in every fragment of music he heard. This was a god he knew intimately, a god made manifest as his beloved, his lover in endless forms. For this god of the world, he shunned hearth and home, wife and children, choosing instead the monkhood of an extreme sensualist.

He knew his hero, Nikolai Vavilov – the towering and tragic figure of Soviet plant science – must have also known this god as he travelled to distant corners of the world a century earlier. Surely Vavilov, who had rendered all cultural differences meaningless in the service of uncovering co-evolution and genetic novelty in agricultural plants, must have considered his field collecting missions as some kind of sacred scientific pilgrimage. Stefano imagined his own journeys in search of biodiversity, especially here in East Africa, as tribute to his dead hero.

With a nod to god in the stars and the memory of Vavilov, Stefano closed his eyes and took a deep breath.

He opened his eyes again, Zahara appearing before him like a vision. She fairly glowed with the heat of her dancing. She carried herself with a lightness, her shoulders still moving almost imperceptibly to the music. He saw his companions had moved closer to the musicians, so only she stood in front of him.

"Tomorrow, you will leave Chochotte," Zahara said. This he heard as a command as much as a statement.

"Yes, Zahara. Tomorrow I will leave Chochotte and its fantastic music and its plants, and the beautiful young woman who knows them."

She smiled at the compliment, unashamed. "You will go back to Italy," she pronounced with her accent of exaggerated vowels. "But I want to be knowing more about your work. Leave me your Field Manual." This slightly more request than command. Stefano often encountered demands for his things from people who understood he would leave their villages and return to a land of unlimited wealth, unlimited goods, a land they might have seen on faded television screens in a restaurant in a neighboring town. Zahara took his big hands in her long fingers and added an unusual promise to her demand. "I will give it back to you when I see you again."

The newly dawned sun had not yet warmed the air when Nataniel and Stefano greeted each other silently from the doors of their gojos. Stefano wanted to leave before the village woke from its taej hangover. Tadesse sat ready in the vehicle. Everything was already packed, save the Field Collection Manual, which Zahara had set next to Nataniel's reference book the previous night.

Nataniel never drank taej, so suffered no hangover. His religion offered no prohibitions, but his own sense of control forbid it; for taej robbed his world of the order he so diligently sought. So his clear head took in the luxury of the cool morning air without his neighbors' company.

Stefano and Nataniel – once strangers – now walked toward each other, embraced with full shoulders, offered hushed thanks and good luck and turned away to walk back into their own worlds.

Neither sensed there was another soul awake and alert in the village that morning.

Nataniel walked to the stream to wash his face, mopping up droplets of water from his sideburns with the corner of his gabbi. He sat back on his haunches, to take in the newness of the morning. He didn't realize that as he watched the world awake, he was being watched as well. Instead, he noticed that with the dry season, the lichen on the big trees had dried into a grey scale. A spider sat poised on its reed-straddling web. Hawks circled overhead. The green of the low bushes – watered by the stream – was still verdant with new growth, except one small plant that seemed to struggle. Nataniel reached out, plucking up the struggling plant, and one of its lush neighbors. Just as he had thought, the small one lacked the little nodules on the roots that made the other healthy. He tossed them aside, satisfied at his correct hypothesis.

He lost himself in speculation about the effect of the tree lichens. *Would boiled dry lichen give the same effect as mashed moist lichen? What did the pigmentation matter? The red lichens were usually toxic, but was that related to the red pigment, or was it coincidental?* At moments like this, he wished his Aunt Darjena were still alive, he would press her for whatever she knew or even imagined about the red lichens.

Nataniel did not hear the footsteps of the only other villager awake this early come up directly behind him. When a steel blade pushed up against Nataniel's neck, his inhalation was genuine surprise, not Ethiopian affirmation.

A hand held Nataniel's head tightly, knees dug into his back.

A familiar voice hissed at him. "How could you do this to us? Ato Worku would watch our children starve, making our coffee worthless for his own profit. Yet you would stoop to cure him. You had the chance to help us, to kill him. When you came here, we protected you, and look how you repay us. You help keep us in our poverty."

Nataniel began an inhalation to speak, an inhalation to give him enough oxygen to turn his head to address his neighbor. As Nataniel's eyes caught those of the man behind him, the steel blade cut the inhalation short. Blood flowed onto Nataniel's white gabbi. One living hand threw a bloody steel blade into the stream, and the other living hand shoved Nataniel's dying body face down at the water's edge

Chapter 6

At times the wailing was deafening. Zahara's cousins had asked for contributions from the village and had gathered enough to pay for three professional mourners from the neighboring village. The mourners beat their breasts, called out Nataniel's name, as they led the procession to a clearing past the southern forest where Chochotte's dead were buried. Six men carried Nataniel's body wrapped in white cotton. Two of Zahara's female cousins held her up as she stumbled alongside the body. She heard voices wailing all around her, but could not discern if her own voice was among them. She saw the people – the whole village had come out of respect – but she could not be sure she recognized any of them. They were all strangers that day, perhaps her father's killer was among them.

Zahara's life had practically started in this place of the dead. Her father had carried her here in his arms to bury his wife, her mother. Childbirth was always risky in Chochotte, but when Zahara's mother bled to death a few days after her daughter's birth, many in Chochotte interpreted the event as a just punishment for a Muslim woman who had married a Christian man. Had others wailed for her mother? Had her father suffered through these same awful sounds? He never spoke of that time except to recall his determination to see his tiny Zahara live. He carried her everywhere, slung her across his back, just as the village women did. He only let her go when Darjena insisted the baby suckle at another woman's breast. 'Your mother was unlucky,' he had repeated over the years, 'but you will be lucky, my little one, you will find your own luck.'

Nataniel's body was lowered into the chocolate colored soil as the wailing reached a fevered pitch. Zahara's legs collapsed under her and she sank to the edge of the grave, an overwhelming hollowness in her chest. *I will be alone now. I will be the only Christian in Chochotte, the only one who knows my father's medicine. How could he be gone like this? What will I do?*

A man's strong arms lifted her to her feet as her father's body disappeared beneath shovelfuls of soil. "You must be careful now, you must stop your father's work curing the sick." Zahara looked up to see Esmail's face. The man who spent his mornings trying to convince his neighbors to plant chat whispered in her ear. "This is the work of Ato Worku's men. It is a warning to the village not to speak of his sickness."

She passed through the next several days as through a waking dream. Everything familiar, but altered. Zahara went through the motions of caring for the people in the clinic gojo, but one by one they left, frightened by Nataniel's murder. With each departure Zahara's field of vision clouded until she saw not the person before her, but the image of her father's surprised face, just as she had discovered it when she went to wash at the stream that morning.

Aside from his image, her senses seemed incapable of registering the world around her. The injeera was tasteless, the *wanniye* birds' cries were silent, the sun offered no warmth. When she wandered to the edge of the forest one afternoon and saw the dark gojo consumed by flames, she could not hear the crackle of the straw roof, or smell the grey smoke that billowed toward her. She knew she should feel some emotion, but could feel only a dull throb in her stomach. She did not even hear when a four wheel drive vehicle drove into the village, or when Ato Worku walked up behind her.

Chapter 7

Washington, D.C.

A n express delivery envelope arrived on his desk, addressed in a flowering script to 'Robert Kresovich'. The label indicated the documents inside had arrived from a hotel in Ethiopia.

Intrigued, Robert turned the envelope over several times, before finally pulling the sealed flap open. Cardboard bowed open to reveal a flattened plastic bag, and a single, handwritten note from Stefano Geotti.

Robert had known of Stefano's collecting work in Africa this year. The Italian had mentioned his plans when they had met at an international science conference in Washington a year ago. Robert had presented a scientific paper about developing drugs from traditional medicinal plants. Stefano had challenged him from the audience with a question about conservation. After the conference, the two had speculated, debated, even boasted about their own work over bottles of wine. Robert's explorations into the chemical mysteries of plants differed dramatically from Stefano's collecting missions around the planet. Despite their contrasting temperaments, they soon developed a mutual admiration based on their shared passion for plant biodiversity and their reverence for Vavilov.

The note, written on hotel stationary, bore the same flowing script as the envelope.

'Robert,

Hello from the land history forgot. Brilliant place. Coffee collections were excellent. Came across intriguing medicinal plant. Locals claim it is powerful, even against their plague. This is more your speciality than mine. I wondered if you would please to take a look at this. Could there be something to it? I have no phytosanitary certificates, so sending these 'documents' personally. The institute director here should to be displeased at my distribution without his prior informed consent. Your discretion will be necessary.

Please contact me at my personal email address, not at my institute.
Eagerly awaiting your insight.
   Fondly,
   Stefano'

Robert raised an eyebrow as he unfolded the plastic bag. The handwritten note, Stefano's cryptic message and unorthodox collection were unusual. But everything else about the sample was textbook regulation perfect. Robert removed the absorbent paper, the same paper that covered the thousands of botanical specimens that came through his lab. Stefano had included a copy of the handwritten collection voucher, listing all the plant's passport data: location, habitat, description, season and date, local name, local uses, botanical description. Between the layers of paper were five flat leaves – as big as his hand and shaped like the leaf of the bodhi tree, but with less of a point.

Robert laid them out on his desk, where they resembled a Warhol painting, repeating shapes rendered in different colors. One was a deep green. One a pale green, with red lines following the pattern of the leaf veins, dead tissue spreading out from either side. The other three were deep green, flaunting crimson streaks in differing patterns along networks of veins radiating out from the stems. These three, Robert marvelled, were striking specimens.

He smelled them. Odorless, no volatile oils. No leaf hairs to limit evaporation, no scale or insect damage. The red veins were most likely due to a virus. Similar colors grace carnations, orchids, tulips – evidence of viral infections to which the plants have adapted, rendering the virus non-fatal, even advantageous in the eyes of humans. The leaf which showed tissue damage surrounding the infection, indicated the virus wasn't completely benign.

Robert sat back in his chair and folded his arms with a smile. Even from a distance Stefano's life of science had an adventurous mystique. The initial virology assays would only take a few hours. But they would have to wait, as Robert attended to the everyday tasks of his less adventurous life of science. Robert reassembled the package, unlocked the low humidity refrigerator next to his desk and slipped the cardboard envelope inside, among other recently received samples.

He was already five minutes late for his lecture at the university. Every semester he talked to the new biochemistry majors about his work, and his career path, which they could potentially follow. He was grateful for the commitment, as it excused him from today's departmental meeting, which promised to be grim. The director of the institute was coming down with news from inside the beltway. He knew the routine. The latest Congressional budget required funding cuts to the National Institutes of Health – again. The natural compound research, especially in the HIV research track, would inevitably be slashed. The director would explain that too few promising substances had come out of the program. If they could align more closely with the cancer track – he would counsel – they might have a better chance of getting their overdue budget increase.

Robert gathered his papers, locked his office and walked out into the lab, into his kingdom. He took a minute to survey the scene on his way out into the corridor.

Josiah, the would-be rock star PhD candidate, was in his usual place at his bench, listening to heavy metal music blasting from the stereo. He placed a dozen sample tubes into the centrifuge and closed the lid, playing air guitar to a hard rock solo with latex gloved hands. At the next bench, three young graduate students transferred the sediment from Josiah's tubes into sample plates, and set them in the automated screener. Beyond the whir of the computer directed motions of the screener, Robert could hear Raj, a post-doctoral student from India banging away at his keyboard, analyzing the raw data from the screener that appeared on his networked laptop.

Robert had built a lab full of promising scientists and bright graduate students using high-throughput screening techniques to screen thousands of plant samples for promising compounds. They worked a hundred times more efficiently than a decade ago, when they had been flush with new monies. But now, just as he had a dozen compounds in the pipeline, a dozen potentially life-saving drug compounds, the politicians and accountants were shutting down the flow of funds.

He announced his departure for the university, "I am going to tell all the undergraduates how glamorous your work is."

"Don't forget the pin-up photo of me in my lab coat," Josiah teased in response. All of Robert's colleagues called out their greetings as he walked out the door. He heard the warmth in their voices, felt comfort knowing he had found his exact place in the world. Only after he stepped out into the long, anonymous corridor, did he feel lost in the layers of the organization. He looked forward to his lecture today, the slides of his samples, his lab, and the stories would tell of the plant chemicals he had discovered.

By the time he returned, the sun had long since set on a short December day and his staff – even Josiah who usually worked late – had left, their scrubbed glassware drying on plastic pegs sprouting from a rubberised wall. Robert closed the lab door, thoughts of the outside world dropped away. He unlocked the sample refrigerator and pulled out the express mail envelope. Swivelling in his chair, he reached to turn on a spotlight, illuminating a small black backdrop he used for photographing samples. He set each leaf in turn against the black velvet backdrop, propped up the greyscale card and metric ruler for scale. He took two photographs of each leaf. Just as he reached for the lens cap, he stopped to admire the intricate beauty of the red veins branching out through the leaf. He thought of Sidney, his wife, who, over the years had admonished him to take pleasure in life's details. He cleared the little theatre of everything but the leaf, the one with the brightest red pattern. He took a photograph.

He glanced at his watch, knew he would miss dinner with the family. Sidney, who had long since resigned herself to Robert's love affair with his work, would not complain as long as he described it later, so she could enjoy this passion vicariously.

He moved into the lab, pressed the stereo's play button. Heavy metal. Josiah Klaus always left his music in the stereo. The young man's last name, the moniker of one of the biggest pharmaceutical companies in the country, had intimidated Robert at first. Josiah's great-grandfather, a pharmacist, had turned to drug manufacturing after watching his wife die of malaria a century before DDT had eradicated the disease in the United States. Robert knew the family business, Klaus Pharmaceuticals, now a global empire, surely provided Josiah with a trust fund allowance several times the amount of Robert's government salary. The young man, nevertheless, endeared himself to Robert. The cocky rock-star act belied an intense work ethic. The two often discussed their careers and their respective hopes as they worked late into the evenings. A shrewd business sense drove Josiah's ambitious pursuit of a PhD in plant biochemistry. Even though he could have won a comfortable job in the company, simply by virtue of his pedigree, he knew the credibility of a successful academic career would give him a competitive edge over his cousins. He had seen his uncle run the company with an arrogance and incompetence that antagonized the company's board. They unanimously deposed him, replacing him with Timothy Crosby, a one-time intelligence services man known for successfully turning companies around. Josiah swore to Robert, one evening, that he would not be the spoiled heir his uncle had been.

This evening, without Josiah's presence, Robert turned the stereo's volume low enough to avoid distraction, but loud enough to maintain the camaraderie of his absent colleagues. His commenced his work with movements precise and assured. He had practiced this procedure so frequently, he could perform the individual tasks in quick sequence, as though dancing around the benches: sterilizing his equipment, preparing the samples in solution so that he could test the compounds they contained.

He took the keys from his belt, unlocked the biohazard refrigerator, and removed the vials of HIV strains they used for screening. Wearing latex gloves and a face mask, he fitted the pipetting syringe with sterile plastic tips. He carefully filled the syringe with the virus laden solution – then precisely dispensed the load in one milliliter increments, partially filling the small plastic wells of the ELISA screening tray. Then he repeated the process, filling the tray with the leaf solution in increasing increments. He stood back, admiring the neatness of the small green wells in the tray. Five rows – one for each leaf, and twelve columns – each a different concentration of plant solution. The sixth row served as a control, filled only with viral solution.

A drum solo banged out of the stereo, and Robert paused in his dance, allowing the chemicals to take their turn. This simple mixing of pulverized plant tissue and virus would indicate whether the leaf contained any compounds that could combat the virus. Plants, the great chemical engineers of the world, had already devised, tested, and unleashed novel chemicals on the insects and microscopic diseases that would destroy them. For millennia, millions of plants had battled their myriad potential destroyers. The two sides maintained a rough evolutionary parity through constant adaptation. Robert's search through the plant kingdom's collective armory could yield weapons to battle HIV's two small strands of RNA: a tiny virus, the quasi living entity insidiously making its way through human cells across the planet.

Now Robert would wait – an hour, ninety minutes maybe – before adding the stain that would reveal the presence of the virus. If the individual wells turned red, the virus was still present at full force. The effect of the stain would decrease as viral levels decreased. Over the years he had observed thousands of dead-end compounds, red stop signs blinking up from the endless stream of ELISA trays. Sometimes a sample teased out an encouraging pink, a promisingly pale wash of stain. Those few samples, often false leads, would be tested in a second assay. From the wide net his lab had cast into the world, from the tens of thousands of samples they had screened: leaves, tree bark, seeds, even an occasional fungus; more than a hundred substances were advancing to further research. A couple of the most promising compounds had already been licensed out to pharmaceutical companies for production and marketing.

Robert went back to his office, sat before his computer screen, unable to force himself to read his email. He gazed up at the map on his wall. He had bought the biggest physical map he could find and tasked one of his former students with tracking the travels of his plant explorer heroes. Pinpoints – a different color for each scientist, perforated the map. Nikolai Vavilov in red. The great grandfather of plant exploration had travelled from his native Russia in the USSR to dozens of red pin points on five continents. Frank Meyer, the adventurous American was represented by a constellation of blue pinpoints through Russia, China, Mongolia and Manchuria. These two iconic crop collectors of the early 20th century were followed by others. Richard Schultes, the great experiential ethnobotanist, showed up on the map as orange pins. He had sought out the secrets of plant medicines in South America, living with the medicine men of the forests, ingesting their magic plants, scribbling in his notebooks. His recent death meant there would be no more orange pinpoints. E.O. Wilson – Harvard's great guru of biodiversity – was represented by a trail of green pinpoints from Fiji and New Caledonia to Costa Rica. He had followed ants across the world, working in rainforests; places where evolution had proceeded in extravagant excess, places where a single tree could host an entire universe of insects and plant parasites, a tantalizing undiscovered pharmacopoeia.

Perhaps, in a decade a new student would be pushing pins along the routes Stefano had ventured; another legend in the world of botany, biodiversity, the kingdom of plants. But for now, Robert thought, Stefano remained a midcareer plant explorer, following in the footsteps of the greats, across a planet impoverished by human 'progress'.

Robert had never seen the places pricked by the colored pins on his map. Nor did he ever want to. He knew about the world's great vastness from the little bits of living things that migrated by the thousands to his laboratory, an island of rich plant life in the middle of the city. Specimens, like botanical messages in bottles, gave him clues about distant places he would never reach. He could guess from the texture of a leaf in what latitude it grew. He could differentiate desert plants from temperate forest plants by smell. He could estimate the level of threat insect invaders posed to a tree by the thickness and structure of its bark. These attributes in turn hinted at the chemicals the samples harbored.

His work would never be completed; he would never be able to follow all the trails evolution had forged through the forests and grasslands. He felt sometimes like Newton, who had described himself "like a boy playing on the sea-shore, and diverting myself now and then finding a smoother pebble or a prettier shell than ordinary, whilst the great ocean of truth lay all undiscovered before me." But the great unknown was precisely what attracted Robert. The sophisticated intricacies of the plant world commanded study, respect, even adoration. Although he recognized a quasi-mystical belief fuelled his career, he never spoke of it directly, not even with Sidney. He preferred the firm, solid edges of facts and quantities to the diaphanous nature of belief.

An electronic timer beeped, ending his reverie. *Cookies are done.* Josiah's humorous exclamation rang through his head with

Pavlovian consistency whenever he heard the beep. He went back out to the lab, to perform the second act of his dance, dispensing the stain into trays. He set the trays onto the agitator, to thoroughly mix the solutions and opened his personal lab notebook to record the results.

Before Robert even removed the trays from the agitator, he knew something was amiss; he must have made an error somewhere. The stain worked properly in the first and second rows and the control, showing up as bright red stop signs. But there wasn't a trace of red in the other three rows. He was irritated. He must have been distracted; maybe he hadn't used fresh stain, or had forgotten to add it to all the wells. He seldom erred in his dance, but then again it had been a long time since he had broken down the assembly line of screening to look at a single sample.

He glanced at his watch. He would have liked to return to eat before the food grew cold in the refrigerator, but he refused to leave the lab with an error. Doggedly, Robert repeated the entire dance. Viral solution, then plant solution in plastic wells, one row for control. Back to his office. Wait.

Robert dozed off, and woke disoriented when the electronic timer beeped again. He stared over each shoulder in turn, trying to recall why he had been sleeping in a fully lit room. The map and the small black photo backdrop reoriented him. He rose from his chair and walked back into the lab, repeating the staining process with stain from a new, sealed bottle. There could be no error this time. He took a slow inhalation. The results were the same. Three rows of brilliant green appeared between three rows of red stop signs.

Robert didn't bother to read any of his emails the next morning. He composed a new message, writing to Stefano at his personal email address,

Thank you for the samples. They look to be very promising. VERY(!) promising. I would like to proceed, but can't do any more until I have a collection agreement with the source country. Can you help arrange the agreement and the phytosanitary certificates and send me a set of documents I can work with in the light of day?

I look forward to hearing from you at your earliest opportunity.
Thanks much.
Robert

There was a knock at the door. Robert minimized the screen before looking up.

"Bob?" Ruth was the only one who called him that, a nickname dating back to an intimacy more than twenty years in their past.

"Ruth. Good morning. How are you?"

"Well. I'm well. I'm just making my rounds, seeing if anyone has anything interesting brewing."

He stood up to shake her hand, stiffened momentarily when she instinctively embraced him. He gestured to a chair. "Have a seat. So have you found anything interesting?"

Ruth unbuttoned her red suit jacket, ignored the chair, and sat on the edge of his worktable, next to a stack of current scientific journals that he insisted on reading in hard copy. "Well the folks in cancer research say they have something from the Malabar Coast that will be the next best thing since rosy periwinkle, and they are getting a flood of marine organism samples. I'll keep my eye on them. But otherwise most of the government folks seem to be hashing through tired old compounds. What about you Bob? You always seem to have something."

Robert knew dozens of pharmaceutical company scouts. Though they liked to call themselves 'liaisons', Robert thought of them more as parasites trawling through publicly funded research looking for substances they could shepherd to market. But Ruth cultivated her relationships with government scientists so they more closely resembled a real partnership, or at least a pleasant opportunism.

"I'll tell you the same thing I told your competitors last week when they took me out for lunch," Robert said. As a government scientist – an ostensibly neutral party in the pharmaceutical pipeline – he was subjected to relentless influence peddling from the top pharmaceutical companies. Ruth represented Klaus Pharmaceuticals, the biggest of them all, the legacy of Josiah's great-grandfather, and he couldn't help but admire the company's turn-around man, Timothy Crosby, for leveraging her experience to Klaus' advantage. "I don't have anything definite." He paused. "There may be some intriguing possibilities on the horizon, but too soon to say." Could she hear the restraint in his voice?

"Possibilities? Like what?"

He paused again.

She reached out and pushed the door. It glided shut on a silent hinge.

"Bob, since when have you been able to keep anything from me?"

"Never."

She knew him as well as Sidney, in some ways even better because she had witnessed the period in his life when his personality was still a possibility, before the outlines of his professional identity had solidified. She could always sense when he was holding back, a perception undiminished by the months that had passed since their last meeting.

"I hate to talk about things before I am sure, you know that," he said. "But..."

"But I got a sample from a colleague, he sent it to me personally, so this doesn't leave my office, right?" He raised an eyebrow. She nodded. "The initial assays are promising, I mean, really promising. I've never seen initial results like this. Not just antiviral activity, it looks like viral annihilation."

Ruth leaned closer, her arms folded at her waist. "Really? Where did it come from? Is it from the Brazilian collections?"

Since she had helped negotiate a ten year billion-dollar plant prospecting deal between the Brazilian government and Klaus Pharmaceuticals, she was always hoping for breakthroughs from Brazil. The groundbreaking deal that promised the Brazilian government drug royalties in return for Klaus' exclusive access to Brazilian forests had made her a star in the pharmaceutical industry.

"Brazil? No, wrong continent. But I can't say more until I get the right papers. If I don't get a proper plant distribution agreement, the non-governmental organizations will string me up for stealing somebody's plant genetic resources. But I am anxious – to put it mildly – to get working on this."

She gave him her crooked smile, the same smile that had attracted him more than two decades earlier. "That's exciting. I will hope for the best for you, Bob. The best for us. Keep me posted, right? When will you get the papers? You know I am dying for something to take back to Timothy and my boys at Klaus. They are insatiable." She gave a low chuckle and swung the door back open. She made her exit with the same self-assured step he had seen when she left him at the university, heading off for her life in the jungles. He had known he couldn't stop that step. So he had never tried.

Chapter 8

Addis Ababa, Ethiopia

Zahara woke with the knock of the maid's hand on the door. For the first time since she had left Chochotte, she woke without disorientation. After six days of waking in Ato Worku's house, Zahara was starting to realize that she wasn't going back to her gojo, she wasn't going to sleep next to her father, she wasn't going to eat her meals with him…ever.

She rose, walked barefoot across Persian carpets into the kitchen. Orange juice had been squeezed into a glass pitcher, just as it had been each morning since she had arrived. There was only one glass set out on the table as Ato Worku had already left for the office. In silence she ate the scrambled injeera the maid had prepared for her.

Silence overwhelmed Ato Worku's house, a sterile lack of noise completely foreign to her. Perhaps he had been so quick to bring her here so she could beat back the silence; perhaps she would make a more pleasing sound than the expensive Japanese stereo in the living room. She had wondered when he called it that – the *living* room. If that was the living room, were the other rooms for the dead?

When Ato Worku had arrived that second time in Chochotte, he had been visibly shaken at Zahara's appearance. The weeping and worrying in the village were not what he had expected for this reunion. When he had found her in front of the burning gojo, he had embraced her, a wave of honest sorrow washing over him. Her long arms had hung limp at her sides. He whispered while her ear was still close to his face. "Come back to Addis with me." He had spoken the words before he even realized their meaning. He saw her now clearly, an orphaned child. "Daughter, it's not safe for you to stay here."

Zahara's cousins had eyed Ato Worku with fear. They feared he was responsible for their sorrow. Rumors that Ato Worku's men had killed Nataniel – rumors whispered first by Esmail – had shot through the village like lightning. But even more, Zahara's cousins feared that Ato

Worku would rage against them if they resisted his offer to take Zahara. The cousins argued amongst themselves for an hour. At last they agreed she should take the opportunity to leave Chochotte. *No one knows for sure who killed Nataniel. At least in Addis, you will have the opportunity to live a different life,* they had whispered, trying to reassure her as they gathered up her few things. Zahara sat numbly in Ato Worku's car, where her cousins placed her next to Nataniel's bookshelf with its contents bundled in an old gabbi.

Ato Worku had come because of the good news he had received. A few days after Ato Worku had returned home from Chochotte, he had worked up the nerve to send an anonymous driver to deliver a blood sample to an international clinic for testing. A different driver delivered the results: HIV negative.

That single piece of paper vindicated his risky decision to seek a cure in Chochotte. Although he could have sought the advice of any accomplished doctor in the world – after all he had lived among the faranji in London since the socialists came to power in Addis – he still did not trust them. In London he had seen businessmen, politicians, movie stars destroyed by revealed affairs or backroom deals. The oily secrets of their lives splashed across the front pages of the weekly tabloids. A man of his stature, he was sure, could not bear the risk of faranji and their publicity. A brilliant but anonymous village witchdoctor was a much safer option.

On an impulse he had taken his car and personal driver back to Chochotte, to express his gratitude. He had thought to choose a site there to build a school, or maybe a church, just for Nataniel's family. The churches he had built in Addis had burnished his public image nicely. He had not expected to return home with Nataniel's grieving daughter.

Perhaps fate – or maybe luck – had delivered Zahara back to the city her father had fled two decades earlier. Either way, it was not her choice.

She had been like a child when she first arrived at Ato Worku's house. Mute with grief, she had barely understood the servants' local accent. They looked at her with pity, showed her how to draw a bath, how to adjust the two levers mixing cold water with hot so she would not burn herself. They showed her how to ring the buzzer when she needed them, how to open the big chilled cupboard in the kitchen to find food if she was hungry between meals. Light switches, locks, windows, door handles, sheets and pillows, every luxury required a demonstration. She received their lessons without responding; only noticing the strange smell throughout the house. The air did not smell like a person, or a goat, not like the smell of a smouldering fire below a rising moon, nor like the smell of damp grass along the stream's edge. Ato Worku's house smelled of emptiness.

He had barely spoken to her the first week. He had observed her with what was – he told himself – a respectful distance. He did not want her to mistake his intention in bringing her here by being too forward. In truth, he feared how she might respond to any overture he might make. Her exuberant spirit could suddenly return and crowd out the loneliness with which he filled his life; just as possibly she could disappear and leave him with a new void in his life.

Exactly one week after she arrived he decided he would ask her to join him for dinner. He had just returned from his office and saw her sitting on her bed, turning the pages of her big reference book. He stood just outside the doorway to her room, hands clasped behind his back. He watched her unfold a worn piece of paper, run her fingers along the words. He took a deliberate inhalation in order to speak. She heard his breath, looked up at him, her eyes clear. Before he opened his mouth she delivered her first words to him as if they were a command. "I want to go to Addis Ababa University, if it is still here."

Ato Worku had influence in Addis. He knew most everyone who wore leather shoes and had a telephone on their desk; though he often pretended to forget the names of those he perceived as beneath him. He preferred to think that everyone knew him. In fact, most people, even people who had never seen him, never known what business had made him rich, knew his name. No fewer than three buildings on Bole Road, the tallest and shiniest three buildings in the capital, bore his name. All the faranjis and the rich Ethiopians who lived and worked in the embassies along Bole Road, knew the buildings housed the development banks, the aid agencies, and the few foreign commercial businesses that ventured into the horn of Africa.

When Ato Worku threw a party, everyone came, everyone had a good time, as his Scotch whiskey collection was unparalleled. With the exception of a few fellow coffee traders, though, none of Ato Worku's guests considered him more than a strategic relationship, certainly nothing resembling a friend. Although he shrewdly exploited the cruel structures of the international commodity markets, he was not personally cruel. He did not speak ill of people. He was not unlikeable – at least not until he got drunk – when he assumed the rude attributes common to most drunk men. He religiously read the front page of the Wall Street Journal which was flown in from Nairobi every day, so exuded a certain business sophistication. When he went to the Sheraton – the city's oasis of five star good taste – he ate injeera with lamb stew, paying an average Ethiopian's week's wages to have the simple food of his childhood. Still a bachelor in his mid-fifties, he worked, travelled and distracted himself with Scotch, loud music and frequent commercial sex. Ato Worku had largely failed at human relationships because behind the cufflinks and the cell phone, the cool demeanor and rudimentary charm, he was profoundly bland.

Ato Worku asked his secretary to put in a call to the dean of Addis Ababa University.

"Would you like me to have him call you on your mobile or your land line, Ato?" replied the secretary – the latest in a long line of secretaries. She wore her long hair fashionably braided in intricate woven patterns across the crown of her head. Despite her beauty, he hardly even looked at her.

"Make it the mobile. This is a personal call. And call my driver; I have a lunch meeting at Le Petit Paris Cafe."

Ten minutes later, Ato Worku was safely ensconced in the backseat of his Land Rover when the call came through.

"Ato Worku, it is a pleasure to receive a call from your office," the university dean said. "How are you these days? You are spending this month in Addis, so you will be here for Epiphany?"

"Yes Abebe, I prefer the holidays here to Christmas in London." The two had met over beers in a Brixton pub one damp Christmas when they were both studying in London. They had maintained cordial relations for nearly three decades based on the discovery that night of their common accent in a foreign country. "And you? How is your work? Your students are behaving?" Ato Worku's question alluded to the political unrest that seemed to brew perpetually at the university.

Inhalation, "For the time being all are well behaved. The university is preparing them all for a bright future," he said flatly. "To what do I owe this pleasure Ato?"

"I have a young woman I know – the daughter of a cousin – she has come to Addis recently. She is very bright and I think would be well served by some time at your fine university, Abebe. But if memory serves me correctly, this isn't the time of year to be enrolling. I figured you would know best how she might start her studies immediately."

"Well of course you are right; this isn't the right time of year. But perhaps something could be arranged. Does she have scores from entrance exams? If not, she can send me her past school records."

Ato Worku ignored the question, he quickly tired of civil servants and their fetishes for papers and records. "Excellent, perhaps we can all meet in your office on Friday? Noon. Then we can all have a nice lunch while you prepare her for her courses."

Abebe hated lunch meetings, especially on Fridays when his wife prepared Nile perch, but the meeting would give Ato Worku an opportunity to see how badly the dean's office needed repairs. Abebe knew he could count on Ato Worku to repay favors. "Yes, please come by with her. And bring those records, so we can process her application."

Ato Worku hung up the phone. He turned up the volume on the car stereo – heard again the American rhythm and blues beat that made him feel younger – and smiled to himself. He found distinct pleasure in making the world conform to his wishes. He felt a flutter in his stomach, a peculiar sensation of nervousness. He could not wait to bring Zahara out into his world. He wanted her to see him in control, here in his element, not as he had been, weak and helpless, in Chochotte.

Chapter 9

The maid brought a new dress and new shoes. Zahara had already filled a shoulder bag with the things she would need to get to the university and back: a notebook with directions, a map Ato Worku had sketched out, the course list that Abebe had handwritten during their lunch meeting the previous week, and a mobile phone. Ato Worku had shown her how to call up his name and the driver's name and dial the numbers. Only a carefully folded paper, her father's university diploma tucked inside the back cover of her notebook, linked her to her old life in Chochotte.

She stepped awkwardly into the passenger seat of the Land Rover, Ato Worku filling up the driver's seat.

He drove out through the labyrinth of lanes that surrounded his protected compound. From his enclave of luxury and wealth, they plunged into the pulsating city. Old Russian Lada taxis, public minibuses with men hanging out the windows – calling out routes for illiterate passengers – occasional herds of sheep, brought in from the countryside to be slaughtered in the city markets, all crowded the roads. The sidewalks spilled over with open air fruit stalls, shoe shine stands, endless rows of shops and offices. City people in western fashions and impractical shoes rushed with purpose along the cracked and crumbling pavement. Zahara felt dizzy at the life swirling around the car.

"The dean has enrolled you in a couple of basic courses, English, biology, and algebra. When you are caught up with the other students, you can add more courses." Worku attempted to chip away at the apprehension he felt in the car.

Only an inhalation interrupted her nervous silence.

"I went to Addis Ababa University myself," Ato Worku spoke to the silence. "It was brand new then, it was called Haile Selassie University. There were Americans from Utah and Oklahoma universities teaching us. We loved the Americans then, we would invite the professors to coffee at the new Ras Hotel. We sat on the sidewalk and talked about the outside world. I hadn't been abroad yet, but everything seemed possible."

"What did you study?"

He continued, encouraged by her words. "Economics. I wanted to know how I could help my country become wealthy. I certainly learned how to create wealth, as you can see." He patted the dashboard as evidence.

Silence. He wondered if he had lost her.

"There's the Ras Hotel, that's where we used to eat outside." Men loitered on the sidewalk selling biscuits and candies from cardboard boxes slung with straps around their shoulders. Ato Worku started to apologize for how shabby the hotel looked now, a ghost of its former glory. But Zahara craned her neck to look as they passed, exclaiming at the whiteness of the outdoor plastic chairs and tables.

"Where did you get the money to have coffee there?" she asked, still looking out the window.

"Money was never a problem with my family. My father was an attorney with the government. He taught me to focus on keeping the family prominent. He made sure I went to university. He was going to send me to America for university, but when the university was built here, it became fashionable to stay." He added, "Not like now."

"My father wanted to send me abroad as well." She seemed suddenly present with him in the car, eager at this newly discovered commonality. "He said a woman with an education could make fate kinder to her, she wouldn't be dependent on a husband. My cousins thought he was full of dreams, and I never wanted to leave Chochotte, never wanted to leave him. I never thought I would actually be going to university."

"You never left Chochotte?" Ato Worku imagined her life behind the wooden gate that encircled the village.

"My father took me to Jimma town once a year. We would have cold Coca Colas and buy things in the market. Once I took a trip with my cousins to Sidamo. We rode with a coffee trader who had business there."

They arrived at the gate to the university. He inched the car through as students begrudgingly gave way to his insistent honking. Zahara leaned her head close to the window glass, looking at all the people, all the doors and buildings on the campus. Ato Worku stopped at the end of the drive, worry wrinkling his forehead. He reached out to hold Zahara's hand and tried to imagine what a father would say to a daughter. "Good luck, don't talk to any of the men. The driver will be here at three. Call me if you need anything." He pointed to a building, "That's Menelik Hall, your first class is in there."

She squeezed his hand, fear flashing in her eyes, and did not move for a long moment. Then in a single gesture she turned, opened the door and stood on both feet. She took two steps forward, slammed the door behind her and strode on her long legs into the crowd of students without looking back.

Zahara imagined all the other students were staring at her. She wondered if they could they see her unfamiliarity with all the right angles, the new notebooks, the tumbling words of the professor's lecture. She ignored them all and looked either at the professor or her notebook. She wrote down as many of his words as possible, phonetically spelling words she did not know; she would ask their meaning later. The first hour passed. She asked the professor for directions to her next lecture – where she repeated her private performance, writing everything she heard. By the third class her hand was exhausted from the writing and her mind was filled with the overwhelming task of making sense of lectures midstream, courses midterm.

When she saw Ato Worku's Mercedes waiting for her, she practically cried with relief. The driver opened the door for her and she slid onto the seat's smooth new leather.

He looked at her curiously, asked "So sister, how was the first day at university?" He would never have spoken to any of the other women who came to Ato's house; the over perfumed, overweight wives of Ato's colleagues, or the over perfumed, underweight women from the bars of Kazanchis. He spoke with Zahara though, because she shared his Oromo accent.

Zahara, unaware of the correct protocol of servants and masters, spoke easily, knowing only that the driver was a safe, familiar presence. "I don't know yet. I had no idea it would be so difficult." He eased the car back out onto the road. "Chochotte school was always easy for me. The government teacher told my father I was the best student he had ever had."

"But that was Chochotte, sister. This is the best education in this country. It will take time."

She could not respond, suddenly overwhelmed with sadness. Maybe it was the way he said Chochotte, as if it were the distant edge of the world. She missed the familiarity of her neighbors, her cousins, the human feel of everything in the village, houses built by a single man, paths beaten by feet and hooves, leather made smooth by wear, only the towering trees suggesting a larger scale of creation. Where was her father? Could he see her now, alone in the vast sprawl of the capital? Was he proud of her entrance into the university? Ashamed that she had come to live in the home of a man he had distrusted? She turned away from the driver, silent tears obscuring the city in its afternoon brightness.

Chapter 10

"**A**to, what is the meaning of 'anarkee'?" she asked, pointing to the unfamiliar word transcribed in her notebook.

"It is chaos, no proper rules, no government. Like when Haile Selassie was overthrown. There were three days of anarchy, A-N-A-R-C-H-Y, before Mengistu's regime was established." He checked to make sure she wrote it properly. "Or when Ethiopia beats Kenya during the World Cup and the fans riot."

"Or when the servants can't get mangoes?" She smiled as she teased him.

"Zahara, mangoes are critical to the functioning of my business," he said with mock seriousness. "What else, what other words have you got?"

She looked back at her notebook, which had become a fixture of the evening meals they shared, a spiral bound bridge connecting their lives. The words she wrote down with her left hand, while eating with her right, stirred up his long forgotten memories of student life. Over the course of the semester he had sprinkled their conversations with his stories: about a woman whose notes he had copied, an inspiring philosophy professor, bawdy rhymes his classmates had composed to help memorize economic terms. By the end of the semester, a more youthful, irreverent Ato Worku appeared to her.

And he observed her sharpening focus, her curiosity about every lecture topic. He took pride in her progress, and took credit for molding her into a modern, educated woman. He so relished these extended meals, and his newfound purpose as her mentor, that he shortened his business trips and postponed his visits to the discos, lest he miss an opportunity to sit with her.

"That is all I have from the English lecture. But Ato, I'm worried about the algebra. It's too hard for me." She pulled her textbook next to her plate. "Our teacher in Chochotte wasn't good at math. He only did sums and multiplication. I can't follow what the professor is doing. I'm sure I will fail the exam."

"Fail? I'm sure you can't fail." Ato Worku looked at the opened pages in her book. The letters and numbers made his head swim. He had hated algebra. He understood the sums of his business – percentages, profit margins, exchange rates; but these letters and numbers represented nothing – no coffee, no money, no interest or risk.

"Let's see what you have here," he said running a finger along the page. The text instructed finding the value of x in terms of y. "Y, well you have y and you need to find x. Y...y...y. I'm not sure that I think y is important," he said leaning back and shrugging his shoulders.

"But Ato, I have to know what to do to pass this course."

"Yes, of course you should pass." He looked at the problem again, tugged his earlobe as he thought a moment. "I will find you a tutor."

"A tutor?"

"Perfect, a tutor." He leaned forward and closed her book. "I will find someone who can work with you privately on the algebra. Someone can come to the house and make sure you keep up with the professor. You won't fail the course."

Zahara's hand tensed around her pencil as she struggled over a linear equation. Elizabeth, her tutor, stood up and said, "Take a few minutes. There's no hurry. Stand up, walk around, look at it again. I won't hover."

Elizabeth stepped away from the big wooden table in the formal dining room where they had sat every other weekday for the last month. She wandered down the hall, past the gaudy bar and the ostentatious living room and into Ato Worku's cluttered home office. Elizabeth noticed her husband's business card, with the emblem of his American investment bank taped to the cradle of the phone on Ato Worku's desk. The bank had offices in the biggest tower on Bole road, and the two men had known each other professionally for years. Elizabeth's husband had mentioned Ato Worku's enquiry to her as an amusement, something to fill some of her long afternoons with something more important than the gossip of the other expatriate wives she knew in the capital.

"Elizabeth?" Zahara called out. Elizabeth returned to the big table. "I should have one answer, alone, right?" Zahara hesitated over her English, uncertain she had chosen the right word.

"For a linear equation? No, there isn't a single answer; in fact there are an infinite number of answers. The linear equation describes a line, a relationship between a pair of variables. It is only the relationship that stays the same, not the numbers."

"So the numbers change?"

"Yes, the numbers are always changing, depending on what point on the line you choose."

Zahara nodded slowly, letting out a slow hum of understanding. "But the relationship stays the same."

"It is sort of like a marriage, or a parent and child. The two people in a relationship both move along in their lives, so the line between them continually changes." She drew a horizontal line on a graph. "Imagine this is me." She drew a second line vertically. "And imagine this is my son. When he was born, we met at this point on the bottom left of the graph. As he grew up, he went this way on the graph. As I grew older, I changed too, in this way, out the graph. But we didn't grow away from each other, our relationship continued, like this." She drew a diagonal line.

"And does the line end?"

"A straight linear equation does not have an end point."

"And your relationship?"

"My son is at college now, almost a grown man, but he is still my son, just like you are still your parents' daughter."

Zahara looked away from Elizabeth, felt a hollowness inside her ribs. "My parents are dead," she said matter-of-factly.

Elizabeth shifted uncomfortably in her seat, unable to ask why or how. "You are still their daughter," she finally said quietly. "So now you determine how the relationship continues."

Zahara closed her book. Looked at her hands and said simply, "I will look at the equations again and show you my work next week."

Elizabeth gathered her things and they walked through the heavy, still atmosphere to the front door. Elizabeth stepped out, inhaled the cool evening air and turned around. "Let's meet next week at the British Council for our sessions."

"What is the British Council? I don't know where it is."

"It is like a library. It would be good for you to get out of this house. I will pick you up and we can go together."

The British Council, near the Piazza, was far from the few places Zahara knew in the city: the university, the Cathedral and Ato Worku's house. Elizabeth's driver dropped the two women in front of a two-storey building that had been new and modern three decades ago. Zahara and Elizabeth passed through the building's double set of glass doors into a cavernous room filled with rows of shelving. Zahara stopped short, just taking in the view of so many books, overwhelmed by the sheer number. She nearly forgot Elizabeth as she began walking down one aisle after another.

Beyond yards and yards of cheap paperback novels, were stacks of books with stiff bindings: books of distant lands, books of plants, politics, people, racks full of glossy magazines and international journals. She imagined the enormous world that would unfurl before her, the nearly infinite knowledge contained in all of the books surrounding her.

Elizabeth did not even mention the algebra they had planned to discuss. She just observed her pupil, with a kind of maternal pleasure. When their browsing converged on the same shelf, Zahara turned to Elizabeth, incredulous.

"There are more books here than in all of Addis Ababa University. Why?"

"The University is funded by the Ethiopian government. This is sponsored by the British government and the British community here."

The directness of Elizabeth's answer, the simple fact of the economic inequality struck her with a devastating force. She suddenly perceived the university her neighbors in Chochotte had held in such esteem as inadequate, unable to provide her the knowledge she would need to make her own luck, to make her way in the world her father had wished for her to see.

In the days that followed, she would come to the British Council over and over again, even without Elizabeth. She would browse all the aisles, eventually learning the library's layout, the order behind the shelving, the clustering of subjects. Eventually she would develop a particular fondness for the rack which held a long row of old National Geographic magazines. She would spend hours pouring over photographs and maps, trying to make sense of a planet she had only vaguely imagined. But more than the maps, she would be attracted to the foldout diagrams of inner worlds – DNA, viruses, the tiny universes contained within a single cell. These she would read word for word, probing each symbol or colored line until she could follow the flow of the whole spread. But on this first night in the British Council, she wandered the aisles, like an awestruck visitor exploring the streets of a foreign city.

Ato Worku returned home late, expecting to find Zahara reading yesterday's edition of the Wall Street Journal, or sitting in front of the television watching the BBC or the local news broadcasting the monotonous stories of coffee and sheep farmers.

Tonight, however, he found her wandering from room to room. She looked lost, even a little afraid. "You don't keep books," she said.

This he heard as both question and condemnation. "What do you mean?" he asked indignantly. "I keep very good books, ask my accountants."

"No. Books, Ato, things you can read, things with words and pictures. I came from Chochotte with two books, but that is more than you have."

He was embarrassed; he did not tolerate others exposing his shortcomings. "International business moves faster than books," he improvised. "I have computers and fax machines. I have access to everything I need to know."

"Everything you need to know to profit from buying coffee cheap and selling it dear."

The accusation slipped from her tongue before she could understand its sting.

He recoiled, blinked in shock. He raised a hand to strike her for her impudence, but she turned away from him, covering her face with her hands. The sight of her as she collapsed to the floor as if under the weight of an unseen burden, transformed his anger.

He reached for her, lifted her to the couch and pulled her in an embrace. "Life is unequal, my dear Zahara. Only God can know why one man has money and another man has a family."

"I have neither."

"You have both."

Chapter 11

In the months since Elizabeth's explanation of linear equations, the algebra concepts had come faster and faster to Zahara. Encouraged by her own comprehension, she did extra problems, stayed up late forcing herself to solve them faster than the day before. When Zahara greeted Elizabeth in the British Council on a warm Friday during Lent, she presented her tutor with a corrected exam, 91% circled at the top.

"Congratulations!" Elizabeth embraced her and then leafed through the exam. "I guess we have accomplished our objective."

Zahara inhaled.

"So I guess you won't be needing my tutoring, but perhaps we can continue to meet here once in a while."

"I would like to ask your help. Not algebra help. I would like you to help me please, for to go to university."

"You are already in university, Zahara."

"I want to go to university in America."

A smile spread broadly across Elizabeth's face. "An American university. Why not? Do you know which one?"

"A good one, where I can study biology and chemistry and medicine. I am hoping you can help me to know where to go and how to receive the acceptance."

"Well we have our work cut out for us then." Elizabeth pulled a notebook from her bag, turned to a clean page, and wrote out 'American university.' She began numbering the page for the steps they would have to take. "And Ato Worku," she said, "is he willing to pay the tuition?"

"It was my father's wish that I should go abroad, and Ato knows the debt he owes my father. I will ask him about the costs when I have the invitation from America."

"See, you are still your father's daughter," she said gently, "and clever, too."

Chapter 12

Zahara and Ato Worku sat quietly together in the Addis Ababa International airport cafeteria, oblivious to the noisy airline announcements echoing through the terminal. He stared at the plate of scrambled eggs and injeera they had shared and tried to comprehend just how he had come to this place, how he had found himself powerless to keep her from leaving.

He had long contemplated his power and influence in the world as a coffee trader dealing in vast sums of money. Because of him, Ethiopia's green coffee beans quietly circumnavigated the globe, part of a global commodity trade second in size only to oil. Worku and his fellow traders discreetly controlled the world – he had thought smugly – offering the critical substance that allowed people to get up and face the task of running the world's largest economies. In moments of self-grandeur, he had imagined a coffee embargo stopping the flow of the stimulating brew in coffee pots around the world. Mid-level clerks would go on strike, demand later starting times, productivity would drop among stock traders and teamsters, international markets would reel, demand for cocaine would soar, the arrogant Western world would come to realize the power they had given unconsciously to Brazil, Colombia, Kenya, Ethiopia, and by extension to him.

But this girl, a simple Ethiopian village girl, had subverted whatever power he had, convinced him that an invitation from an American university validated his efforts as her mentor. Her departure to America would be a logical next step in their mutual success, she had explained to him. He had enthusiastically agreed, even boasted of her enrollment to colleagues. But now, as the final minutes before her departure dissolved in the airport cafeteria, rather than congratulating himself on the success of his protégé, he could only scold himself for his weakness, letting her go so easily, willingly ushering her vitality out of his home and onto a plane.

Without ceremony – he was not accustomed to gestures of affection – he put a small box on the table. "These are for you. They were my mother's."

Zahara, equally unaccustomed to such gestures, simply opened the velvet box out of curiosity. The hinge squeaked to reveal a pair of gold hoop earrings, the ornate etchings of an Ethiopian jeweller worn, but visible in the soft yellow metal. She smiled and hung one and then the other in her ears. She was unfamiliar with the weight; most of her life, the holes her aunt had pierced in her earlobes had been filled with a loop of simple black thread to match the thread around her neck that marked her as a Christian. She swung her head back and forth so the metal knocked pleasingly against the sides of her neck.

"They look beautiful," Ato Worku said. "Please wear them all the time," he said with a note of resignation in his voice, "so you will remember me."

She only nodded, not trusting her own voice. In her eagerness to leave for university, intoxicated by the thrill of opening a door to another life, she had not anticipated the pain she now felt, sitting in a plastic chair about to abandon the only man in Addis who had known her father, a man who had welcomed her into his world. She reached out for his hands, to feel the warmth of his skin.

"And I expect you to write to me often, fax me, it's faster. You have the number." Ato Worku, almost embarrassed by the caress of her hands, picked up her boarding pass. "Make sure the flight staff get you onto your connection."

She ran her mind over the checklist of procedures he had explained to her about airports and government officials. She imagined a series of obstacles she had to hurdle before they would allow her into their gleaming country. She stood up and moved in front of him, towering above his chair. With a hand on each of his shoulders, she leaned down to kiss his cheek.

"Ato, thank you for all your kindnesses. Of course I will think of you often, my father in Addis. My papa would thank you too."

He could only scowl as he reached to hand her bag to her. She took it from him and slung it over her shoulder, feeling the weight of Stefano's field collection manual and a guide to the District of Columbia University she had packed for the flight. They walked together to the baggage screener, Ato Worku's hand on her upper arm. Wordlessly, she kissed him good-bye once more and then she and her bag moved in concert through the walkway and x-ray. A metal detector squealed over her belt buckle and then she was gone.

Chapter 13

Addis dropped away from view, a grey wound on the undulating landscape. The surrounding fields and forests emerged like the designs of stained glass windows in every shade of green. She had no idea her country looked like this, so beautiful, everything so small. She could hardly believe that their lives – covering the land with crops, living on the fringes of forests, all their struggles – could appear so silent and serene. She saw rivers cut into the land, deep gorges crackling out from the vast Lake Tana. Sunlight glinted off water, off the tiny silver specks of corrugated iron roofs. Every contour of the land was covered in the green velvet of vegetation. Had she ever seen such a luxurious thing? Soon the land fell away into low browns of dust and desert as the high shelf of western Ethiopia gave way to the desolation of Sudan. She wept. She had had no idea what she was leaving. She looked around the cabin for some way back, someone she could tell about the mistake she had made. But there was only the huge Nigerian woman next to her – already asleep – and the binding tightness of the seat belt across her hips.

Only the constant droning of the engines hinted at the progress of the journey. Hours of flying over the dull grey blue of the Atlantic, with no physical landmarks, no solid ground to offer perspective only heightened her sense of isolation, dislocation. Although hundreds of Africans surrounded her – Ethiopians, Somalis, Sudanese, Eritreans, Nigerians – accompanied her to the faraway land of America, she could not imagine their stories. The man who had been invited to an Islamic conference in Ohio, the woman visiting cousins in New York who planned to request political asylum, the young woman with dreams of supermodel fame, the stately gentleman returning to his Colonial three bedroom in Connecticut after a depressing visit back to his motherland, the man in jeans with a forged Somali passport stiff in his back pocket were all worlds apart from her. Even more distant were the couple of faranjis sitting among the Africans, haggard and resigned in their minority status, confident they were returning to their own people after tours of duty in Africa; Africa is what they would call it in America; for 'Africa' conjured up the outline of a great dark continent, so much more easily understood than 'Ethiopia' or 'Sudan'– specific places with histories and cultures that no one back home knew or cared about anyway.

Zahara carried on an elaborate rhetorical conversation with her father, who now seemed closer, as the distance increased. She – speeding through the stratosphere, he – moving only microscopically, his individual molecules decomposing to animate the myriad flora and fauna of Chochotte's soil. She wondered for the first time if he had been afraid to leave Addis Ababa, or rather, if he had been afraid of starting a new life in Chochotte.

Fear is a useless emotion, he would have said, she imagined.

But even after Mengistu's regime fell, you didn't return to Addis. Were you afraid of returning? Or afraid of leaving Chochotte?

This, he declined to answer, or perhaps she refused to answer for him, to imagine him as a man with fears.

You're right Papa, fear is a useless emotion. Had he really said that? Maybe when she had crawled up to him at the crash of thunder, her tiny feet pressing against his upper thighs, or maybe when he had thrown her into the stream so she learned to swim with the boys. If not then, surely when he had taught her to catch horned beetles with her bare hands. Or maybe he had never said it, had only let the meaning hang between his inhalations.

I was busy with my work; you were busy working with me, Zahara. A life of science requires stability, time to observe, to learn. The secrets of the world are not revealed in the blink of an eye, those who are busy travelling, those with unsettled lives only know the surface of things.

Her knees knocked against the red and orange upholstery of the seat before her. She lifted her hips and set her legs at a new diagonal.

But Papa, my life was unsettled by fate. She took up her own side. *I have to move, I am doing what you said I should, I will become an educated woman.* His approval – and only his – mattered to her, because she admired him, who he had been. Her desire, simultaneously crushing and liberating, would never be satisfied. She could imagine his approval, but would always suffer from the shadow of doubt.

She looked up at the projected map in the cabin that offered an imaginary arc of flight. They were close now. She looked around. At some point the passengers had been transformed. They no longer looked like the Somalis, Sudanese or fellow Ethiopians who had boarded with her. Now they were within the gravitational pull of America. Now their identities reflected the fashion of the ground beneath them, a hint of hip hop around the waist of jeans, a briefcase infused with suburban sturdiness. Headscarves disappeared. American names rolled off tongues. Whatever had bound them together, whatever common experience of Africa, of Addis Ababa that had been obvious twelve hours ago was now just vapor. It would evaporate when they walked off this plane and were absorbed into the America they imagined or knew, mythical or mundane.

Chapter 14

Washington, D.C.

"It's a beautiful spread, Dr. Ruth," Josiah gave her a wink, loved that her nickname brought to mind the slightly scandalous sex therapist who made the talk show circuits.

She winked back, amused at the opportunity to flirt with a university boy.

In the space of an hour he had watched her transform the lab from a work site to a sort of post-modern lounge. Cuban jazz music had replaced the hard rock in Josiah's stereo. A couple of spot lamps covered with silk scarves beamed mood lighting out of the ventilation hoods. The work surfaces of the black benches offered the buffet: trays of high end cheeses, roasted vegetables, and crusty breads, dwarf pears and blackberries, good chocolate, and of course, champagne – not cheap syrupy stuff, real champagne. Instead of champagne flutes, she had ordered a case of 250mL glass beakers, a humorous nod to the lab setting.

The whole scene testified to her adaptability. She could share a meal of mashed root from a communal pot with indigenous men in loin cloths as easily as she could share the soup du jour with corporate executives in monogrammed shirts and cufflinks. What men admired most about her, the men around the pot and the men sipping expensive soup, was her adaptability, her ability to make them feel as if she belonged with them, belonged to them in some effortless way.

Robert hung by his office door for a moment, savoring for a moment the way she had taken control of the lab, simultaneously adapting to it and adapting it to her purpose. This little celebration over their collaboration cleverly advertised both his achievement and the financial extravagance that she could offer – on behalf of Klaus Pharmaceuticals – for promising research. For him, the partnership served as a validation of his methods, a reward for nearly two years of work.

Ruth looked at the big white faced clock on the wall. She never wore a watch. Five 'til five. "Bob, we should open the door, people should be coming."

He turned the smooth steel handle and pulled open the big white door with its rectangular window of wire reinforced glass and the computer printed party announcement taped to the outside. When Bob turned back to look at her, he noticed that she had hung his framed photograph of the green leaf with the red veins from the cabinets above the food, spot-lit as if it were the patron saint of natural compound research.

The party was in full swing by the time Sidney arrived, the lab awash in men wearing khaki pants and primary colored sweaters – the unofficial uniform of official scientists. She found Robert in the middle of a cluster of chemists, next to the ventilation hood at the far end of the lab. Two men heatedly debated the differences between natural alkaloids and synthetic copies.

"But by the time you isolate the active compound, you may already have lost unknown synergistic effects with other substances in the plant," said a man with shaggy red curls.

"...a chemical compound is a chemical compound, theoretically there should be no difference," responded a visiting Chinese scientist.

Sidney knew from years of dinner table discussions with Robert, the arguments in the natural versus synthetic compound debate: if a synthetic compound varied from the original, in even in the twist of a single protein, a drug's usefulness could be significantly impacted, for better or worse. Source plant materials, on the other hand, usually contained such small amounts of active substances, that the market could demand wholesale deforestation to secure adequate supplies, or cost-prohibitive plant production programs. She enjoyed the intellectual glamour of the issues he debated, always a welcome contrast from her workdays spent baking experimental bread at the USDA food labs, measuring relative proportions of proteins, carbohydrates and fats.

Sidney greeted her husband and glanced around the room to see who had come. Sidney caught Ruth's eye from across the bench. Ruth ducked out of her conversation with an emeritus professor and came to Sidney's side.

"Sidney, so good to see you, it's been a long time." They shook hands, a four handed embrace.

"Ruth, you'll have to come to dinner soon. We are thrilled that you are going to be collaborating on Robert's new compound." An honest affection between the two had replaced long-faded jealousies. Their obvious differences had bred a confidence in each that there was no common arena in which they could compete.

"You're not the only ones," Ruth said. "I have convinced my board to go full force with this one. Our R&D portfolio for HIV drugs was struggling, but Bob's work puts us in a really strong position, and it is exactly the kind of breakthrough that Bob's natural plants division needs."

"You've heard about the last funding round then?" Sidney asked.

"Of course, it breaks my heart."

"One of Robert's graduate students decided to switch his thesis project because they couldn't get the money for lab space. Could this collaboration fund his project to get him back?" Sidney felt no shame in advocating for his needs.

"I did hear that. We should be able to slide enough money around."

A man in a pinstriped suit and crisp collared shirt walked in the lab, paused and scanned the room with a stone-faced expression. Ruth looked up, obviously surprised by the man's presence. "Sidney, please excuse me, that's Timothy Crosby from Klaus. I wasn't expecting him here."

"Of course. You have to make the rounds. Let Robert know when you are free for dinner."

The man's face opened into broad smile when he spotted Ruth walking toward him. "Look at you," he reached out and grasped her elbow in greeting, turning her around so she stood next to him. "You even know how to throw a party in a laboratory," he pronounced the last word in the British style, stressing the second syllable, subtly registering his low opinion of the room's dynamics.

"Yes, clearly this la-BOR-a-tree is exciting," she said, mimicking him. "I didn't know you were coming, didn't know you even knew where Robert's lab was."

He looked down at her, arched one eyebrow. "I make sure to know a lot of things that might surprise you."

She stepped back, unbalanced by his tone.

"And I wanted to get a sense of Robert's territory," he leaned in to whisper to Ruth, as one would tell an inside joke, "wanted to see where Klaus' next billion dollar drug is coming from."

Chapter 15

Zahara closed the door to her dorm room, turned the key in the lock and walked deliberately down the stairs and out the building's main entrance. She cut across the quad toward her lecture hall on the far side of campus. After two weeks of consulting her maps and repeatedly asking directions, she could now make her way around campus without hesitation.

America, so obviously different from Addis Ababa, had nevertheless defied all Zahara's expectations. The taxi driver who had driven her from the airport shocked her by speaking English with an Amharic accent and giving her the address of an Ethiopian church in the city. The dormitory she shared with an African American political science student, with its painted cinder block walls, was not as opulent as she might have imagined. But then the everyday places – public bathrooms and bus stops – appeared formal beyond their purpose.

The excitement and euphoria she had anticipated in the weeks before her departure from Ethiopia had not materialized. She had first felt American soil beneath her, had first breathed in the air of Washington, D.C., had first heard the American accented announcements in the airport through a protective shroud of numbness.

So now, as she walked town the tree lined footpaths, past lecture halls and libraries, she viewed all of the different kinds of people from some inexplicable distance. Students of more skin colors, hair colors, and shoe colors than she could have imagined did not notice her in turn. Occasionally other students would smile at her, but nobody initiated conversation with her.

She had decided last night that she would enter the coffee shop she had seen on campus. Just a few steps off the sidewalk the shop appeared like a vision of warmth and community. She opened the glass door reverently as one might enter another's church. The atmosphere that swirled through her senses exceeded the impression offered through the glass from the sidewalk. There was furniture – as if she had walked into someone's living room – there was music, there were cookies the size of pies in cheerfully lit glass cases and people eating chocolate croissants twice the size of her fist. A black signboard with colourful writing chirped about the coffee of the day: Ethiopian coffee from Sidamo. The familiar smell of coffee filled her lungs.

She ordered a cup.

"Anything else? That'll be $2.75" the girl behind the counter said. Zahara held out three dollars to her as if paying homage at the altar of coffee. *Three dollars to take me back to my country, three dollars for the memory of roasting beans on an iron griddle, three dollars for the stories my father told me over tiny shared cups of coffee, three dollars for a taste of the days before everything changed.* The girl handed Zahara her receipt, looked irritated when Zahara did not move. The girl had to explain that customers must wait for their coffee at the far end of the counter past the case with pie-sized cookies.

Zahara moved, trying not to look awkward. She waited at the counter, beside a basket overflowing with packages of Sidamo Ethiopian coffee. She picked up one of the packages; hard as a brick, vacuum sealed in plastic so shiny she thought she could see the reflection of her eyes. No smell. The price tag read twelve dollars fifty cents. Twelve hundred fifty cents, three hundred Ethiopian birr, enough to keep her and her father eating injeera, their beloved sour pancakes, for a year.

"Ha!" The sound erupted from her, unbidden, shattering the respectable chatter around her. People looked up from their newspapers, paused in their coffee covered conversations, to look at this tall woman laughing at a plastic bag of beans. *Americans! Crazy! They are paying twelve dollars fifty cents for a bag of coffee, as if it were gold.* "Ha!" She looked around at the faces that had turned to look at her; disturbed, indignant, curious. She moved toward the door, without sugar, without cream, weaving her way past the Americans and their mugs of overpriced coffee.

Out on the sidewalk the coffee's bitterness pierced through her numbness. Her father would have scolded her if she had burnt the beans as these had been. She felt her three dollars had been stolen. Instead of enjoying a brewed visitation to her country, visions of the coffee beans themselves haunted her. Beans in the calloused hands of her aunts and uncles, beans assembled into bricks of gold in coffee shops across this city. She looked at the cup in her hand, and let it fall into a concrete garbage can.

Shame. Shame that she had wasted three dollars. *Do not worry that we are not rich with money, we are rich in spirit,* her father had told her as he mended his own shirt, as he fed her gristly lamb stew for Epiphany. Shame at the memory of Chochotte's women – not a gram of gold among them. Shame at the knock of the gold earrings against her neck – and this life that Ato Worku's wealth had made possible. She wanted to escape, to get out of her own body. She wanted to leave this shame, this untenable life behind. But with every step, her feet followed. With each breath, air expanded the lungs still inside her chest. She walked faster to make it to her class on time, trapped within her own skin.

She walked into Franklin lecture hall, just as she had done a half dozen times before, and picked a seat in the middle of the fifth row. As she opened her notebook to the biochemistry section and reached for a pen, her professor announced that he would not be giving the lecture today. "Instead, we have the honor of a guest lecturer," he said. "Dr. Robert Kresovich from the National Institutes of Health is here. I ask him to come every semester to give my class a feel for what a real live working biochemist does for a living. He's been getting pretty famous recently, so I don't know if I will be able to keep convincing him to come and give this lecture. But as long as my luck is still good, please welcome Dr. Kresovich."

A middle aged American man came up to the podium. He pointed with a remote controlled clicker and a photograph of a lush jungle flashed on a screen at the front of a hall. "Plants!" he said. "Plants are the richest single source of medicine in the world. Nearly 25 percent of the medicines we consume today are substances that were originally invented by plants. Plants around the world have done incredible work testing and refining chemicals. The work for a biochemist like me, is finding those plant tested chemicals that are also useful against human diseases."

Robert's images of South American jungles abruptly switched to images of his lab – with its dozens of high tech machines that – he explained – screened mass quantities of plant samples. It all looked so complicated; Zahara tried to imagine what might happen inside the machines that filled the lab in the photos. He continued lecturing against backdrops of photographs taken through microscopes, photographs representing genetic fingerprints, photographs of strange and unfamiliar things.

Dr. Kresovich continued, "We have had some successes with our high throughput screening techniques, but this is the one we are really exited about." He pressed the remote control again.

She gasped.

Inhalation. Surprise. Affirmation. Oxygen to sustain her concentration. She was face to face with a giant projected image of the green leaf with the scarlet veins. The same leaf that she and her father had gathered in Chochotte. Her shame melted away. The students around her looked to see what was wrong, what had happened. Even Dr. Kresovich looked up to see if there was some emergency. No one knew what that anonymous gasp meant. But Zahara knew exactly what she was seeing. She felt – for the first time since she had arrived in America – a familiarity, an overwhelming certainty that she knew exactly where she was.

She could hardly concentrate on the rest of the lecture. She put her notebook back in her bag. Even before the lecture was over, she stood up and climbed over half a dozen students to get to the aisle. Eyes turned to watch her, but she did not notice them. She walked deliberately to the front of the lecture hall to stand and wait for Dr. Kresovich to finish.

When he finished and the lights came back to full, he saw her. He smiled distractedly, put up a finger – indicating she should wait one minute – and started speaking to the professor. She did not move. She stood perfectly balanced on two feet, she made no gestures of nervous impatience, did not fidget with her bag or move an imaginary hair into place. She just stood waiting.

Robert was surprised that she did not step back, slightly irritated at her implied insistence. *Do I know her?* He excused himself from the professor and turned again to Zahara. She stood there like an African queen. He did not actually know any African queens, but imagined if he did, they would look like this. Her skin looked like velvet, the color of the bitter powdered chocolate of expensive truffles. Thin, curving hips seemed to hover above her legs – impossibly long legs – and her eyes looked down on him from above spectacular cheekbones.

"Hello. What can I do for you?" he said, trying not to feel intimidated by her physical presence.

"I'm here because of the leaf photograph in your lecture. It's from my village."

"I'm sorry?" He heard her words, but could not comprehend any rational meaning behind them. He knew the world from which his samples came, knew that it shimmered upon the earth like a series of miracles. Aside from Ruth's stories about the semi-mythical Indians of South America; men who could shoot a blow dart into the eye of a flying bird, men with sharpened teeth, tribal people who worshipped plants and the spirits that inhabited them, Robert understood the world of his samples to be inviolably separate from the world of humans. Particularly separate from the world of people who – on any given day – would show up in a lecture hall and stand before him.

"I know Stefano Geotti. Do you?" Zahara demanded.

Robert stood completely dumbfounded. She thought he might not have heard her, so she offered, "He is an Italian."

Robert leaned his head slightly forward, "I'm sorry, have we met before?"

"No. Not yet. I am Zahara Katani. I'm an Ethiopian international student."

"And you say you know Stefano Geotti?"

"He came to my village, Chochotte. It was more than two years ago. I told him about the leaves of that tree, the one you are having in the photograph."

"Please, can we step into the corridor?" he was stalling for time, trying to find his bearings in this disconcerting conversation.

She pushed open the door at the front of the lecture hall; most of the students had already filed out the back. He was looking at her intently, curiously. "Zahara, like the desert?"

She nodded.

"Please tell me a little bit about yourself."

In the coolness of the corridor she felt something unknown in her chest. The first flutter of proof that she existed in America – someone was listening beyond the first few words she said. So she spoke, short declarative sentences at first, "My father was the doctor in Chochotte.

He was first a pharmacist. He taught me things no one else knew. Things about plants, about healing." As the faranji continued to listen – she wondered if they were still faranjis in their own country – her speaking gained momentum. "First he was in Addis Ababa, where he finished the university. But when the socialists come, he did flee to the highlands. I was born there. My mother was from Chochotte, but she did die when I was born. There still is no clinic in Chochotte."

Robert nodded, concentrating on the formal pronunciation of her words, imagining the things they represented. She tumbled on. Robert gathered that her father had done his own prospecting in the forest. He had followed the common folk remedies he had learned from an old woman, but then came the sickness. "I guess it was HIV," she said. "We had no way to know for sure. No one called it that, maybe when you call a disease by its name, you give to it power. Maybe the people who came to Chochotte really did not know. First, they all died. I hated it when so many people came, only to die. We must to send word for their relatives to come and take the bodies back. But then one man lived and my father was so happy. He told me what he had done, he used that leaf. It is very strong medicine."

At last she had swung around to the point where their lives intersected and Robert was able to speak. "Your father was right. I have been looking at thousands of plants, looking for anti-viral activity. And I do know Stefano Geotti. He is the one who made it possible for me to study this. This is the most exciting thing I have worked on. It could be a very important medicine for keeping people alive."

"My father didn't only keep people alive, he made the illness to go away."

Robert smiled, the slightest bit of condescension turning down the corners of his mouth. "So far no one is talking about cures, Zahara. The best we can do is keep the virus at bay."

"No, I am sure, the illness was gone."

"Your father is still using the leaf medicine for HIV?"

"My father was murdered."

This caught Robert off guard. He started to reach for her hand to comfort her, but paused mid gesture, as she threw his balance even further.

"But he would say to you that you only have one part of the medicine he used to drive away the illness. Without the rest, you will only kill people."

Chapter 16

"Ruth," a colleague stuck his head in her door, "did you get the draft design for the clinical trials?"

"Yes, thanks. I have just opened it. I should be able to send my comments along tomorrow."

"Tomorrow?" he said, "I am hoping to send them back to the FDA by close of business today."

"All right, let me see what I can do," she said.

Through the windows of her corner office – Timothy's recent reward for her research discovery – she could see the noonday sun reflecting off a slice of the Potomac. On her desk stood a picture of her – nearly twenty years earlier – with her beloved mentor, Dr. Schultes. In those days, Bob, jealous of the attention she lavished on her professor, had complained *he* was her lover not Schultes. Next to the picture a silver tray with her business cards confirmed her current status: Ruth Toll, Director - Natural Compound Research and Development. The woman in the photo would never have imagined the view from a corner office.

Ruth had been one of Schultes' brightest protégé's at Harvard. She had followed his example with ambitious abandon. She spent as many summers and research stints as she could in as many wild backwaters as she could reach by dugout or on foot. He himself was regarded as a renegade in the early years of his work. In a time when synthetics from sterile laboratories held the promise of cures for every disease, his grungy field notes and penchant for ingesting the hallucinogens that illiterate shamans offered him seemed unorthodox, at best.

But when those sterile laboratories started confirming the effects written in his field notes, he became something of a pharmaceutical guru. And she became one of his most devoted followers. Whenever she came back to the university, she published prolifically, as if her survival depended on it. She wanted the world to know what was in the places she had been.

Schultes, who knew the pharmaceutical industry's constant need for new ideas, might not have been surprised that her ambition landed her a corner office at Klaus.

She moved aside the other work she had been doing to focus on the clinical design trials. A light on her phone lit up with a ring. "Yes?" she answered.

"Dr. Kresovich is on the line," Ruth's secretary chirped, "He says it is urgent."

"Thank you, put him through."

"Ruth, it's Bob. Are you in the middle of something? I think we need to talk, there is someone you need to meet."

"Now? What is it?"

"It's either awful, or incredibly good luck. Can you meet me, meet us, at the Irish pub? Now?"

"Who is it?" she asked, irritation hovering in her voice.

"It's a young woman from Ethiopia. We may have problems with our compound. Just say you'll be there, please."

Bob, always letting his fears get to him. "I'm sure everything will be all right Bob. What do you need me for?" She marvelled that he had never outgrown his constant need for calming and reassurance. In the last year of their relationship she found the more she knew of his fears – fear of flying, fear of her flying, fear of foreign countries, fear of strange food, and on and on – the more she wanted to go to places where no one worried about the things Bob feared.

She glanced out the window, figuring from the noonday sun that she could probably meet Bob and his young woman, calm him down and be back in time for her afternoon meeting. The trial designs would have to wait. "Which Irish pub, Bob? O'Reilly's?"

"Uh huh."

"Order me a shepherd's pie and a Guinness, but I will be gone before dessert."

"Fine."

She reached for her bag, her essential travel accessory with its pockets for everything; notebook, pen, passport, Swiss army knife (with corkscrew), extra pair of underwear (she was prepared for every possibility), and the obligatory phone and files for navigating the world of Klaus Pharmaceuticals.

On her way out, she knocked on Timothy Crosby's open door at the end of the corridor, leaning into the CEO's corner office. "Timothy, I have a lunch appointment. I'll be back for the board briefing."

"All right, I expect you won't be late." For a moment he envisioned closing the door, pressing her up against the wall and running his hands over her hips. Instead he ran a hand over his closely cropped hair. "The board is eager to hear about Robert's compound, and I will be sure to mention your skills as an impresario, even in a la-BOR-atry."

She smiled at his compliment. "Yes, I won't be late." She turned away, feeling his eyes on her backside as she swiped her magnetic card over the security door next to his and walked out. Their mutual admiration had elicited a few remarks from her secretary. His buttoned-up brilliance, packaged with good looks and designer suits perfectly complemented her adventurous worldliness. With patents on the company's best selling drugs set to expire in a few years and a dearth of new drugs in the pipeline, he had offered her an outrageous salary, hoping to harness her instincts and Latin American contacts to drive their flagging research and development. A year later Klaus Pharmaceutical shareholders continued to approve of the unconventional choice, buoying stock prices. A successful turnaround.

Zahara drank large quantities of dark brown beer because the food was so salty. Her thirst persisted, but she felt warm and dreamy tucked into a dark, high-backed wooden booth between two faranjis. Ruth. Like in the Bible. Zahara liked the way the woman sat down next to her, acted as if they were already friends.

"So Zahara, what's Ethiopia like? I haven't been to that part of the world, yet. Got stuck in this hemisphere I guess."

"It's green. Yes, so green, and lots of mountains."

"Do you miss it?" Ruth had seen people from third world villages, confident and knowledgeable in their home setting, fairly crumple when they had come to the US for the first time. But this girl seemed confident, if a bit humorless.

"Of course I miss it; I miss my village, my father. But he isn't there anymore."

Robert cut Ruth off before she could ask Zahara more about her father. "Ruth, Zahara's father was very close to our work. In fact, you might say he was responsible for our work."

Ruth raised her eyebrows.

"My father was the closest thing we had to a doctor in my village. He had studied at Addis Ababa University, he was a pharmacist. The leaf that you are working on, it did come from my village. When he started using it on the people" she hesitated, "the people with HIV, who came to him, some of them survived."

"Yes, I think Bob has found the same thing."

"But they not only lived, they were," she hesitated again, "cured… when my father used the leaf medicine. But you need to know there was also something else, without that, they died, maybe from the medicine, not the sickness."

"Zahara, HIV is an incredibly sophisticated virus. No one has found a way to cure it yet. I'm sure you're father has helped people, but you can never be sure about a cure."

"My father was sure."

Ruth leaned forward, cocked her head in a way that reminded Zahara of chickens examining grain that turns out to be pebbles. "Were you able to do blood tests to confirm?"

Zahara didn't answer the challenge. The pressure in her bladder was giving her dreamy state a decidedly unpleasant edge. "Excuse me," she said. Robert slid out of the booth and pointed toward the restrooms as Zahara slid past him, stood up and walked away.

When he sat back down, Ruth looked peeved. "Bob, what's she saying, her father had some other miracle drug? Do you know how many slightly educated 'medicine men' come up with cures that are completely bogus?"

"No, that's not my specialty."

"Well let me tell you. I knew an old medicine man that a whole village depended on who claimed he could drive out malaria spirits. People he 'cured' would look better for a few days, go out hunting, and fall down dead in the forest. OK? HIV is even trickier than malaria. Most traditional medicines are the result of generations of trial and error. But HIV is still a young disease. Her father may have stumbled on something, the same thing we have. But not by design, he got lucky."

"Why not? He was trained as a pharmacist."

"Bob, please. Where was he trained? The local university? I read obscure magazines, you know? Third World Resurgence, FolkWays, the

Wisdom Bee, little rags that colleagues in the field pick up sometimes. They are chock-a-block with technologies that villagers can duplicate, things they don't need to buy from international corporations. There are usually one or two cures for HIV, some guru in southern India, some renegade veterinarian in Thailand, distributing their cures for free. But they aren't real. They're just hopeful myths for desperate people. It's a shame because those guys can discredit legitimate and useful traditional knowledge."

She cut herself short, looked up with a smile as Zahara walked toward the table. Ruth noticed other people in the restaurant looking up at the grace of Zahara's long gait, in jeans too stylish for a village girl.

"Dr. Toll, yes?"

"Call me Ruth."

"Dr. Ruth, what is your work? Dr. Robert said you could explain better."

"Well, I am what is called an ethnobotanist or an ethnopharmacologist. I specialize in studying traditional plant medicines used by different cultures, especially in places far from western medicine."

"So you help heal people in those areas? You work with the sick?"

"Not exactly." Ruth took a swig of beer, "I work more with the healers. I document their medicines and how they use plants and natural ingredients."

"Then what happens?"

"In the past, I have brought back plant samples. They go to a laboratory and other scientists – people like Bob – analyze the materials to see if there are active chemicals in them."

"To make medicines out of them?"

"Exactly." Zahara's quick grasp of the process impressed Ruth.

Zahara, still – save for the expansion and contraction of her lungs – paused for a moment preparing her words. "So do you know how to care for a person who is sick? Can you bring water for a person with fever? Have you cleaned a person of his filth?" Zahara leaned closer to Ruth, lowered her voice out of respect for the dead. "Have you held the hand of someone afraid of their sickness? Cared for them until they dead? Held orphaned children who trusted you to save their mother?"

Zahara's unexpected challenge silenced Ruth.

"This is what I did with my father. Can you know how our lives changed when he came to know how to make medicine for these people?

Thanks God. People were cured and walked away with their families. If you want to help people, you can listen to me, to know what my father knew. But you cannot tell me it did not to work. He was murdered because it did work."

The air between them drained of any warmth. Ruth could not look Zahara in the eye, focused instead on Zahara's gold earring. "I'm sorry. I meant no disrespect to your father." She glanced at Robert's watch. "I hate to say this, I want to talk about this more, but I have to get back to a board meeting." She turned to Robert, "Bob, thanks for calling me. Can we continue this over dinner, tomorrow maybe?" She attempted a smile. "We can all meet at my place."

"I can't tomorrow. Sidney and I have plans. But maybe you and Zahara can meet without me. She and I have already talked all of this through."

"Zahara? I can pick you up."

"If you think it's necessary."

"Necessary? The conversation or the ride? Both are necessary. Here's my card. Please call my secretary and tell her where I should meet you. Sorry, Bob. Say hello to Sidney." She was as ready to leave as she had been to come. Bob and Zahara sat in an unsatisfied silence as Ruth paid the bill on her way out.

Chapter 17

B ack in his office, Robert sat in front of his computer, a blank outgoing email before him, desperate to know more about what Stefano knew. Had he collected the fungus Zahara claimed was essential? Was she right about its ability to mitigate the toxicity of high doses of leaf extraction? Robert's own toxicity trials were still weeks away from producing any meaningful results.

In principle, Robert had no faith in folk wisdom. Western scientific inquiry had yielded more miracles than any other method. His faith in the scientific method bordered on religious zeal. Good drugs had been found in wild plants and animals that no shaman or medicine man knew about; rosy periwinkle to treat cancer, calanoids from a Malaysian hardwood in HIV clinical trials, AZT derived from a chemical in a Caribbean sea sponge. Humans had been endowed with an intelligence to discover the secrets of the natural world, and western science was the most evolved demonstration of that intelligence. In his belief system, credentialed scientists were the only priests he could trust.

But there was something in what Zahara said, or maybe it was the way she had said it. She had a certainty from seeing with her own eyes, feeling with her own hands. She had an elegance that completely baffled him. He wondered how she had arrived here from an Ethiopian village, but had not yet bothered to ask her.

His fingers banged out an email to Stefano that was not altogether coherent, nor altogether polite. He was afraid. What had appeared to be a great breakthrough drug – and a huge boost for his career – now teetered on the precipice of some unknown. He knew of potentially good drugs – drugs that could save peoples' lives – scrapped because they proved toxic in a few test subjects. He didn't know if he could survive such a disappointment. He wanted to get home to see Sidney. He hit send and stared at the screen for a minute. If Stefano were at a computer somewhere in the world at that moment, he could see Robert's note and reply immediately. But the computer oracle offered no wisdom. So Robert tried to bundle his crashing career scenarios along with his uneaten lunch into his black nylon lunchbox. Sidney would unpack both the food and the fears and deal with them.

Zahara stared at the green lights of her roommate's clock glowing 3 am. A thin line of light seeped in at the base of the door, the thumping music down the hall had stopped at least an hour ago.

Three weeks in America. And today was the first time she had had a real conversation with Americans. She felt like all the students at the university knew each other, the people in her dorm flitting back and forth between each others' rooms like bees to blooms. They all dressed alike in new clothes, carrying futuristic looking bags with books and cell phones. People had said hello, asked Zahara her name and her major. When they heard her accent, they would ask where she was from. When she told them, they ran out of questions, looked at their watches and said they were late for class, or had to meet someone, or had 'tons of reading to do. See you later.'

Her isolation settled into the bedsheets, enshrouding her like the dead. An isolation born not of loss, but of an obliteration of her past. Her father – stolen from her. Her village – not even on the maps in this country. Her country – nothing more than a twang of guilt to the people she met. She had not taken off the gold earrings since she arrived, felt their hardness against her neck as she lay in bed, a thin link to a familiar place and a man perhaps lonely for her. Although she had written to Ato Worku almost everyday, she had not yet sent the letters. She would send them when she could describe her life her in a way that would make him proud.

She rolled onto her side, heard her roommate's regular breathing in the bed across the room. She saw pairs of shoes lined up under the bed, a chairful of unworn clothes. She reminded herself to close her eyes. Sleep would never come with all this staring about. She closed her eyes, only to see the image of the leaf in her mind's eye. The leaf grew into the whole tree, one of the trees that had sheltered Nataniel, Stefano, the people who had populated her old life. Maybe she had made a mistake, maybe she should have stayed in Chochotte, never gone to Addis, never come to this cold place where she knew no one, where everyone was rude in their politeness. *At least in Chochotte I knew where I was, what I was doing, I had my cousins, my family. I have betrayed my father, abandoning him in the Chochotte ground.* She felt the pressure behind her eyelids, forcing out two tears that ran down the left side of her face and disappeared into her pillow.

Chapter 18

Thailand

While Robert's message to Stefano sped through fiber optic cables across the planet, Stefano suffered from the chili fire of northeastern Thai food, far from the nearest computer screen. His discomfort brought great amusement to his hosts, old women with blood red lips framing blackened teeth – the result of years of betel nut chewing. Stefano, nearly twice as big as any of these tiny women whose families had been eking out a living on the stingy soils of the *Isaan* plain, nevertheless felt as helpless as a small child. The old women laughed with open mouths, handed him little balls of sticky rice. After three days here, he still had to be reminded that rice would tame the chili burn better than water.

Aside from this gastronomic excitement, the villages in the region were notably dull. The music of Isaan – almost exclusively sad ballads – consisted of pining over faraway loves and the grinding poverty of the region's rice farmers. Most Isaan women either fled or were lured to the bars of Bangkok, Pattaya and the southern tourist islands as soon as their bodies curved enough to excite the opposite sex. Young, ablebodied men soon followed, to drive taxis in the capital. The remaining population – mostly old women, children and drunk men – made for pretty limited social exchanges.

Thankfully, the mission had been professionally fruitful. Stefano had collected nearly two hundred samples of rice varieties. Most had come off the heads of scraggly little plants that barely battled their way out of soil so salty, it could season popcorn.

Stefano understood that priceless genes, selected by generations of observant farmers, made such agricultural feats possible. Isolate those genes, engineer them into wheat and suddenly a whole dry swath from North Africa to western China would bloom into a breadbasket. Plant breeders sought genes like these, genes adapted to salty soils, like a holy grail. Did the old women around him have any inkling, Stefano wondered, what they had stewarded in their rice baskets through all those lean years, those sad times when their children begged for more rice to eat with a bit of salty fish sauce?

He popped another rice ball in his mouth, nodding with gratitude to the woman who had offered it from her open palm. As the chili burn radiated out from his reddened lips he digested the irony of evolutionary adaptation. Genetic riches offered by the poor.

He wiped his hands on a bandana, signalled to his hosts he had had enough and stretched his legs out from his perch on a tiny plastic stool. Tomorrow, he and his translator would drive to the regional airport in Khorat and make the quick hop back to Bangkok with their samples bundled into plastic trunks. Soon enough he could leave the laughing old ladies of Isaan for the giggling young beauties of Isaan in Bangkok.

Bangkok's elevated commuter rail, more than a decade in the making, whisked Stefano through the city's skyscraper canyons, in air-conditioned comfort high above the gritty streets. He tried to remember his last visit to Bangkok – probably for his institute's regional conference in the mid 1990's. He had found the Thai scientists adept at adapting existing technologies for their own purposes, if not inventing their own. But his lingering memories of Bangkok stemmed from the senses, not the science.

He had experienced the city at that time from street level. Watched in the early morning as young Buddhist monks walked the streets during their daily ritualized begging. Crass-looking street vendors, selling skewered pork had placed rice and vegetables in the monks' bowls, under the long shadow of gleaming high rise buildings where bankers in western suits had funded wild speculation in the real estate market. Stefano had perceived in those pre-crash boom years the permissiveness, the flair for the outlandish and the extravagant that made Bangkok irresistible for tourists and tycoons alike.

After three station stops, Stefano stepped out into the oppressively hot air and down three flights of stairs to the seething energy of Patpong, Bangkok's infamous red light district. That first time in Bangkok, he had come here and pressed through the flow of people and knock-off goods and felt himself carried away by a river of possibility. Anything could be bought for an evening: a Rolex watch for ten dollars, a Louis Vutton briefcase for twenty and a smooth skinned young lover for fifty. So he had purchased all these seemingly innocuous pleasures.

Patpong's two blocks had not changed, the garish neon signs undimmed by the economic crash. Stefano floated again along a river of possibility past dozens of quasi-legal establishments with evocative names like the Pussy a Go-Go. He stepped into the Siam Girl Galore, allowing his eyes a minute to adjust to the dim light. Chrome-topped tables surrounded spot lit stages where slender girls of otherworldly beauty gyrated their hips against metal poles. Patrons could request the company of a girl from the *mamasan*, identifying one individual from another by the numbers pinned to their bikini bottoms.

Stefano ordered a Thai beer, surveyed the stage and requested Number 51 – attracted as much by her complete lack of guile as by the perfect roundness of her breasts or the ideal proportions of her hips and waist. She seemed to drift over to his table, where the mamasan loudly reminded her in Thai to ask for a Coke to start running up his tab. He asked her name. Number 51 just smiled. He asked her where she was from. Number 51 smiled again. Number 25 floated over in her red satin bikini and knee high leather boots. She ordered a Coke, then translated back and forth into broken English. Number 51, also known as Noi, he learned, had just come to Bangkok from Isaan, a village near Khorat. She had just turned 18. Number 25 smiled, put her arm around Noi's waist. "Does Mister like her, want to pay bar fine?"

Stefano chuckled to himself that the girls referred to the transaction as a fine, like some kind of penalty for his desires. He pulled out four bills for the mamasan – the image of Thailand's king peering out at him from the banknotes. Stefano easily recognized the monarch's image from the signs at the gates of royal sponsored agricultural projects around the country. He chuckled again that the image of such a virtuous monarch graced this exchange for pleasure services.

The mamasan smiled at her four kings. "You lucky man. Noi new in bar. She virgin."

He looked at Noi, she smiled and walked away, displaying her stunning backside to him. The mamasan turned to him. "She get dressed and come back."

"I'll wait outside. Thank you." He smiled ruefully at the mamasan's claim of virginity. He had heard it the last time he had passed through Patpong. Instead of the naked pleasure of deflowering a virgin, he had ended up with a painful bout of the clap.

In the hotel room, he turned off all the lights, save one lamp by the bed. He liked to be able to see a women, to enjoy the play of shadow on skin. Noi quickly began to undress. Stefano stopped her. He sat on the edge of the bed and tenderly removed each article of her clothing, carefully placing them on an ottoman within reach. He ran his fingers over every inch of her body, silently appreciating each curve and crevice. He did not rush, but waited until the tension left her body and he could sense she would receive him without resistance. He picked her up and placed her on the bed. She rolled back and reached for her clothes, pulling a condom out of a pocket he had not noticed. She began to open the package and reached down for him with a practiced gesture.

He started to question her. She looked up at him and said, "Me, no HIV. You? Me don't know."

He grinned at these first words of English she had spoken to him. The last Thai girl he had enjoyed, had none of Noi's saviness and had allowed him in unsheathed. He waited for Noi to finish with the condom before taking and giving his fill of pleasure.

Chapter 19

S tefano had not been near a computer in three weeks, so now – the morning after a night of pleasure – he faced two hundred and fifty messages in his inbox. He always hated this re-entry into capital cities, such a contrast from the departures. There were inevitably messages from his mother (asking when he was going to settle down), a series of announcements about the most recent system-wide report from the head office and a dozen monotonous looking queries from institutes he had visited. Today he noticed in addition to the usual messages a whole series of correspondence from Robert and a woman named Ruth Toll.

He opened the most recent one, from Ruth.

"Dr. Geotti,

We are interested in returning to Chochotte, Ethiopia, in order to retrieve field specimens we believe will be critical for our work. Are you available to work with us on a consultant basis (not through your institute) and make the trip to Chochotte in the near future? Time is of the essence, we eagerly await your response.

Best regards,

Ruth Toll

Director Natural Compound Research and Development

Klaus Pharmaceuticals"

The message, straightforward to the point of bluntness, intrigued him. He imagined the woman who wrote it resembled the schoolmarms of his childhood – matronly and strict.

The messages that followed, in reverse chronological order, revealed a series of desperate pleadings from Robert interspersed with responses from Ruth, intended to assuage his panic. At last he reached a response from Ruth to Robert which struck him as pivotal.

"OK Robert, I can see that she may have a point. I have met with Zahara three times now, and think I can assume that the other

substance may have had some key synergistic effect. According to her, the substance is derived from a tree fungus, she describes it as a bright orange scalloped fungus. As it only appears for a few weeks at the end of the rainy season, we will have to plan a trip accordingly."

His heart skipped a beat when he read the name. Zahara. His Zahara? From Chochotte? Had this Ruth met with the same girl? Ruth made no reference about travelling to Ethiopia. Was Zahara in the U.S.? Stefano tried to imagine some plausible scenario to explain the seemingly impossible.

He looked up from his computer screen to survey the hotel room as if to find some answer there. He saw his computer atop the antique teakwood desk, Thai silk pillows on the leather sofa, the skytrain gliding by outside his window, breathed in the faint scent of Noi's perfume on his skin. Zahara's arrival in America was perhaps no more improbable than his arrival in this scene of royal Thai elegance. Perhaps she was no more destined to remain in Chochotte than he was destined to till the soil of his father's farm on the banks of the Po River.

Stefano instinctively began a note to dash off to Robert and this stranger, Ruth, asking about Zahara. *'What is she doing, is she well?'* he wrote. *'It wouldn't surprise me if Zahara has figured out a way to go abroad, she is intelligent and resourceful for sure, but is America what she had hoped for?'* Then he stopped himself, thinking Robert and Ruth might misconstrue his genuine admiration for the girl as a romantic interest. He hit delete, remembering Ruth had asked him to make a return trip to Chochotte. He had not been able to return to Chochotte for the forest conservation feasibility studies. The institute had sent another scientist, while he continued his collecting in Kenya and Tanzania. He would be pleased to return to Chochotte so he could see what his colleague had done in his stead.

Stefano forced himself to read through the remaining messages and then ordered room service. He allowed himself to turn his thoughts again to Zahara only after he brought himself up to date with the latest machinations of the head office and devoured a plate of noodles.

He spent an hour composing a message he hoped would sound suitably disinterested.

"Ruth and Robert,

Have received your many messages. I am delayed in replying, was in north eastern Thailand for previous three weeks. Made interesting rice collections, what nature has withheld from the soil, she has compensated for in genes, both plant and human...

A return to mountainous majesty of Chochotte may be possible, I must to complete some reports for the institute, and find another colleague to deliver a paper at a upcoming international breeding conference, but then may take a temporary leave. Under what auspices you will be collecting? Will Zahara be participant in the trip, as she has the most knowledge of the plants in question?

Ciao from Bangkok,
Stefano"

Only then did he realize he was still unshowered and undressed at noon, so he rose and walked to the bathroom, glancing at the bed. No blood stained the sheets. Noi was no virgin – the condom a wise precaution, he thought in passing. His thoughts then turned to his desire for fresh mangoes and a foot massage.

Chapter 20

Washington, D.C.

She looked up from her packing to watch Zahara, who had arrived at the apartment this evening unannounced. She had told Ruth to continue with her preparations, walked gingerly to Ruth's crowded bookshelf and focused on reading every title.

Ruth turned her father's compass over in her hand, the brass bezel shiny from years of use. Her father had always carried it with him on his hikes in the forests of Minnesota, though his innate sense of direction almost never failed him. She had always coveted his compass and when he eventually gave it to her – with great ceremony upon her high school graduation – she carried it like a talisman. The compass had accompanied her on all of her travels, faithfully pinned to her travelling bag, providing her a metaphorical sense of direction as much as a sense of true north. She had hardly seen it, however, since she had joined Klaus Pharmaceuticals, the same year her father suffered a fatal stroke. She pinned the compass on the worn travelling bag she had pulled out of the closet, along with her field boots and the olive green pants that had been her standard uniform throughout South America. She would wear this uniform again in Ethiopia – in the field again after a long time, too long a time.

"Are you sure you don't want to come along on the trip?" Ruth asked Zahara, interrupting her silence. "The expenses are no problem. There is still time to decide."

Zahara looked up, startled. "To Ethiopia?" She inhaled, then exhaled. "Thank you Dr. Ruth, you are kind. But for me, Chochotte is impossible now." She pulled a book from the bookcase – *The Shaman's Apprentice* – and sat on the floor, the book in her lap. "I must be in my life here, my classes. My mid-term exams are coming." She opened the book and looked down. "And my father is gone now. To be in our village without him will break my heart." She turned the pages of the book as if she might find him there.

Ruth knew Zahara ached for her father. She almost envied Zahara's grief, so seemingly constant. Ruth's own father had hardly existed in her life aside from the compass. He had maintained the strict English formality of his ancestors – seldom expressing pride or praise, and almost never expressing affection. She had sent letters home from every place she travelled. She labored over friendly yet formal missives – ultimately unsuccessful efforts to persuade her parents of the value of her undignified professional pursuits under the guidance of Schultes, a man they considered eccentric at best.

She carried her father's intimate distance into all her relationships. Although immediately friendly, almost familiar with people, Ruth never let others tread on her self-sufficiency. None of her many lovers knew her more intimately than Schultes, who never expressed a moment of physical desire for her. In his office and in the field, she had confessed to him her aspirations, her fears, her passion for their profession. After her ill-fated relationship with Bob she had defiantly proclaimed her two-month rule to Schultes. She would never keep a lover for more than two months – two weeks if it was in the field – long enough to experience the euphoria of falling in love, but not long enough to become disillusioned by his faults. Schultes had only smiled.

Ruth turned back to the closet, retrieving an old pair of boots by the laces. She examined them, well worn, but still sturdy. She glanced at Zahara's feet.

"Will these fit you? They are great boots, but I don't use them anymore."

Zahara closed the book and picked up the left boot with curiosity.

"Try it on. If they work for you, we can go for a hike tomorrow, before I leave." Why hadn't she suggested this earlier? "If not, we can go out and get some new ones for you."

They fit well, and Zahara walked around the room, her ankles laced up with the casual rigidity that she had come to associate with life in America.

The next day Zahara followed Ruth silently as they stepped into the state park, the Virginia woods aflame in autumn colors. She looked up at the trees, feeling life, the totality of creation surround her for the first time since she had left Chochotte. The warmth of the afternoon sun enveloped her like an embrace.

Ruth, distracted with thoughts of Timothy Crosby's latest email, engaged in an internal debate. Had his message to her been a veiled sexual proposal or merely an offhand suggestion for a weekend meeting before she left for Ethiopia? She would not allow any sexual intrigue to distract her before this trip. She turned to ask Zahara about her village, only to realize she was alone. Zahara knelt a dozen meters back, examining red berries on a low bush, her pockets bulging with tree leaves and shrub stems she must have collected in the space of just a few minutes.

Zahara stood up and turned around – a woman transformed. Her skin glowed with a light Ruth had not seen before.

"My father always wondered about the red pigments. He stayed away from them, because they were usually toxic, except of course the red coffee berries. What do shamans in South America say about red pigments?" She strode to Ruth and quickly past, not waiting for an answer. Ruth trotted to catch up.

Zahara handled leaves, stroked grasses as if they were old friends. "This is almost the same as the shrub we used for to stop vomiting. Do you ever come here for plants?" She laughed, almost giddy as she grabbed a handful of small grasses gone to seed.

Ruth, so stunned at the broad smile exposing Zahara's white teeth, couldn't bring herself to explain that in America park forests were for pleasure and plant collecting illegal.

"Dr. Ruth, when you go to my village, please remember everything. You will be my eyes in Chochotte. You will tell me how it looks. Please check my father's grave. You will need to look at the trees, tell me how they look. Watch for the falcons and eagles, the turacos and hornbills, tell me they are still there. Look for the spiders, the beetles, the ferns, the flowers. I miss them, I did not realize how I miss the air of Chochotte, it is alive. Like this place, not like Addis, not like Washington." She put her hands up to her face and inhaled deeply. Ruth thought Zahara was taking in the fragrance of the plants she had touched. But her slender shoulders shook and Ruth recognized the silent sobs Zahara's long fingers attempted to conceal.

Ruth placed her arm around Zahara's shoulders, guided Zahara's head to rest on her shoulder. The young woman inhaled deeply and gave sound to her mourning, filling the space around them with a deep moan. There was nothing to say, no words of comfort Ruth could offer, so she said nothing. And in her silence, Ruth allowed the intimacy of Zahara's grief to settle. When Zahara finally pulled away and revealed her reddened eyes, Ruth simply replied, "Of course, I will remember everything for you."

Chapter 21

Addis Ababa, Ethiopia

R uth arrived at a hotel perched like an oversized mansion atop a hill, surrounded by trees, walls and guards. Inside, leather sofas and high lobby ceilings suffused an impeccable international five-star blandness, making the hotel remarkable only for its location in the center of a dysfunctional, grindingly poor city. According to her guidebook, Addis Ababa had gained some prestige by hosting the Organization for African Unity headquartered in a sprawling, decrepit UN complex. And although the main avenues were chock-a-block with foreign embassies and international organizations, the city remained a third-world backwater capital, where a foreign visitor would struggle to find an international newspaper and only three businesses could accept a credit card. The hotel was one of them.

The woman at the reception desk handed Ruth's corporate gold card back to her.

"I am expecting a colleague, a Mr. Geotti, has he arrived yet?"

The woman consulted her computer screen a moment and looked up, "I'm sorry madam, he has not checked in. Would you like to leave a message for him when he will arrive?"

Ruth gazed at the woman's face, dark pupils contrasted against stark whites, copper skin covered a long fine nose and graceful cheekbones. Her striking features were so similar to Zahara's, Ruth almost thought they might be cousins. She looked down the counter at three other women, hotel staff smiling and chatting with customers over recessed computer screens. Amidst this incredible display of exotic physical beauty Ruth felt acutely pale and plain, ordinary.

"Madam?"

"Yes, when he checks in, please ask him to call me in my room."

"Yes madam."

Ruth carried her own bags to the elevator and the room – a habit that flummoxed bell boys in good hotels. Since she travelled with so few things, she would not risk letting anyone misplace them.

In the room, she took off her clothes. After the long flight, with a six-hour stopover in Cairo, she only wanted to shower and sleep. Disoriented by the jet lag, her mind told her it was the wee hours of the morning, but the clock hands pointed to the late afternoon. Time dislocations had not figured in to her previous field work. South America, Schultes had often told her, offered the advantage of season lag, instead of jet lag.

She let the hot water of the shower run down her body, enjoying a luxury that would be unthinkable as soon as she was in the field. She pulled back the curtain to see herself in the full mirror, checking for the reality of the plainness she had felt in the lobby. She saw in her reflection the rather angular face of a well kept woman. Her body still held its curves in place, no children had distended her belly or tugged at her breasts. She had maintained her weight and her muscle tone – not out of vanity, but because she had spent so much of her adult life in the field, hiking and hauling equipment. She turned her body so she could catch the still-high curve of her buttocks. She concluded her form, although admirable for a woman of her age, was nevertheless unremarkable.

She pulled the curtain closed again and looked for a long time, not at her reflection, but directly at her body. She observed the legs that had carried her up mountains, down river gorges, into the canopies of distant forests, and now to the horn of Africa. She touched the hands that had touched shamans and their plants, then wrote field notes and scientific articles. She felt again the strength in her body, the self assurance that caused men to both fear and admire her. With satisfaction – and a bit of shame at wasting so much water – she turned off the taps and stepped out of the shower and into a terrycloth robe.

Without even combing her hair, she collapsed on the bed and surrendered to fatigue.

The phone rang, interrupting her incoherent dream. She answered before she was fully conscious.

"Hello?" pause, "Dr. Toll? There was a message to call you."

She heard a man's voice with a thick Italian accent. She did not know anyone who spoke like this. "Sorry? What time is it?"

"Apologies Dr. Toll, it is past midnight here, but I am just arriving from Hong Kong, so it will seem still early for me."

"Ah yes, Dr. Geotti. It's early for me too but on the other end of the day. I should be getting up. Shall we meet now? No, wait. Give me 15 minutes."

"Yes good, I will be waiting in the lobby."

The elevator doors opened, revealing such an imposing figure that at first she didn't know whether to take a step out or a step back.

His laugh, proportionate to his frame, filled the elevator. "Are you Dr. Toll? So now I have surprised you a second time."

She laughed at her own reaction, "Ruth. Please call me Ruth."

"Please come, Ruth. I was going back to my room for some papers, but now you are here." He took her by the arm, clearly not the arm of the schoolmarm he had expected from her curt emails, and walked toward a big carved wooden table next to the bar. "Do you drink red or white? They have a nice Chianti, the Italians may colonize this place after all."

"Chianti is perfect. How was your flight?"

"Fine, enjoyed the duty free shops in Dubai. But I was disappointed to fly into Addis in the dark. When you fly in the daytime the fields of this country look like a Byzantine mosaic. So I missed that pleasure." He glanced up at the waiter who had arrived, "A bottle of Chianti, please."

She smiled at herself, remembering Bob's warning not to try to keep up with Stefano's wine drinking.

"So you have met the young Zahara. Did she tell you about Chochotte?"

"Ah, yes. In fact she sent along maps of Chochotte that she has drawn out. According to her, there are only a few areas where we should be scouting for the fungus." Ruth pulled a bundle of papers out of her shoulder bag. She handed Stefano a laminated line drawing, with circle gojos and footpaths, notes and arrows.

"Fantastic! Zahara sent plastic maps!"

"Actually I laminated her maps," she said. "It's a habit, in case the field conditions are wet. She also made this drawing, so we could recognize the fungus." She showed him a pencil and crayon drawing of a crescent shaped fungi, colored bright orange.

"Were you able to determine the name of the fungus, or get an herbarium sample?"

"No. There has been very little work on the highland Ethiopian flora, so I don't even know the genus. But Zahara was emphatic that we would recognize it when we saw it. She said all the other fungi in Chochotte are green or brown or dull grey. This is the only orange one, and she said it feels rubbery between your fingers and tears easily in strips radial to the point of attachment to the tree."

"All right, certainly I have collected plants before with less information than that." Stefano glanced at the other papers. "She sent these other papers for us also?"

"No these are for her uncle here, letters she asked me to deliver."

"Her uncle in Chochotte?"

"No, here in Addis. Zahara had said we should see him first, that he would help us arrange our transport out of the city. She also sent a message for you."

"Really, what was that?" his heartbeat quickened.

"She said you shouldn't worry, your field collecting manual is in good condition and she will return it to you when she sees you again."

With that, he let out a laugh that echoed between the marble walls – a laugh he repeated over and over again – as he enjoyed wine, conversation and the company of a fine woman sitting next to him.

Chapter 22

When Ato Worku's black sedan pulled up to the hotel's main entrance in the morning, Stefano put a hand to Ruth's shoulder. "I forgot something in my room, I'll be right back."

The hotel bellman opened the back door of the car and Ruth stepped inside. She greeted the driver, who said hello, then nothing else. In the still, silent car, Ruth felt the tug of jet lag and the lingering effects of the previous night's wine. She had just closed her eyes when Stefano, suddenly next to her, said, "Ok, excellent, thank you for waiting."

"What's that?" she asked seeing the plastic bag next to him.

"Scotch whiskey and Swiss chocolate. A man who sends a car like this most definitely will drink Scotch. I always buy Scotch in the duty free shops, in case of emergency."

The car pulled out of the tree lined hotel drive and onto a wide avenue. "I have only these to offer him," Ruth said, touching envelope with letters and photos she had brought from Zahara.

"Any uncle will enjoy news from his niece more than booze, but at least my hand will not to be empty when we arrive. Now Ruth, tell me what you know about Zahara's uncle."

In all of the previous night's roving conversations, she had not mentioned him. "I don't know much, other than that his name is Worku Demisse, and Zahara told me he is a wealthy coffee trader. As far as I can tell, he is her patron, he helped to arrange her studies in the U.S."

"Aha, I see, so that is how she came to America. And you have been in touch with him?"

"Not directly. Zahara arranged everything by fax and phone with him. He does not use email, I imagine he is one of those men who have built businesses without ever learning to type. Anyhow, the last fax said we should meet with him directly to firm up all the logistics."

The driver turned onto Churchill Avenue and Ruth turned her attention to the city. She recognized the name of the street from her guidebook, knew it ran like an artery through Addis, pulsing through a city battered by political unrest from within and famine from without.

From here high on the hill of the run-down Italianesque neighborhood of
the piazza, Churchill Avenue brought them down through blocks where
children wrapped themselves in dirty gabbis and *shammas* to sleep
on the sidewalks – bare feet sticking out of their mummified dreams.
They flowed through a few blocks where shops opened doors for absent
tourists, offering grey wool rugs from the countryside and paintings
of St. Mary, Ethiopian style. They inched through traffic before the
self-important façade of the Ministry of Immigration – where crowds
milled about the shoddy buildings, no doubt hoping to escape from the
country. They finally emerged, almost triumphantly, from the crush of
slow moving, outdated cars, at Jomo Kenyatta Avenue.

The driver turned left on the wide avenue named to honor the
leader who had ousted the British from neighboring Kenya. Stefano
pointed out the vast stone amphitheatre of Meskel Square, which –
just a week before, he explained, had been filled with the energy of a
million orthodox Christians gathering for the annual Meskel festival.
Ruth had seen the guidebook photos of troupes of the faithful, dressed
in scarlet, violet, green and gold embroidery, parading in song through
the plaza, cheering the giant bonfire, a symbol of Jesus' true cross, as
though it were a rousing match of football.

None of the majesty of the festival remained today. The car fairly
sped through the enormous, almost desolate plaza before turning left
onto Bole road, and then left again into a series of smaller and smaller
lanes. As they slowed over a badly pot holed alley, a steel gate in a
concrete wall slowly swung open ahead of them, revealing another
Mercedes and another wall crowned with unspooled razor wire. Stefano
let out a cascading whistle as the gate closed behind them. Ruth looked
at him curiously.

"A coffee trader?" he said in a low voice. "Looks like *Signore*
Worku is THE coffee trader." He gestured toward the house that had
been out of view from the gate. Oversized potted fan palms framed a
two storey carved wooden door. A marble walkway snaked along the
edge of a black tiled swimming pool, white bougainvillea and tree
sized poinsettias nearly camouflaged the razor wire beyond.

The imposing front door opened to reveal a young manservant,
who smiled and led them over Persian carpets and under crystal

chandeliers to a sitting room. They sat on leather couches beside Ato Worku's well stocked glass and chrome bar.

Ato Worku emerged from behind a closed door, paused for a moment as he walked toward Stefano. Standing before his guest, he stretched out a hand in greeting, then craned his head higher and higher as Stefano rose to his feet.

"Welcome to my country. I am Worku Demisse." He raised his left hand to join his right in Stefano's grip.

"Thank you Ato Worku. I am Stefano Geotti. It is a pleasure to return to your country again. I am happy to be welcomed to your beautiful house."

Ruth noticed Ato Worku's diamond studded watch slip out from a gold cufflinked shirtsleeve as he held Stefano's hand. The sparkling stones reinforced her unease, her instinctive distrust for this small, round man who lived in such opulence.

"And we look forward, of course, to return also to Chochotte," Stefano said, continuing to shake Ato Worku's hand.

Ruth thought she saw a flash of recognition in Ato Worku's eyes, before his smile evaporated and his expression suddenly clouded. Abruptly he turned his back on Stefano and addressed Ruth.

"And you madam, this is your first time in Ethiopia?"

Ruth stood up and accepted Ato Worku's greeting, two kisses, European-style. "Yes. I'm Ruth Toll, Ato..."

"Yes, I know. Zahara has told me," he interrupted.

"...and yes, it is my first time in Ethiopia, my first time in this hemisphere in fact."

"Good, good," Ato Worku said distractedly. "Let us have some coffee and pastries. You can't come to Ethiopia and not have coffee." He motioned to his manservant who quickly disappeared behind a door, presumably to fetch refreshments.

"Wonderful," Stefano said. "And Ato Worku, I have something I hope you will enjoy, as I can see you are a man who knows many Scotches." Stefano nodded to the bar shelves filled with crystal bottles, leather covered boxes and a few very expensive looking dark wooden cylinders. Stefano held out his bottle of Scotch in one hand and chocolates in fancy gold foil wrapping in the other.

"Yes, very good. Thank you." Ato Worku cocked his head, signalling the young manservant – who had reappeared. Ato Worku did not touch Stefano's offerings before the manservant accepted them and disappeared again.

"Now please, sit down," Ato Worku sat next to Ruth, attempting to obstruct Stefano's view of him. "Tell me what I can do for you, and tell me about Zahara. The house seems so quiet without her," Ato Worku's eyes wandered around the room as if seeing her here again.

"She lived here with you?" Stefano sounded incredulous. He could not reconcile this house with all its right angles and hard surfaces with the vitality and grace he had seen in Zahara's dancing.

"She was here for two years, a bit more maybe. She came just after her father was killed."

No one spoke.

Stefano wondered about a man like Ato Worku who would have allowed a brother like Nataniel to languish upcountry. In most traditional societies, even in Italy, no wealthy uncle would let his family struggle in Chochotte's deprivation. He would have at least hired brothers and nephews into the business as a form of family patronage.

Ruth broke the awkward silence by handing Zahara's letters to Worku, "She asked me to deliver these to you, her letters from Washington."

"Ah, finally the letters. Zahara told me on the phone they were too many to fax." Ato Worku's face revealed no expression, but he reached eagerly for the thick envelope, stroked it almost affectionately. He sat back, leather creaking, and rested one arm on the back of the couch.

"And for you, my friends, what can I do for you?"

Stefano remained uncharacteristically silent.

Ruth leaned forward to fill the silence again. "Well, I imagine Zahara has told you that we are scientists, we are planning to collect some field samples for our research. We have clearance from the Environment Ministry. What we need mostly is transport to Chochotte, and translation. Once we get there we are well prepared, as Stefano has been there before, he knows the headman."

"Yes, Stefano has been to Chochotte," Ato Worku said under his breath. Then he cleared his throat, tapped the back of the sofa with his fingers, "Transport is no problem, you can take my Oromo driver and my vehicle. But Chochotte is a meager place. I'm sure I don't need to tell you, this is a vast and beautiful country, let me take you somewhere else. Sidamo has wonderful coffee forests, or to the headwaters of the Blue Nile at Bahar Dar. No trip to Ethiopia is complete without a trip to Bahar Dar."

"Yes, I have heard it is wonderful." Ruth flashed her crooked smile at his unexpected suggestion of a diversion. "Perhaps if we finish our work in Chochotte, we will have time to travel to Bahar Dar." Her smile faded as she continued firmly, "But Chochotte is our real focus. It is important that we get there."

"I'm not sure you understand that this is a complicated country," Ato Worku said condescendingly. "People speak more than fifteen different languages in Ethiopia. The people in Chochotte are Oromo, Muslims, not like the Amharas here in the capital. There has been some trouble with the Oromos lately, claims of ethnic discrimination. It's all just domestic politics, but it's better that you go somewhere else."

"Ato Worku, I can understand your concern. We are familiar with ethnic and political conflict. I have travelled in Colombia, Peru, Nicaragua – all places where domestic politics have killed thousands of people." Ruth continued deliberately, "Stefano was in Afghanistan during the Taliban time. We are not naive about the dangers here, but we both think travelling to Chochotte is worth the possible risk."

Ato Worku did not respond, so she continued.

"I appreciate your warning, but Chochotte is critical to our work. I am sure you can understand we have come a long way already. Zahara was certain that if anyone in Ethiopia could help us, it would be you."

"I see. Zahara told you that." He fidgeted his shoulders, as if suddenly uncomfortable. "Yes, well let's see what I can arrange. You should have a proper escort then." He pushed himself off the couch and stood up just as the manservant arrived carrying a silver tray with porcelain coffee cups and pastries. "Unfortunately I have a morning meeting I must attend to. Please enjoy your coffee without me. I will send word round to the hotel soon." He nodded his head at Ruth and Stefano and moved to leave before either responded. "Thank you for coming," he said curtly from halfway down the hall.

Ruth and Stefano languished in Addis Ababa for three days. Ato Worku sent faxes to the hotel suggesting routes to alternative destinations. Every time Ruth called his office, his secretary said he was in a meeting. Out of frustration, Ruth left a midnight message on an answering machine "kindly informing him" they were hiring another car to take them to Chochotte.

Chapter 23

The next morning, Worku's white Land Rover appeared at the hotel entrance. A second car with armed escort waited just beyond the hotel guard post. After a hurried cup of coffee, Ruth and Stefano quickly packed their gear in the car, and hopped in, to slowly crawl through the city's morning traffic, away from the better neighborhoods.

The city seeped in through the windows. Ruth felt the chill of the grey morning, intermittent rain showers fell like dirty lace against the windshield. At several stoplights beggars approached the car, hands outstretched, hands with burn scars, hands with purple lesions, hands dulled by the grime of a life beyond the reach of running water. Shop signs seemed to reflect the city's dreariness: *Dinosaur Fashions* sold men's suits, *Satisfactory Printing* displayed textbooks photocopied in their entirety, and the *Global Technology* shop – tucked into a ramshackle building flanked by fruit vendors under plastic tarps – offered cell phones in dusty plastic bags.

Ruth despaired at the pervasive dirt, silently blamed Ato Worku and Ethiopia's elite who would allow the city to fester in this kind of filth. She thought of the dirt in South American forests, a rich combination of decaying plants, industrious termites and life giving nutrients. This city's dirt, indeed all the dirt she had seen in the urban centers of the third world offended her as a toxic mix of car exhaust particulates, rotting food and human waste. For a moment she closed her eyes, trying to obliterate the city and its ugliness with memories of her neighborhood in Washington with its conventional American wealth.

She reached for her compass, silently castigated herself for her weakness. She looked at Stefano. He looked like a boy on his way to a carnival. He had oiled and combed his hair back, an effort that struck her as a ridiculous vanity.

"Did you see that?" Stefano asked. "The big statue in front of the hospital, it is the black lion." He practically cheered. "The black lions are extraordinary, only black manes and tails. Different from the lions in Kenya. The emperors used to crown themselves with the black manes of lions – nature's own status symbols. The Rastafarians call this the Lion of Judah."

A woman with a child in her arms rapped on the window. Stefano rolled down the glass and pressed a small banknote to her hand. From the rear view mirror Ruth could see the driver raise his eyebrows.

"Have you smelled the money?" Stefano grinned, "It smells like sheep, for all the modernity of the city, you are never more than a step away from village life. It makes the whole country so vital. Everyone knows living things, animals, plants, insects."

Ruth gave an ironic smile, repeating his phrase "modernity of the city" under her breath. They passed a vacant muddy lot where a herder stood with a scruffy flock of sheep browsing at their barren urban pasture. She caught the herder's eyes as they drove past. His eyes, clear and alert – surprised her by softening into a handsome smile. She instinctively smiled back.

"One minute, please?" the driver said into the rear view mirror.

Stefano nodded, "Yes, *ishy*. Please, my friend, tell us what is your name?"

"I am Mohammed Yashewe." Stefano shook his hand and introduced Ruth.

Mohammed pulled the car alongside a vegetable market as the driver from their escort vehicle hopped out to haggle with a vegetable vendor over a huge pile of leafy twigs. After a few back-and-forths he walked away with three small bundles. He handed one to Mohammed through the window, and slid back into the car behind them.

Stefano leaned forward, tapped the driver's shoulder and held his hand out, requesting a few twigs. "Mohammed, OK?" The driver smiled, curiously watching Stefano, and put the car in gear.

Stefano leaned back, handed Ruth what looked like the branch of a dwarf citrus tree. "Chat, it's chat. You know it?"

She shook her head. He pinched off a few leaves and popped them in his mouth. Through the chews he said, "Ethiopia's favorite legal narcotic drug. They export a huge amount to the Somalis and the Yemenis."

In true Schultes style, Ruth followed Stefano's lead, grinding fresh tender leaves between her teeth. "It's bitter."

"Mm-hum. Typically you eat something with it, or drink a sweet soda."

They drove along in silence, munching mouthfuls of leaves as roadside goats searched in vain for shoots of grass. Soon the city's crowded buildings gave way to villages with wooden shacks and then green fields dotted with circular gojos.

After the grey of the city had passed, Ruth thought the sun shone brighter as their horizon greened.

Colors punctuated the landscape: yellow flowers, red winged birds, brown children walking along the roadside, a purple sweatshirt, a flamingo pink dress, a bright blue jerry can.

She stared out the window, noticing the plants people kept near their homes. She reached out for Stefano's forearm as she asked about the banana trees.

"False banana, actually." He made a dismissive gesture with his hand, "Ethiopians make an absolutely tasteless kind of unleavened bread out of the starchy stem. I don't understand why they grow it instead of sorghum or millet, it's no more nutritious and it reduces the art of food to dismal utility."

His flowery words and the chat euphoria induced a smirk as she looked at him. She noticed a few grey hairs flashing in the darkness of his sideburn, and suppressed an urge to run her fingers through his hair.

Mohammed suddenly slammed the brakes to avoid hitting a mule that had been shooed out of the ditch by its owner. Ruth noticed beads of perspiration dotting Mohammed's forehead from the considerable effort required to maintain any speed without colliding into the flow of people and livestock travelling every stretch of the road.

The gentle undulations that surrounded Addis segued into rolling hills and then mountainous extremes. Soon a seemingly endless series of switchbacks brought them in and out of deep ravines. As they crossed a rusting patchwork steel bridge – more empty space than supportive span – Mohammed announced, "The Omo River. We are now halfway to Chochotte."

The riot of green: green trees, green fields of maize and sorghum, green hillside pastures where gabbi-covered shepherds tended sheep and goats and – to her surprise – horses, shoved aside any memory of the grey of Addis.

The distance between villages increased until Ruth imagined they passed through an uninhabited world, a luxurious kingdom of vegetation.

Only the growing fields and browsed pastures hinted at absent farmers
and herders – perhaps working just beyond the next ridge. Then almost
without warning, villages coalesced into a town. The streets muddied in
a poor imitation of Addis, while trucks laden with commodities bound
for the capital lumbered past.

"Where are we?" Ruth asked Mohammed.

"This is Jimma town. Chochotte very near to here."

They drove for another twenty minutes, making turns at unmarked
intersections. Stefano craned his neck, looking for anything familiar.
"This I remember, yes…yes," he said as they passed a small block shaped
mosque and a row of shack front shops. They turned onto a narrow
road, and at last the car came to a stop in front of a scattering of gojos.
Mohammed turned around to look at his passengers. "Here is Chochotte."

Stefano sat speechless. Ruth saw all the eager anticipation of the
day's drive drain from his features. "This is not Chochotte." Stefano
declared. "We must be lost."

"No sir, I have come here before, I know sure."

Stefano and Ruth stepped out of the car, she breathed in the fresh air,
felt the late afternoon heat. She looked at Stefano who stood stock still,
as if he had received a physical blow. He pointed to one gojo, slightly
bigger than most and said to himself, "This must be Ibrahim's, the
headman's home." He turned in a full circle to take in the entire scene.
"Chochotte is gone."

"What?" Ruth replied.

"This was the village," he said in a low voice. "All the trees are
destroyed."

Every tree, every coffee bush that Stefano had seen on his previous
visit had been chopped down. Before him lay only field after field of
tender green chat.

A few villagers noticed the vehicles, but did not approach.

"Let's find the headman" Ruth said. Stefano did not move. She took
his arm in one hand and gently pushed his back with the other. "Come
Stefano, let's see what we can find."

They walked toward Ibrahim's gojo. The men from the second vehicle
followed, guns slung across their chests. Ruth turned around and put up
her hand, shaking her head. She waved for only Mohammed to come

with them. She had approached hundreds of headmen, and she knew a show of force always added tension to an already uncertain meeting. Her respect for headmen and elders, for the typically democratic and effective village structures they headed, bordered on reverence. A headman's character, whether honest and hardworking, or arrogant and lazy, reflected in the character of the entire village. She walked with Stefano, head slightly bowed, ready to express deference to whatever authority controlled the village.

Before they reached the gojo Mohammed called out a greeting. A haggard middle-aged woman appeared at the entrance and said something in Oromo.

"Mohammed, please ask her if Ibrahim is still here. Please tell him I am the Italian who was here two years ago."

Mohammed translated. The woman frowned, and went inside. When she returned, she waved them through the entrance.

In the dimness, they heard a labored breathing. A frail looking man with a wiry grey beard lay on a tattered woven mat – the same mat where Stefano had lain in a typhoid delirium two years earlier.

"Ibrahim?" Stefano lowered himself to his knees next to the man. The old man reached his hands out in greeting, Stefano tried to embrace him, shoulder to shoulder. At the awkward angle, the embrace only seemed to embarrass the old man. The woman came to his side, struggled to raise him to a sitting position. Stefano stayed next to him, held his leathery hand. "Ibrahim, this is my colleague, Ruth. She is from America, and we have come again to look at Chochotte's plants. Mohammed, please."

Ibrahim nodded at Mohammed's translation and held out his free hand to Ruth. She shook it, looked into his watery eyes. "Hello, good to meet you. I have heard much about Chochotte from Zahara."

Ibrahim recognized the name before Mohammed began translating, and the corners of Ibrahim's mouth turned up in an attempt to smile. He spoke to Mohammed.

Mohammed turned to Ruth. "He says you are welcome in his home. He wants to know how you know Zahara."

Ruth explained Zahara's journey from Addis to Washington and her studies at the District of Columbia University. While Mohammed relayed the story, Ruth produced a photograph from the bag slung around her waist. In the photo, Zahara and Ruth stood arm in arm, surrounded by the red and orange trees of a Virginia forest. Ruth handed it to Ibrahim, and he held it close to his face. He passed it to the woman. Stefano reached for the photograph when she finished looking at it. He could just make out the smile he recognized. This glimpse of Zahara in America revealed a woman older and more refined than he had known; seemingly darker next to Ruth's fair skin, but with all of the village roughness polished away by the city.

Stefano remembered walking in the forest with Zahara. He looked up again, "Ibrahim, Chochotte's farmers are no longer growing coffee? Where are the trees?"

Ibrahim's sigh caught in his throat. "This is an unhappy story, do you want to hear it?" he asked through Mohammed.

The woman left them to tend to a charcoal fire near the entrance. She threw a handful of green coffee beans onto a flat iron pan.

Mohammed translated Ibrahim's long story imprecisely, but expressively. He described the scene shortly after Stefano's departure. Nataniel had been killed near the stream. Some in the village believed his murder was a sign from Allah, but disagreed about what the sign meant. Some thought it was a bad omen, a portent of sickness – because of their weak faith – so began to pray day and night. Others thought Nataniel had been murdered because the village had welcomed the sick and outsiders. So a group of men burned the clinic gojo and forbid outsiders from sleeping in the village. Ibrahim found these explanations superstitious, "only from demons" in Mohammed's words.

Ibrahim seemed to digress to describing the Chochotte of years past. Chochotte had been relatively prosperous, the coffee crops had allowed them to buy plenty of food and clothes. All of the children had gone to the school. But as the coffee prices fell, the luxuries disappeared and hunger stalked, the children's bellies "grew big with their hunger and the elders became weak" Mohammed said.

Then Ato Worku had appeared. By then there was fierce debate in the village about whether to continue with the nearly worthless coffee crop, or to plant something else – a cash crop, or grains they could eat. When Stefano visited, many became proud again of their traditional coffee and viewed Ato Worku as the cause of their increasing poverty, some even called him evil. When Nataniel was killed, a huge amount of money was found in his pocket. A man named Esmail took this as evidence that Nataniel had been conspiring with Ato Worku against the rest of the village.

Here Ibrahim threw up his hands and took a deep rasping breath. He glanced over at the woman who looked up from her work pounding the deep brown roasted coffee beans into a powder in a mortar between her feet.

Nataniel had come to Ibrahim when Ato Worku gave him the money for curing his sickness. Nataniel offered it all to Ibrahim, but he had told Nataniel to keep the money until a council could be formed to decide how it could best be spent. Ibrahim had tried to explain to Esmail and the village that the money was intended for everyone's benefit. But Esmail was a charismatic man, "strong and loud, with many following his powerful words". He convinced most of the villagers that Ibrahim had led the village into its poverty and he could not lead them out. The only way to improve their situation would be to destroy the coffee that was making them poor. So, after the harvest, Esmail led a systematic program of crop conversion. Over the last two years, the big trees had been cut down and sold to a logging agent in Jimma. Smaller trees were burned in great smoking underground fires to make charcoal. The coffee bushes that had once given them everything were cut and bundled for fuel. Even the trees from the protected coffee area the institute had established had been destroyed.

When the trees were sold, money started coming into the village. With great hope, everyone planted chat. Children were sent back to school, elders began to regain their strength from the extra food they could purchase. Esmail declared himself headman.

Mohammed looked from the old man to Stefano and back again. Stefano took both of Ibrahim's hands in his, "You are right, this is a very unhappy story. I am sorry to hear about your troubles."

"Mr. Stefano, you understand what this means?" Mohammed looked apprehensive. "Madame Ruth, this man is not the headman, he cannot welcome you to the village. You must go to the new headman, it is not safe for you here in Ato Ibrahim's house."

"All right Mohammed," Ruth motioned to the woman boiling coffee, "we will have coffee with Ato Ibrahim first and then we will go to Ato

Esmail. Or Stefano, if you want you can stay here and I will go to see him myself."

"No, we will go together. But I don't know what will be the use of staying here. If there are no trees, there is no tree fungus."

Ruth spoke in a low voice, "At least I can go to Nataniel's grave for Zahara."

A sudden shouting outside focused everyone's attention on the door. They heard footsteps and a man cast a long afternoon shadow into the room. He shouted at Ibrahim in Oromo. The old man looked up in disgust, answering in slow deliberate tones. The conversation continued back and forth for several minutes. The woman had receded into the darkness of the gojo. Mohammed followed the conversation, a growing apprehension evident on his face.

The man gestured dismissively toward Ruth and Stefano. Mohammed fairly whispered, "This is Esmail, he says you have to go, you cannot stay here tonight. Especially the Italian, he recognizes you from before."

Ruth responded calmly. "It is nearly night. We cannot drive now, at least he could let us stay for the night and we will leave in the morning." Ruth made a step toward Esmail, held out her right hand. "Mohammed please tell Mr. Esmail, Ato Esmail, we apologize for the misunderstanding. We would be very honoured if we could discuss with him our reason for coming to Chochotte."

Mohammed began to translate, but Esmail shook his head vehemently. His shadow seemed to expand along the dirt floor. He turned around to see Ruth and Stefano's armed escorts, two AK-47 wielding men, blocking his way out the door. Stefano saw Esmail's hands clench into fists and Ruth wondered whether the escorts Ato Worku had insisted upon were a godsend or a provocation.

"Ato Esmail, we don't wish to cause problems for you or the village," Mohammed translated Stefano's words quickly. "We would just like to take a walk around the village and we will leave in the morning."

Without turning around Esmail spoke. "You can stay the night, but not in any of our gojos, you must stay in your vehicles, and leave at sunrise." He gestured to the armed men, waving them out of his way, and they stood aside to let him pass. Then he spun on his heel and in disgust, kicked a pile of wood kindling into the gojo before walking off.

Ibrahim made a harrumph, and sunk back down to his mat. Ruth shook her head in amazement. Mohammed looked palpably relieved the confrontation had not escalated. Stefano broke the stillness of the air with a giant laugh. "Stefano!" Ruth scolded him, laughter would only exacerbate Esmail's anger. But as he continued – the next wave of laughter even louder – Ruth saw that he was not looking out at Esmail, but at something in his hand. He had picked up a chunk of tree bark that Esmail had kicked to his feet.

"I think we should not need to walk around the village. Our friend Esmail has brought us what we came for." He handed the bark to Ruth, and even in the near darkness she could see it was covered with a bright orange fungus – the small rubbery feeling scallops that Zahara had described.

Chapter 24

S tefano and Mohammed shoved aside the equipment in the back of their vehicle, taking out the biggest of Stefano's still-empty collecting cases and placing them on the roof of the car. Ruth tried to gauge the available space in the back of the car. "It will be a tight squeeze for the three of us, but it's only one night," she said shrugging her shoulders.

Ruth walked away from the car and toward the stream, following the murmur of water in the quiet of the night. Stefano dispatched one of the armed men to follow her. As she reached the edge of the water, she could see the light of the nearly full moon reflected in the quickly moving current. She put her hands in, drawing water to wash her face and arms. Each time she submerged her hands they disappeared into the opaque fluid. She had seen many sediment laden streams like this in South America, especially in Brazil. Streams that had run clear enough to spear hunt fish from shore, turned cloudy brown and gritty after new roads and clear cutting allowed the rain to flush soil to the streams unimpeded.

She looked to the other shore and tried to imagine what the stream would have looked like flanked by trees; tried to imagine Zahara here, and her father. Ruth had no idea what Nataniel had looked like. Zahara had no photographs of him. She sat back on her heels, drying her face with a bandana while she listened to the crickets. Her skin erupted in goosebumps as if from a chill, but no breeze moved the few ferns along the shore.

Esmail's skin also rose in goosebumps, as he watched Ruth from a distance. She sat in the exact spot where Nataniel had sat just before his death. And just as on that day, Esmail's heart beat faster as his hand tightened around the steel handle of a blade. He took a step forward. A twig snapped. Both Ruth and her guard – the guard to whom she had been oblivious – instantly reacted to face Esmail and his knife. Esmail looked at her and then at the muzzle of the other man's gun. He spat out a few guttural words of Oromo and was gone.

"Mohammed said he and our other driver will be keeping the watch until we leave in the morning." Stefano stood at the back of the Land Rover and held out his arm to hurry Ruth into the vehicle.

"If we live that long," Ruth said as Stefano closed the door on the night behind them. "I had thought Ato Worku was exaggerating when he said it could be dangerous." She pulled out a thermal blanket, and lay down. Her feet just touched the back door.

"You can't imagine how this pains me," Stefano said. "I felt this village before, saw it sing and laugh and dance. I was among its trees and plants." Stefano lay on his back, raised his knees to shorten his body so he could fit in the cramped space. "I feel we have passed through a crack in reality as though the place that was here before has been replaced with...with what? With something else, like the reflection of a broken mirror."

She heard his voice quaver. "I wish I didn't understand how you felt. I have seen this same change in a dozen villages in the Amazon. You always feel the shock and the grief, even though you know the deforestation is coming."

"It's good Zahara is not here," Stefano said in a low tone.

Ruth squeezed his forearm in an instinctive gesture of affirmation. "She knew she shouldn't come. I had encouraged her, thought it would be good for her. But on some level she knew this place was gone to her."

"I was with her for just a few days," Stefano said. "But it was clear to me that she was extraordinary. Not just intelligent, but she had some wisdom, or intuition, or maybe it was just her confidence. It makes you want to be in her presence."

"I have known people who have that quality. There was an old man in Bolivia, a Chiquitanos man. He had no teeth and spoke no English, but I was so attracted to him, I didn't want to leave his side." She could see Stefano only in profile, backlit by the moon. "It wasn't a physical attraction, it was as though he had some connection in the world that I couldn't see, that I wanted to feel. He communicated with everything, the trees, the birds, me. I didn't have a translator in that village. But the old man was so clear about communicating descriptions of what his plants did, how they worked in the body, that when I looked at my field notes when I got home, I had put quotations around his descriptions, as if I had understood them verbatim."

"Ahh, the mystery of the plant kingdom." Stefano looked directly at Ruth, "The way it binds us."

Ruth averted her eyes. "I think most academics, or classical scientists, just scratch around the edges of that mystery. I spent years at the university because I wanted to prove that my Chiquitanos man's intuitive knowledge had a connection to our lab work...was...how can I say it? Schultes used to call it..."

"divine science."

"So you know. You know Schultes?" She looked directly at Stefano again.

"You can't work in this field without knowing Schultes. Your old Chiquitanos man, that is how I felt around Zahara, but she is a young woman. So I also felt a desire..."

Ruth braced herself, expecting a confession.

"...in English you say...paternal love?"

Ruth smiled to herself, relaxing her shoulders.

"It was different..." Stefano trailed off.

Ruth finished the sentance silently "...than this."

Stefano rotated his shoulders, grunted with discomfort. "This space is very small, please excuse me." As his hips followed the twisting motion in his spine, his legs pressed against hers.

"Of course." She rolled on her side, pulling her knees up so the curve of her back fit against the outline of his chest.

She felt the contrast between the warmth of his body, the comfort of his presence in the car, and the tension of the suspicious cold night air beyond.

Chapter 25

Just before dawn Mohammed and Stefano went to see Ibrahim again. The woman was already awake, starting her cooking fire. The old man greeted them weakly, held out his arms toward Stefano, who sat again by the old man's side. "Mohammed, please tell him we are leaving, it is not safe for us to be here."

Mohammed translated, gesturing toward the car and the stream. Then Ibrahim spoke for a long time, not to Stefano, but to Mohammed. Stefano waited for a translation. But Mohammed only said, "He is sorry for the trouble. He feels ashamed. He wants to know if you have what you came for."

"We have something, but I am not sure it will be enough." Stefano produced the bit of kindling wood he had picked up the day before. "Has he seen this, or would he know where we can go to find trees with this orange fungus?"

Ibrahim shook his head.

"The old man says the last load of Chochotte's trees went to Jimma town a month ago."

Stefano persisted, gently, "Does he know who they were sold to? A company? A name?"

Mohammed spoke again with Ibrahim. "It was Esmail who did make the sale. He can only remember the lorry taking the trees had a blue color, and an Ethiopian flag in the front window."

"I see." Stefano looked into Ibrahim's eyes. "Is there anything we can do for you? Anything we can get for you?"

Ibrahim put a hand to his chest. "I am an old man now," he said through Mohammed. "It will be a relief to leave this world. It is too different from what I knew as a child." He pointed to the woman at the door, "But my daughter, she will be alone. Her husband died of the illness after Nataniel was killed. The rest of the family left for Addis when Esmail cut the trees. It is only she and I that refused to leave our Chochotte. Please pray for her. Al hamd'Allah. Mas salaama – go in peace."

Stefano gathered the old man in his arms. Held him for a long time, felt the rattling of Ibrahim's lungs through his own skin, before he lay him back down. The woman stood over Stefano, put a hand on his shoulder. When he looked up, she just nodded at him with a sad smile. Stefano reached into a pocket and brought out a folded envelope he had filled with banknotes. He handed it to her, nodded and walked out as Chochotte's few remaining birds began their sunrise chatter.

Ruth asked one of their armed escorts to walk with her to the south end of the village. Zahara had described where Nataniel's grave should be in relation to the trees in the southern forest. Without the forest, Ruth could only walk south and look. She and her guard walked the narrow muddy path through the chat fields single file. Eventually, they passed through the chat to weeds and long grass. Only the lumpy earth seemed to indicate the area could be a burial ground. Zahara had said she had placed a small wooden cross on Nataniel's grave. Ruth had no idea under which small hillock or sunken area Nataniel might lie.

A flock of Nile geese flew overhead, the first birds Ruth had seen fly over Chochotte. She took a few steps to her right and then turned to walk to her left. A wave of uncertainty stopped her. On whose graves did she tread? What did she know of the lives lived by the dead below her? Who would she be offending with her ignorance of Chochotte's cemetery customs? She squatted where she was and plucked a bunch of grass and small white flowers. If she couldn't say for sure how Nataniel's grave looked, she could at least bring this back to Zahara. Ruth felt a pressure behind her eyes and tried not to let the man see the tears she fought; tears for a lost grave – tears for a man she had never met.

Chapter 26

Beautiful hand painted Pepsi-Cola signs had proliferated along bad roads in Jimma town. Amidst the mud and ubiquitous ragged plastic grain sacks, the town appeared to worship the great international soda. The oversized, precisely rendered Pepsi-Cola logos covered whole buildings, including a small restaurant where Ruth, Stefano and Mohammed sat at a wobbly table waiting for a breakfast of scrambled injeera.

"Pepsi and Coke should start a political campaign," Ruth mused aloud, "they have a bigger global reach than any entity in the world. They are more united than any religion. And those guys have perfect local market knowledge. In Mexico they make the little plastic holders restaurants use to keep flour tortillas warm, Pepsi and Coke tortilla holders."

"In Thailand," Stefano took up the thought, "Coke advertises on the tarps that cover the three wheeled tukk tukk taxis, and in China they advertise on the little plastic chopstick holders in all the restaurants."

Mohammed said nothing, only looked toward the street.

"So Mohammed," Ruth said with a false cheerfulness, as if they had not just fled the destruction of the very village they had traveled so far to see, "tell us where you learned such good English."

"In school. Here in Jimma."

"Here?" she said, trying to mask her surprise.

"After the 7th form all of the books we study are in English, so we must learn English. I speak English with Ato Worku. He does not speak Oromo and my English is better than my Amharic."

"How did you meet him?" Ruth asked.

"I was working in the bus depot, I was manager." Both Ruth and Stefano waited for more, so he continued. "One night Ato Worku came, he was angry, too much angry, hitting the office door. He came to Jimma to see the coffee crop, but his plane back to Addis cancelled."

"There is an airport here in Jimma?" Ruth said, surprised again. "But there are no paved roads in Jimma."

"The air routes in the country are better than the roads," Stefano explained. "Because of the mountains, flying can be easier than driving.

Of course if you fly you don't get to enjoy the real views of the country."

Mohammed nodded. "He say someone must take him back to Addis by morning. He was having a driver in Jimma, but driver said he will not drive at night. Dangerous. Ato was too angry, so I said I will drive to Addis."

"And you did?" Ruth asked.

"Yes. It was very difficult, no lights. You saw the roads we drove to come here, very bad roads. But Ato, he sleep, you know, as a baby. So when we get to Addis, he say he wants me to be his driver."

"So you didn't come back? Did you have a family here?" Ruth had assumed Mohammed, in his late 20's, had a wife and children.

Mohammed looked out to the road, ran a hand over his head. "I had a wife, but she died. She was sick just after we marry. No children."

Stefano nodded silently. He had seen that death was a companion in most of the world, a member of the family – coming for strong wives, cherished children, old men and boy soldiers. Only in the West did people seem surprised when the most certain of life's events came to pass. Stefano sighed, expecting Ruth to say something overly comforting, something too sweet like his mother would say, something that would only make Mohammed's grief worse.

But Ruth said simply, "I'm sorry. Do you know what made her sick?"

Mohammed shrugged his shoulders and shook his head. A woman with long kinky unbraided hair came to the table with a big tray of scrambled injeera and a bottle of carbonated water with three glasses. They ate in silence.

The deep rumbling sound of an engine spilled into the restaurant from down the road. "Sometimes I dream of living in a world before the invention of the internal combustion engine and plastic." Ruth shouted irritably.

Stefano raised his glass of water, as if to raise a toast to the thought, just as a huge lorry passed in front of their Pepsi restaurant. The lorry cab, the same color blue as the Pepsi-Cola signs, filled their entire view for a moment as it lumbered past on the road. Once he could speak over the noise Stefano said, "The internal combustion engine…both blessing and curse," then stood up suddenly, toppling his chair. He sprinted out of the restaurant and along the road, following the lorry as it groaned up a hill. He nearly knocked over a woman with her child when she stepped into the road, but his long legs covered the distance with surprising speed. Children called out, "You! You!" as he passed – half greeting, half accusation. He continued, oblivious to their cries and to the mud he splashed with each pace onto the sacks of lentils, teff and dried fava beans displayed along the street. He focused only on catching up with the lorry's cab. When he saw the Ethiopian flag in the windshield, he called out "Fermata, fermata!" reverting instinctively to Italian.

A man stuck his gabbi-turbaned head out the passenger side window, shocked to see a huge faranji running after the lorry. The head retreated inside, appeared again, and again disappeared. Stefano heard the engine rev higher as the driver downshifted, perhaps slowing down to stop, or just to climb the hill. Stefano reached the top of the incline just as the lorry did, and both came to a stop.

The driver leaned forward on the steering wheel to see out the passenger side window. His expression wavered between alarm and amusement. Stefano breathlessly grabbed onto the rear view mirror to steady himself. He laughed, only able to get out the words, "Chochotte, Chochotte?"

Stefano pointed to the bed of the truck, a blue plastic tarp covering the cargo flapped in the breeze, revealing dozens of irregularly shaped logs.

Mohammed, sprinting after Stefano, slowed several yards from the top of the hill.

The turbaned passenger turned around to look at Mohammed and shouted something to him. Mohammed smiled and shouted back. As he reached the lorry, the door creaked open and a tall slender man slid out. They embraced each other and engaged in a spirited exchange.

Ruth followed Mohammed up the hill, nodded and smiled at the men. She squeezed Stefano's upper arm, teasing him, "This is a great Italian sport? Running after lorries?"

"These are trees from Chochotte. I think." He turned to Mohammed, who was gesturing to the faranjis and to the payload of the lorry.

Ruth saw how refined Mohammed looked next to the lorry driver and his passenger. Small distinctions, clues she had overlooked in the city, now stood out in stark relief. With their plastic sandals and deeply creased dirty hands, they deferred to Mohammed with his Chinese-made leather Nikes and clean smooth hands.

While Ruth and Stefano waited for Mohammed to include them in his conversation with the two men, a whole crowd of men and boys gathered around them. Most said nothing, just waited to see what would happen next. The crowd adhered to an unspoken order; the smallest boys ducked to the front, the tallest stood at the outside edges, and although everyone pressed against each other jostling for a good view, they all maintained a respectful distance from the faranji spectacle.

Mohammed ignored the onlookers, as he at last came to his English. He pointed to the turbaned man, saying "He is my uncle's son-in-law. They are on their way to Addis. They wait here in Jimma three weeks already for parts to come from Addis to repair the lorry."

"And the trees?" Fifty pairs of eyes followed Ruth's arm as she pointed toward the trees.

"Yes, they are from Chochotte. I told them that you want to look at the trees for the orange..." he grasped for the word "the orange..."

"Fungus" Ruth said.

"Yes, fungus. So they say they want money. But I say no, you are my friends, no money."

"How much are they asking for?" Ruth asked.

"No, it is OK, you are my friends. They will wait."

The drivers were already untying the frayed plastic twine that lashed the tarp to the bed. The crowd watched curiously as the three lorry chasers climbed on to the load of trees and examined them. After a few moments, the woman – to the Ethiopians, she acted like a man – pointed to something and reached down into a space between two trees. She laughed as her hand came back holding small knobs of orange fungus. The big man came to her side and they struggled to roll the uppermost logs aside. Instinctively, half a dozen men from the crowd came to help. One by one they removed the skeletons of Chochotte's coffee forest, propping them against the end of the lorry so the faranjis could hack off bits of bark.

"It's not exactly collecting in your 'majestic mountain' forest," Ruth said to Stefano, "but I guess it is a kind of success."

He put his arm around her shoulders and laughed. The Ethiopians laughed in echo.

Papers covered almost the entire surface of the table in Ruth's hotel room: collection vouchers for the fungus specimens, export authorization forms from the Ethiopian forest ministry, the biodiversity institute, the foreign ministry and the trade ministry, and finally permits from the American plant quarantine officials to allow the collections into the U.S. Stefano, familiar with the reams of forms plant collecting required, filled out most everything. He passed on only the documents that required Ruth's signature.

After gathering the papers into neat piles, he announced, "Well, Dr. Toll, I think we are finished."

She refilled his glass of wine from the bottle they had ordered from room service. "There is just one more thing, Dr. Geotti." She pulled out a five-page document. "It feels ridiculous to ask you for this, but I need you to sign this. It's a non-disclosure agreement from Klaus Pharmaceuticals."

He leafed through it. "Can you translate? Legal documents are like baroque music, which I neither enjoy nor understand."

"It just says that you will not speak with anyone about the nature of this trip; what you collected, what purpose the collected specimens will be used for, by whom, or that you have had any dealings with my company. It looks like you are signing your life away, but it's just a formality that my legal department sent with me."

"You promise to me I'm not signing my life away?" he said, adding "Dr. Toll?" with mock formality.

"My word."

He signed the last page of the document with a flourish of his left hand. "Ruth?"

"Yes?"

"Have you emailed your office yet, to let them know we are back in from the field so quickly?"

"No."

He smiled and pushed his chair away from the table. "Ato Worku said you can't leave Ethiopia without seeing Bahar Dar. It is the rooftop of East Africa, where the Blue Nile starts, the water that runs downhill to make the Mediterranean blue. It is a fantastic place."

"So are you proposing a trip there?"

"No, I am proposing an adventure, to another place where you can touch the face of the earth. With me."

Chapter 27

Bahar Dar, Ethiopia

Ruth and Stefano pedalled along on bicycles rented from the hotel. They veered around ambling goats and deep potholes in the road, much as Mohammed had done on the roads between Addis and Chochotte. Here in Bahar Dar, though, Ruth waved to each person they passed, smelled each animal they brushed up against. Amicable hellos and bleats greeted their unexpected appearance on the undulating road.

At a fork in the road they pedalled toward the right, as the hotel manager had instructed them, so they could visit one of Haile Selassie's former palaces. They left the foot traffic of the main road and followed a quiet, tree-lined avenue along the wildflower-strewn bank of the Blue Nile. As the road veered away from the river and ascended a hill Ruth tried to downshift the bicycle gears, causing the bike chain to rattle and skip gear sprockets in complaint. Eventually she gave up the hard pedalling, stopped the bike, despite the non-functioning brakes, and walked the bike uphill.

Stefano followed suit, laughing as he caught his breath. "Did you ever imagine, *Dr. Toll*, that your work would include enjoying the Ethiopian countryside with a low quality bike and an Italian companion?"

She laughed, nodding at a lone sheepherder coming down the road shocked into stillness watching the two faranjis pass. "And you, *Dr. Geotti*, did you ever imagine you would have a grand tour through the Ethiopian countryside compliments of such a companionable American woman?"

"I always acknowledge that all things are possible in this world. But no, neither your generosity, nor your company I had expected." He touched his right hand to his heart and smiled at her.

At the top of the hill, a locked gate blocked their access to the palace. Ruth leaned her bicycle against the metal rails of the gate. "We missed it," she said with disappointment. "The palace is closed." Stefano did not respond. She looked up to see him, back on his bicycle bumping along a grassy field beside the palace fence to the edge of a bluff, oblivious to the rusty chain and padlock around the gate. He turned around, shouting for Ruth to follow.

"We can't get into the palace," she said when she reached him. "It looks like it is no longer being maintained."

"No matter. Come look."

He took her hand and pulled her up on a stone outcrop so she could see past the low trees that fringed the field. She gasped, taking in the view. Far below them the Blue Nile snaked into the distance. Upstream, the late afternoon sun reflected in the glass mirror calm of the river's source, the huge Lake Tana. Mist shrouded Bahar Dar's town, dwarfed between the lake on one side and the expanse of green fields on the other.

Birds glided over the river. Animals grazed in the distance and the crickets began their evening chant. "What is this place?" Ruth asked herself, as much as Stefano.

"There are fifty countries on this continent," Stefano said with a sweep of his hand. "But for me, Ethiopia is the jewel. The world sees only the suffering of the famines in the desert. So all of its richness is hidden as a secret."

She slid her hand into his, nodded her head and inhaled the view until it filled her lungs.

He reached for her waist and brought her to him. She turned her face and rested her head against his chest as they watched the last of the sun's liquid orange spill below the horizon. She felt the heat of his body in the places where they met: their hands, her cheek, her breasts, the small of her back. The dampness of their clothes, the vital warmth of his smell, and the feel of his breath through her hair took on an exaggerated significance, heightened by the great expanse of air around them; the empty space of possibility.

Without a word they began to fill that space.

The ground supported the curving of their bodies into each other. The still-warm air blanketed their skin. Instinctively they opened into each others' bodies. They generously included the world around them: the earthy smell of the ground, the colors of the sky, the sounds of distant birds, until they were lovers not only for each other, but with the whole of life around them.

When they lay still, she ran a finger along the length of his spine, "You have been to this place before?"

"I have been to this place many times in many countries. The places where the genius of creation is so obvious you want to weep and laugh together."

She rested her open palm on the depression between his shoulder blades.

He took in a deep breath and whispered into her ear, "But I have never seen Bahr Dahr before. And this is the first time I have had a lover who is able to see the world as I do."

The chill of the evening's deepening darkness hit her like a wall as they rode their bicycles back down the hill. She perceived the road only as a dark absence of trees, unable to avoid the potholes and rocks which jangled the bike, and then her bones. Invisible clouds of gnats flew into her eyes and mouth. She clenched her jaw in fear, and fought back the impulse to call out his name for help.

For the next four days, the unnamed fear visited her again and again; during a boat ride on Lake Tana, after a conversation with the Christian monks in a tiny island monastery, as the two of them sat squeezed together on a local bus – sharing roasted wheat grains with the other passengers, as they made love on a narrow wooden bed in a roadside guesthouse. Each time the fear came, she refused to acknowledge it, refused to allow it entrance into their world, refused to welcome the unwelcome guest.

Only when they stood in separate lines at the airport – her sealed box of field collections next to her bags – could she identify the source of this fear. Ruth looked at Stefano's frame, the strong line of his jaw, watched his easy movements, and finally acknowledged the fear, the fear that she would never see him again.

He rejoined her after checking in for his flight to Rome. "So the trip was a success," she said as both question and affirmation.

He nodded to the box at her feet, "Successful indeed. You should be able to continue with the pharmaceutical work."

"A professional success. And personally?"

"More than I could have imagined. I took you into new territory in Ethiopia." He reached for her hand and placed it over his heart. "You took me into new territory here."

Chapter 28

Washington, D.C.

Zahara felt as if she had been holding her breath for two weeks. And now, as the passengers from Ruth's flight descended on the escalator, she began to feel dizzy from the airless waiting. She sat down in a chair and looked at her watch: 2 am.

She has spent most of the past two weeks on campus, studying and imagining her country, imagining Ruth and Stefano there. She had left only to attend the Sunday services at the Ethiopian church in Arlington and to visit Robert and his wife for dinner at their house. They had asked Zahara questions, hardly knowing how to reply to her answers. Their worlds intersected only through a strange looking leaf and a woman they all considered a friend.

Zahara thought she saw Ruth at the top of the escalator, then lost sight of her behind a Sudanese woman in a yellow sari.

Ruth, coming down the escalator, saw an elegant woman rise from a chair ahead of her, and only after a few seconds recognized Zahara moving toward her through the fog of her disorientation. Ruth closed her eyes and took a deep breath, trying to summon the energy to speak before the escalator delivered her to the baggage claim level.

As Ruth opened her eyes, Zahara took the sealed box from her, they stepped away from the escalator and embraced. "So you were able to collect it? You found it where I described?" Zahara asked eagerly.

"Yes, sort of. I will tell you about it when I'm not so tired."

They gathered her luggage from the carousel and walked out into the crisp fall air to hail a taxi.

"Tell me what has been happening here," Ruth stalled for time, unable to speak now about Chochotte.

Zahara talked, unleashing two weeks of observations as if she had waited her whole life to talk. She described her studies, how she enjoyed the plant physiology course, how she struggled to understand organic chemistry concepts, perplexed by her professor's strange accent (from Boston – he had told her when she asked), her shock and delight at the trees' autumn colors – so unlike the eucalyptus trees that surrounded Addis Ababa, shedding their bark, not their leaves. She recounted how she had collected a whole bouquet of colored leaves to bring inside her room. She may have said more, but Ruth barely perceived anything beyond the ragged hole she felt in her chest.

When Zahara paused in her monologue, Ruth put her hand on top of Zahara's. "Please talk about Stefano," she said.

Zahara smiled. "You got to see him. It will be two years past that I saw him in Chochotte. He was so intelligent, knew so much. He was so interested in our plants. Everything he called, 'fantastic'. I wanted to know about things like he did. I wanted to know about each one of the tools he carried – and he did explain them to me. He is not same as other faranji. He stayed with us in our village, in a gojo, and ate the same food with us."

"How long was he there?"

"I think seven days, maybe more. I didn't want him to go, I wanted him to stay for to be my teacher. I kept his book so I could remember. I think of him every time I open a textbook, and if I think I will not succeed, I think I *must*, to know so much like him, to make my father proud."

Zahara saw the hint of a smile on Ruth's face. Zahara asked, "Do you think it is strange to think so much about a person you only see for a few days?"

Ruth looked up to see her reflection in the rear view mirror. She could see her eyes clearly, but saw no visible indication of the lump constricting her throat. "No, I don't think that's strange at all."

Chapter 29

R uth's days flew by, between long, brooding nights. She focused intently on her work, shuttling between her office and Robert's lab, following every detail of the research.

"I have good news today," Robert said when she pushed open his office door.

"Excellent, tell me." She followed him as he walked into the lab and stopped in front of a bench with a series of round petri dishes.

"The toxicology tests seem to be bearing out what Zahara described to us. At some point, the compound ultimately causes the cells to die." He pointed to a half dozen dishes with a thick dark brown glaze inside.

"These are the dead cell cultures?" Ruth asked.

"Yes," he walked around to the other side of the bench to another shelf of petri dishes with bright red surfaces. "But when we add a low concentration solution made from the fungus, the leaf compound's toxicity is mitigated. We can continue to treat cells with the leaf extract until the viral levels can no longer be detected. Then when we stop, the virus does not return."

"A cure."

"It seems to be," Robert said, barely able to suppress his excitement.

"That is fantastic!" she said, picking up one of the petri dishes to examine it more closely. "Last week I sent a sample of the fungus to a tropical mycology specialist at the USDA. He identified it as a previously undescribed species, related to *Daedalea quercina*. I persuaded him to name it *Daedalea quercina katanii*, after Nataniel Katani."

"Zahara's father – seems appropriate."

"So are you getting consistent results with the fungus solution?" She put down the dish she had been examining and leaned against the bench.

"Well that is not so easy. I haven't been able to identify the specific chemicals in the fungus that are at play. I don't know how it works, I just know that it does work."

"We have time to understand that, right?" She placed a hand on his shoulder in a congratulatory gesture. "The point is that we have an effective combination."

"Well the problem is that if I don't understand how it is working, I can't isolate the active compounds. Until that happens, we have to use the original source, we have to keep grinding up the fungus."

"So you are going to have a supply issue."

"Exactly. And maybe a production problem. If there is more than one active compound, synthetic production might be too complicated and too expensive to be practical."

"But the natural compound is working." Ruth crossed her arms and pursed her lips, focusing on the petri dishes before her. "Could you tissue culture the fungus, so you would have an ongoing supply of the whole fungus?"

"Probably, but that's not my specialty. I can't do it in my lab. I'm not even sure if what we have left of the fungus we have been keeping under refrigeration is still alive. We have plowed through more than half of what you brought back, so if we are going to start a tissue culture program, we will need to start it pretty quickly, or the research could be stalled."

"It sounds less like a question of 'if' and more a question of 'how'."

"I think so." Robert tucked his hands into the pockets of his lab coat, nervously fiddling with an unseen object inside. "You will need to think about whether you want a tissue culture program housed here at National Institute of Health's tissue culture lab, or whether you want it to be in-house at Klaus."

"I can ask around our labs and see if we have the capacity to even do it, or I could put out a call for proposals," Ruth said.

"Why don't you approach Phil Krueger here at NIH? He runs the tissue culture program. Once he gets a successful protocol, you could easily move the program to Klaus to keep up production."

"Can you call him now? I still have time this afternoon, maybe we can just stop in for a few minutes."

Robert flushed a little, he hated being rushed into action. "Phil has a reputation for being busy to the point of inaccessible, I think it is better if I drop him an email." Robert had always faulted Ruth for her impatience, he knew she had always faulted him for his caution.

She waited.

He sighed, walked into his office, picked up his phone and asked the switchboard operator to connect him with Phil Krueger's office.

Ruth followed, listened to the first few moments of the conversation and suddenly noticed the world map above Robert's desk and the red pin marking Ethiopia. She checked the map legend. Red for Vavilov. The great Soviet plant collector had been there? She had read about his expeditions in Peru and Brazil, but must have forgotten that he had been to Ethiopia. Had they been to the same places?

Robert hung up. "He has a meeting with a student in half an hour, but if we can come right now, he can talk with us."

Robert and Ruth walked down three corridors to find Phil's office empty. In the time since Robert had hung up the phone, Phil had already returned to his laboratory. They passed through a set of double doors into a climate controlled, mirror lined room that housed a world of miniaturized plants and strange little colored plumes growing on white gel in glass flasks under florescent lights. They walked past a dozen rows of packed metal shelves to find Phil jotting notes with one hand, a flask of tiny banana trees in the other.

Ruth reached across a cart full of flasks and petri dishes to shake his hand. "Dr. Krueger, I'm Ruth Toll…" she paused for a moment, surprised at his long black braid, worn cowboy boots and jeans, amidst the sterile glare of the lab, "…it's a pleasure to meet you."

"Right. I'm Phil." He did not put down his pen or the flask to shake her hand. "Robert, excuse me. I'm just pulling out the plants that have to be recultured. Sometimes they insist on outgrowing their homes. You can't imagine how difficult it is to induce them into a state of suspended animation. But I'm listening – so shoot."

Robert glanced at Ruth, clasped and unclasped his hands, and cleared his throat before starting. "Ruth and I are working with a fungus that we need to multiply."

"Yeah, so?" Phil continued to move flasks.

Robert started again. "We are hoping…we, we thought of your lab… we would probably need a hundred grams a week, initially. But we would want to develop a protocol that could eventually be used on a production scale." Robert noticed himself in the mirrored wall behind Phil. He self-consciously ran a hand over his receding hairline, a gesture reflected back to him from every wall. "We thought, well, maybe you could start the program here in your lab and develop the protocol."

Phil finally looked up. "Robert, a hundred grams? Depending on how fast we can induce growth, that should take fifty to a hundred flasks. Look, at this place. Do you see space for another fifty flasks? Between the fungal infections, and skin cells and everything else – not to mention these crazy banana trees I'm growing for some postponed cancer research, it takes five technicians working full time just to keep order. If you're looking for a favor, you are looking in the wrong lab." Phil pushed past them to the next row of shelves.

Ruth turned to talk to Phil across a chrome shelf. "No favors. We would offer a budget. We would draw up a service contract."

Phil finally paused in his movements and looked up at her. "A contract? And I would need another technician."

Ruth did not respond.

"At least a half time person."

"I'm sure we can work something out." She turned to Robert, "Can you bring over samples tomorrow? Phil, once you have a look at them, then drop me a note about what you think would be involved and propose a budget. You can reach me here." She passed him her business card.

"Ah, Klaus, the pharma giant. You guys are tough, I applied for a job there years ago, couldn't even get an interview."

"Obviously before my time," Ruth said with a grin. "I'll look forward to hearing from you."

Ruth and Bob walked out of the lab's warmth. Ruth brushed a drop of sweat from her brow. "OK, so let's see what he says." She hurried him down the corridor and gave him a quick hug. "I have to make my big pitch to the board tomorrow, and still have more work to do on my presentation."

"Right," he said to her back as she walked away. "Good luck and let me know how it goes." He had barely gotten the words out before she tossed a wave over her shoulder and disappeared around a corner.

Chapter 30

R uth stood at the head of the long conference table, facing twelve, mostly grey-haired men in dark suits. Men who had ceased writing, ceased fidgeting, and now looked intently at her. She paused as she flashed the final image of her presentation onto the screen. In a gritty photo, she stood with Stefano and Mohammed, atop a pile of timber on the back of a semi-truck, surrounded by dozens of Ethiopians.

"So we may have been just in time with our field collecting. And if we are able to pursue this research with the full support of the board, we may be just in time to save the lives of millions of people with HIV, people like this man's wife, who died just as their life together was beginning."

The room was silent for a long moment. She held her breath, unmoving.

And someone breathed out and said "Damn...damn fine work." A few men chuckled, as the entire room broke into applause. She exhaled, tugged at her French cuffs.

Timothy Crosby observed how sharp she looked today in a tailored black suit, the perfect contrast to the rugged image of her in Ethiopia projected on the screen.

She took a drink from her glass of water. "Well this is where we are so far, I would be happy to take your questions."

Timothy Crosby looked at his notes and underlined a few words. "So let us be clear, what you're talking about is a cure, right? Not just a therapy treatment."

"Yes. Our research indicates that the combination of compounds would completely eliminate the virus, not only in the blood, but also the lymphatic fluid, semen and bone marrow, to the point where the probability of relapse or transmission approaches zero."

A slow smile spread across Timothy's face, as he looked around the room. "Gentlemen, Ruth, this is an extraordinary day. We are looking at the future, and we are set to make it." His smile quickly gave way to an expression of fearless intensity obvious to each man in the room. "I will proceed with the surest of intent. Klaus Pharmaceuticals is the only company that will develop this drug regime. It will be costly and likely difficult, so we cannot afford any copycat competition." He lowered the pitch of his voice so it resonated deeply in the room. "I'm sure I don't need to remind you that you all signed non-disclosure agreements before we heard Ruth's presentation. I have the greatest confidence that we shall all honor our commitments," he looked again at Ruth, "including our commitment to better the lives of people living with HIV."

Timothy rose from his chair and walked to stand beside her. He placed his palms on the table and leaned forward, displaying his physical dominance over a table full of men old enough to be his father. "Take a day or so to digest what Ruth has told us before we bombard her with questions about the details and the action plan."

Rather than launching into the standard litany of questions about risk and profitability and market share, the entire board remained silent before his forceful charisma. They capped their fancy French fountain pens, checked their cell phones, closed their attaché cases, and walked out the door in expensive leather shoes.

Ruth had braced herself for a debate. She shut her laptop with unexpected relief. Timothy slid a hand across her shoulders. He whispered in her ear, "You are amazing." He stepped back a bit, "Let me take you out for lunch."

At some point between the soup and the catch of the day, Ruth began to comprehend the full measure of today's success with the board. Timothy had brought her to a private club popular among senators, presidential appointees and their king-makers. He had been chivalrous, opening doors for her, taking her coat, graciously introducing her to an administration official whose name she vaguely knew who asked after Timothy's father.

Over three courses and a very good bottle of wine, she listened to Timothy review each of the director's personalities and temperaments. "As if you knew them all, you played to all their needs. You, a woman, a beautiful woman, explaining to them their opportunity to be important and adventurous and rich all at the same time. Right on target."

Timothy pushed his wine glass aside and leaned in as if to speak to her in confidence. "You realize Ruth, that this drug could make us millions – I mean personally – you and I could earn millions if it works." He sat back in his chair and tossed his napkin on the table. "Or it could break the company."

"Break the company?" she asked skeptically.

"This would be a high risk drug. It's complicated because it's not just one compound, so the number of possible outcomes we don't control increases exponentially. If it isn't just right, it could go terribly wrong."

"But that's the whole point of the clinical trials, to make sure it does work right."

"Ruth, this isn't like an anti-retroviral treatment that someone keeps taking indefinitely. It's a one shot deal, like a vaccine. If we make a treatment that extends the life of someone who is already HIV positive for a couple of years then we're heroes. But if something happens and our drug kills someone – even one person – the litigation could be big enough to bring the whole company down, or at least shut down the program."

"Isn't there a way to hedge the risk, to limit the liability? I mean, Salk's polio vaccine caused polio once – but that hasn't kept everyone from inoculating their children."

Timothy looked up as the waiter set a plate of tiramisu in front of him and coffee in front of Ruth. "That was more than fifty years ago. Now it would be impossible for Salk to bring a vaccine to market as fast as he did then. The laws have changed, I shouldn't have to explain to you that we as a company are liable for anything that goes wrong."

"So do you think the risks are too high?"

"I have run the scenario past our general counsel. He thinks if we can successfully file patents for all aspects of the drug regime – there can be no leaks before then – the reward would probably be worth the risk and the cost of R&D. But this is a completely different ball game than the latest cholesterol drug."

"Obviously." Ruth thoughtfully fingered her necklace – an ornate silver cross she had bought outside one of Bahar Dar's monasteries. "But I didn't get into this business to develop drugs that would save us from lawsuits. I am surprised to hear you being so alarmist, Timothy."

"I'm not being alarmist, just realistic," Timothy said, almost defensively. "I will do anything it takes to bring this drug to market."

He looked directly at her. "Anything," he said with a sudden fierceness. He looked away and turned his plate of tiramisu for the best angle. He looked up to change the subject, "So tell me about the cross."

Her fingers wrapped around the cross before she sat back in her chair and let it go. "Well actually, I'm not a very religious person. I found this in Ethiopia, in an extraordinary place. I wanted a reminder." She thought of Stefano.

"Go on."

She forced herself to redirect her thoughts. "The Christianity in Ethiopia is an ancient and elaborate tradition, it would hardly be recognizable to my Protestant parents as Christianity. It felt like some places in Brazil...where you can see forms of Catholicism so adapted to the indigenous culture, the Pope would call them blasphemous."

"I was in Rio last year for Carnivale, that didn't look very Catholic to me, but I haven't been in the bush. It's not exactly my style." Timothy stabbed his dessert with his fork.

"I love to be in the field. If I am in the city for too long, I start to feel as if something is suffocating me."

Timothy clasped his well-manicured hands under his chin, and looked in her eyes, "Who did you travel with?"

"Usually alone."

"And you weren't afraid of going alone?"

Ruth raised an eyebrow to his question. "You mean because I am a woman?"

"No. I mean just being alone."

"No. Being alone has never made me afraid. And I always knew once I got to where I was going I wouldn't be alone. I made connections, friendships, in the villages I went to. In some places, I got very close to the people I worked with. I could go to a dozen villages in South America and people would welcome me in as family."

"And what's the appeal of their lives?"

How could she explain to a man like Timothy Crosby – a man who was never away from his mobile phone, a man who checked Klaus Pharmaceutical's stock every hour, a man who travelled in precise, first-world comfort – the appeal of what looked like a dirty, brutish, superstitious existence?

"Time," she said.

"Time?"

"Time, in the sense we measure it, can disappear in a forest village. There isn't time. There is only an unquantifiable sense of motion, of life going forward. No…not forward…a sense of life going around, of hunting and eating, of laughing and playing, of sickness and healing, birth and death. If I have had any fear in the field it was a fear that that timelessness would be destroyed. Roads would come in, trees would come down and the people I knew would be dominated by time the way our society is."

He sat back in his chair and looked thoughtful. "Hmm, if I could imagine how that would feel, it would probably be something like bliss."

"Yes, it is something like bliss."

The waiter came to the table, "Is there anything else I can get for you?"

Timothy didn't look at the waiter, only smiled at Ruth and said, "Just the check, please." He pushed back his French cuff bringing his oversized platinum watch into view. "Well it seems we have let your South American jungle time invade our world. It's almost three. I have a conference call in thirty minutes."

She smiled her slightly crooked smile full of irony and said, "Exactly. It's time."

On the way to the door he ran his hand again along her shoulder and said into her ear, "We have a lot of work ahead of us. We must be both urgent and patient, and we will not discuss this with anyone outside of Klaus. No press, no friends, no one."

She turned to look at him, surprised at his stern expression, so incongruous with the warmth of his hand on her shoulder. "Of course."

Ruth did not go back to the office, deciding she deserved a break for the rest of the afternoon. When she arrived at her apartment rays of winter light stretched across the living room making long, late-afternoon shadows. Timothy's comment rattled in her head "*No, I mean just being alone.*" She took off her coat, sat on the couch and felt the silence, felt her aloneness. She fingered her cross, thought of Stefano. When she had bought it, he had bought a similar one for his mother, "*So she knows I am not only a heathen,*" he had said. She hadn't heard from him in the two months since they had parted in Ethiopia. There was no professional reason for them to communicate; the legal and payroll departments were taking care of all the professional details. But still... she would have expected some communication. She reminded herself they had no commitment, they had not discussed the future.

Acutely aware of her aloneness, she stood up and called Zahara to invite her for dinner. Zahara was free, and Ruth hung up relieved at the prospect of company.

As she put the phone back in its cradle she noticed a slim paperback volume in the bookcase by the phone. *Five Continents*, Nikolai Vavilov's expedition notes. She pulled it out. She must not have looked at it since receiving a copy at a conference nearly fifteen years ago. Her heart skipped a beat as she read Stefano's institute in Rome had published this first translation from the original Russian. Stefano must have a copy of this same book. She scanned through the list of expeditions: Iran, Afghanistan, China, Japan, Syria, Abyssinia, Spain, Brazil, North and South America. Of course. In 1927, Ethiopia would have been called Abyssinia. She flipped to the map of his expedition route. The jagged contours of the map were crisscrossed by the zigzagging line Vavilov's caravan had travelled on foot. He had been mostly in the east and north of the country, not in the southeast near Chochotte. But their routes had crossed in Bahar Dar. The realization sent a shiver up her spine.

By the time Zahara rang the bell, Ruth was engrossed in Vavilov's description of the countryside and the plants he had collected. Zahara's complexion appeared ashen, because of the short winter days and long hours at her books. But her expression brightened as Ruth greeted her with an embrace.

Ruth held her hand as she led her to the sofa. "Come, look at this. These pictures are from Ethiopia in 1927, but so much of it looks the same. Look, they are all wearing gabbis, just like now."

Zahara examined the pictures, held the book tightly on her lap as if it would disappear if she let go. She turned to the front cover. "Oh, Vavilov. Stefano talked about this man. He was the scientist who agreed with us that coffee did first come from Ethiopia."

"So you know about him. There is a passage here where he talks about coffee, but it was coffee from Harer, not Chochotte." Ruth started to turn pages.

"Ruth, tell me about Chochotte, you said almost nothing about it after your trip to my country. Please to tell me about the trees and the birds."

Ruth pulled away from the book. She had managed to skirt the subject of Chochotte by talking about Ethiopia in general: the drive, the plants, the *asmari* music. The only reference she had made to the events in Chochotte had been to tell Zahara about Ibrahim's illness and Esmail's status as the headman. Ruth could not bear to tell an orphan that the home from which she was exiled no longer existed.

"You know I can't explain it any better than what you hold in your memory. You remember where the footpaths lead through the forest, the sounds of the birds in the morning, how it smells when you stand at the edge of the stream."

Zahara winced, "I remember the smell of my father's blood at the edge of the stream."

Ruth sat mutely, unable to acknowledge the horror of his murder. Then gently, deliberately she angled away from Zahara's pain. "What do you call those little brown birds that look brilliant gold when they are flying?"

"The ones with beautiful song?" Zahara closed her eyes, remembering. "We call those wanniye."

"Wanniye?" Ruth tried out the word.

Inhalation. "Ruth, I would give anything to be back in Chochotte. Of course I have been very lucky, I am very much proud to be here studying. But my life is full only with books. I have nothing in my hands from God, only man's books. I wish to be able to touch Chochotte's life again." She ran her fingers over Vavilov's black and white photos and tried to remember the feel of Chochotte's soil under her feet.

Chapter 31

"Phil, in your budget, you have a line item – ten thousand dollars for lab equipment upgrades," Ruth spoke into her speakerphone. "What does that mean?" He could not see how she raised one eyebrow skeptically or the note she had scribbled on the hard copy of the budget: 'opportunistic padding'.

"You saw how pressed for space the tissue culture lab is. The ten thousand would cover the installation of sliding shelves. That way I can pack in almost twice the shelf space." He sighed, she thought she heard irritation over the phone line. "It is either ten thousand for new shelves, or half a million for an additional lab."

"Just hold on Phil," she picked up the receiver to speak more directly. "We both know this single project doesn't require a new lab, and any new shelves would be used long after this project is over."

"Right, but your project is the proverbial straw breaking my camel's back."

"I understand, but don't think Klaus should…"

He interrupted her, "The half time technician I included in the budget, that would be exclusively for your project."

Ruth paused, sensing an opportunity. "What if I were to offer to agree to the actual cost of the shelving – I'm sure it will be less than ten thousand – if you agree to train a technician of my choosing?"

"Listen, I'm running a tissue culture lab, not a how-to course."

"A tissue culture lab pressed for space."

"Who do you have in mind? I don't suffer fools," he said impatiently.

"A biochemistry student, a woman named Zahara Katani."

Chapter 32

Kara Kala, Turkmenistan

Sweet-sour pomegranate juice dripped down Stefano's fingers from the deep red fruit in his hand. He had deftly cut the fruit's leathery skin to reveal hundreds of seeds, nestled in elaborate honeycombed sections. "Look at the architecture of nature, fantastic!" Stefano's translator – an Uzbek woman named Muhabbat – repeated the comment in Russian to Dr. Ivanovich Cohen.

Dr. Ivanovich, as they called him respectfully, flashed a knowing smile. He had cultivated an unparalleled passion for pomegranates in the forty years he had spent in the orchards of the Soviet deep south. A Russian Jew, exiled from his native Leningrad, he had found a promised land in Turkmenistan. Here, in the mountainous oasis of Kara Kala, he had lovingly created a living collection of more than a thousand varieties of pomegranates, including dozens meticulously hybridized by his own hand. Like Stefano, Dr. Ivanovich had traveled far and wide, to the furthest reaches of pomegranate territory, to collect seeds and cuttings. From his agricultural research station, he had sent out the seeds of improved varieties to populate the vast commercial orchards that supplied the arid villages and cities of the lowlands with the juicy, blood-red orbs.

All day Stefano feasted on the pomegranate varieties Dr. Ivanovich offered him, infected by the older man's passion. As they moved slowly through the collection, Dr. Ivanovich described each variety's characteristics, while Stefano experienced their flavors and textures.

Dr. Ivanovich's motivation for the aesthetic tour sprung from a profound concern for the future. With the collapse of the Soviet Union, funding from Moscow had dried up. The collection, once a jewel in the impressive network of crop collections Vavilov had spawned, now thirsted for water as Dr. Ivanovich could no longer afford to irrigate his orchard.

He was banking on Stefano to publicize the station's desperate situation within Stefano's institute in Rome and raise funds from the deep pockets of the western foundations he had only read about.

That night, however, Stefano could barely raise his body enough to walk the well-worn path between the little wooden house where he slept and the outhouse next to Dr. Ivanovich's turkey coop. The pleasure of the day's pomegranates roiled through his intestines, as the stars wheeled brightly through the sky. He could hear only the sounds of water running weakly through the irrigation channel along the edge of Dr. Ivanovich's yard and his own coughing in the chill night air.

Dr. Ivanovich's wife, Emma, patted her stomach sympathetically as she served Stefano goat milk yogurt and dry bread for breakfast. He drank a little tea, the leaves masking the salty taste of the local water. Stefano would have preferred to leave his stomach alone for a few days, but today's agenda included a drive to a remote mountain ravine and a hike down to a valley where Dr. Ivanovich knew the pomegranates grew wild. He would need some water in his system. Stefano thanked Emma with a forced smile.

Outside, a burly Turkmen man with an oversize woolly sheepskin hat and cheap formal shoes labored over the crank start Soviet-made van that would transport them to the ravine. As it roared to life, Stefano, Dr. Ivanovich, Emma, Muhabbat and the agricultural station's handyman took their seats in the back.

They drove out of Kara Kala's orchards into the dry scrubby highlands. The hills had been crisscrossed with the grazing trails of generations of goats, exposing the tired looking soil to the wind and infrequent rain.

Inside the van, the passengers shouted over the noise of the engine. Dr. Ivanovich explained that the domesticated goats, with their split lips, pull up plants – including wild pomegranate seedlings – by the roots, leaving the bare ground where no seeds will sprout vulnerable to erosion. The wild pomegranates, which had once grown across most of these hills, now persisted only in the steepest ravines, where herders could not lead their flocks.

Emma nodded knowingly. Dr. Ivanovich told them Emma had typed up an academic paper he had written about the danger of the growing flocks. In fact, he said, she had typed all of his papers over the years, translating his flowery Cyrillic into their typewriter's block letters

– whenever she had time between writing her own papers. She had studied the wild grapes of the area and had published nearly as many articles as he had, he explained, admiration shining from his eyes.

The van came abruptly to a stop, at a place indistinguishable from the miles of denuded hills they had just driven through. They all stepped out into the quiet. Stefano saw nothing exceptional, save an empty turtle shell and a few discarded porcupine quills.

Dr. Ivanovich led the group away from the van, to a path only he seemed to discern. Gradually, they descended down the side of a hill until they passed through a narrow rocky passage at the bottom.

Stefano caught his breath as the rocks spilled out below him, into a wide valley, carpeted in green, bounded by steeply rising cliffs. Dr. Ivanovich, encouraged by the sight of the valley, scrambled down the rocks, calling out for the others to follow. He knelt down alongside a waist-high shrub. *"Punica granatum,"* he said in Russian-accented Latin, and then "wild pomegranate," the rare words of English spoken with an impish smile. Emma stood by his side, smiling as if she had spoken the words herself, as if they saw the valley through the same pair of eyes.

The others gathered around Dr. Ivanovich to pay homage to the plant, the ancestor of his beautiful hybrids, a finely adapted plant thriving on the rare trickle of water trapped and hidden in the cracks of the rocks. The few small fruits on the tree – no bigger than walnuts – had already cracked to reveal red seeds. Dr. Ivanovich jotted a few lines in his notebook, underlining the date and the number of fruits on the tree.

Emma, who had walked on ahead, called out from the valley floor. She walked through a thicket of squat trees and vines. Wild apricot, wild cherry and her specialty, wild grapes, grew together. She casually plucked tiny ripe fruits and handed them out to the group, as though she were hosting a tour through her own garden.

Stefano ate them all, despite his fragile stomach, and groaned with delight. The fruits, produced from scarce rainfall and rocky soil, swelled with flavors so concentrated Stefano felt he was tasting them for the first time. He clicked a few photographs and then walked out into the widening valley floor.

He knelt down and plucked a leaf from one of the countless green plants that covered the ground. "Oh!" he shouted, *"Eruca, eruca sativa*," he said in Latin, "rocket – in English – arugula," he explained to his colleagues who were beyond earshot, he realized. He gathered up a handful of leaves into an impromptu salad and popped them one by one in his mouth. "I love this, you can't imagine how I love this. A whole valley of rocket!" A little squeal of pleasure escaped from his throat. He looked around, as if expecting a response. He could no longer see his colleagues, who must have passed to the opposite side of the thicket. He laughed, held out his camera at arm's length to take a picture of himself and his spicy wild salad greens.

His laughter triggered a cough, reverberating against the valley's walls of rock. In the silence that followed, he felt the echo inside his own chest. A sudden hollowness overwhelmed him, a sense of isolation that he perceived as a physical pain centered in his heart.

The sheer force of it knocked him off his feet, pushed him to the ground where he sat still, held by gravity to this single spot of earth, under a nameless expanse of sky. He felt the few rocket leaves still in his hand, uneaten, unshared. He felt his delight in this Eden-like place, unnoticed by another, evaporate. He was alone.

"*Spasiba.*" The Russian word of thanks reached his ears like a whisper over his shoulder. He turned to look behind him. Emma and her husband stood facing each other, just next to a grape vine. She placed a few fruits, evidence of the valley's generosity, in his open hand. Briefly, almost imperceptibly, his other hand stroked her fingers in gratitude as she withdrew her arm. The effortless gesture, the graceful habit of their common life, their shared vision, suddenly revealed to Stefano his own poverty – the absence of a partner, another who could share his world as he knew it.

A woman stepped out from the thicket to join the pair. She flashed a slightly crooked smile. For a moment, Stefano saw Ruth's smile, before it disappeared into the face of the Uzbek translator.

That evening they all gathered around the long wooden table in Dr. Ivanovich's 'institute' – as he referred to the decrepit one room hall. Despite the cold draft, Stefano felt his cheeks burning with fever. Dr. Ivanovich detailed the funds required to maintain the collection, the supplies and staff necessary to promote and distribute plant materials beyond the growers in Russian-speaking central Asia. Muhabbat took notes in English, and then turned to Stefano, expecting a response, ideas about how to secure international funds. Stefano did not respond. He could barely focus his eyes on the table. He looked up at the ceiling, faded Soviet hammer and sickle emblems still decorated the corners. A dusty black and white portrait of Nikolai Vavilov beamed down on them with a magnetic, somehow intimate smile. *We are Vavilov's heirs, following in his footsteps.* Dr. Ivanovich and Muhabbat looked at Stefano, curiously. He must have mumbled this aloud.

"What?" Muhabbat asked.

"Vavilov," Stefano said. "We are all..." he coughed, "...his heirs." He coughed again and again until the contractions of his diaphragm overtook his whole body. A breaking sound from deep within his lungs rang sharply in the institute's cold air. Stefano's shoulders slumped over the table. His companions shoved their chairs aside and reached for him. He looked down at the table and saw a rich red. Beautiful, he thought, the color of pomegranates. He put a hand to his mouth, shocked as he felt the warmth of blood escaping from his lungs.

The torturous drive through the mountains back to Ashgabad seemed endless. Between bouts of chills and fever, Stefano twisted himself into awkward shapes trying to accommodate his oversize frame to the tiny backseat of a rattling Lada. The green oasis of Kara Kala vanished into a lunar landscape, uninhabited, unforgiving; a stark geological reflection, he imagined, of his emotional landscape. As the Turkmen driver navigated the car down to the plain, Stefano felt himself freefalling through his carefully cultivated independence, which he now bitterly recognized as loneliness.

He tried to focus his thoughts on Ashgabad. He wanted only to reach the capital so he could feel some connection, so he could send a message to a woman in the heart of another distant capital.

Chapter 33

Tissue Culture Lab, Washington, D.C.

Zahara walked into the warm lab, past the shelves to the ventilated hood at the far end. She repeated the process Phil had begrudgingly taught her only a week ago: cutting tiny pieces of a bright orange fungus with a sterilized blade, and setting them to grow in petri dishes she had filled with a growth medium. Here in the privacy of the lab, she touched a life that connected her with Chochotte.

Once she had assembled six petri dishes, she marked them with a red grease pencil, *Daedalea quercina katanii*. She stepped off her stool and carried them, as if in offering to her father, to the shelf where the other petri dishes sat nestled between glass jars of miniaturized pine trees.

Some of the first dishes she had prepared already held little puffy new growths, Phil had called them 'calluses', on the sites where they had been excised with a scalpel. She marvelled at the miracle of life, displaced, yet continuing. Others dishes held only shrivelled brown specks. These had either been dead from the beginning, or had suffered under a regime of water and chemical nutrients not to their liking.

She glanced up at the clock and saw it was already nine o'clock in the evening. Her organic chemistry lab report – due the next morning – waited, still unfinished in her backpack. She hurried to clean her work area under the hood. She heard the click of her shoes as she walked across the spotless tiled floor, returning her materials to the storage cabinets, and wondered what her father's shabby plastic sandals would have sounded like beside her. Guilt suddenly stabbed at her chest, and she wondered again the questions that plagued her. *Am I doing the right thing? Should I have come here?* And as if in answer she remembered her father's words, *Give thanks to God for whatever life you have. Remember; to whom much is given, from much is expected.*

Chapter 34

Dubai, United Arab Emirates

The desert sun, so unlike the late autumn sun Ruth had left in Washington, reflected off the towering glass skyscrapers with nearly blinding intensity. She had told the Indian taxi driver to take her to the Emirates Towers Hotel. As they flowed along the highway clogged with expensive cars she shaded her eyes to read again the printout of Stefano's email.

Ruth,

Have fallen sick in Turkmenistan. Blood in the lungs. Leaving for Dubai and good doctors. Come, please, you are the only one I want to see. The one I have to see. Emirates Towers Hotel. Sending my love, feeling yours.

-S.

The message had been sent just fourty-eight hours ago, and only moments later she had made the flight reservation. Now, driving along the line of skyscrapers sprouting surreally from the desert, her impulsiveness struck her as ridiculous. She crumpled the paper in her hand, leaned forward to ask the driver to turn around and take her back to the airport. He did not notice her in the rear view mirror as he reached forward and turned up the radio volume so the afternoon call to prayer reached her ears from some distant minaret, calling the faithful to gather. She reached for the Ethiopian cross that hung from her neck, as she remembered hearing the same melody in Jimma, after they had gathered the *katanii* fungus from Chochotte's fallen trees.

She leaned back in her seat and smoothed Stefano's note out on her lap before folding it neatly and sliding it into her purse.

She told herself she was ready for whatever would come.

When Stefano opened the door of his hotel room – she had presumed she would not need her own – she realized she was totally unprepared for what she saw. Despite the luxury hotel terrycloth robe, he appeared ragged, pale, even small. She had imagined an impassioned embrace when they first saw each other, but he just sighed when he recognized her.

"Oh it is you, good. I wasn't sure if you would come." He took her hand and led her to the suede sofa in front of the floor-to-ceiling windows. "Please sit down." He shoved aside a pile of used towels to make space for her and then looked out on the new construction areas assaulting the surrounding desert.

She looked around, taking in the five star elegance masked by a patina of decay and chaos. Clothes, empty wine bottles, bottles of prescription drugs, newspapers cluttered every surface. Stale air stagnated before a silenced air conditioning unit.

Speechless, Ruth's stomach lurched at some unknown danger. He looked at her, then saw the room, seemingly for the first time. "God, it's a fantastic mess, isn't it?"

She let out a half snort, half laugh. "Extraordinary that you could do all this in between maid service."

"I told them not to come. I wanted to be alone."

"Then why did you ask me to come? What's going on?"

"Can I pour you a glass of wine? I think there is still a half bottle of Bordeaux somewhere." He picked up a corked bottle, "No, that's the Chianti. I didn't like it." He picked up another bottle from the bedside table, held it up to the light, shook it to confirm it was empty. "Wait, I know I had it." He walked into the bathroom, and called out, "Here! It's here." He came out with a twisted, triumphant smile – glass in one hand, bottle in the other. He walked toward her, pouring. He handed her the glass and crumpled to sit at her feet, like a beaded string toy, suddenly released of its tension. He put a hand on her knee, waited while she drank deeply from the glass and then held her breath.

"It's TB, the doctors say I have tuberculosis."

She exhaled, strangely relieved. She raised her glass in a toast. "OK, so you should be in good hands here, tuberculosis is easy enough to treat. It's not like it was a century ago when you would be sent to a sanatorium."

"Ruth, think. I have TB. This is the twenty-first century. I am an otherwise healthy man. And I have TB."

She put her glass down, took in a deep breath and slowly nodded. The color drained from her face and her stomach lurched again.

Tuberculosis, the dreaded lung disease of the early twentieth century, had staged a very modern resurgence as an opportunistic infection, a companion disease to HIV.

Stefano rested his head on her knee. She felt the thickness of his hair, and an image of the Ethiopian sky seen beyond the warmth of Stefano's shoulder flashed to mind. The room seemed to reel and her head felt light with the memory of their bodies. "Have you been tested?" she nearly whispered.

He shook his head under her hand, unable to look at her. "I didn't want to be alone for the results." He coughed, his shoulders shaking. "And I thought you should be tested too."

She looked toward his watch on the bedstand. How long had she been in this city? Was it early morning or late afternoon sun? Time. A sudden desperate need to know the time overwhelmed her.

"We can go to the hospital tomorrow." He took her hand, "Let us live with uncertainty for a little longer."

Ruth looked at Stefano's hands in hers. She breathed out fear and breathed in uncertainty, ignoring the depths of fear beneath. Slowly time evaporated, and she felt only the motion of life going round.

The nurse spoke with an Eastern European accent – Bulgarian, perhaps. She led the man and the woman into separate rooms and put plastic swabs under their tongues. The latest tests required no blood, no sending samples off to a lab, no overnight wait. Within a few moments a result could be matched to an anonymous number. Positive or negative. The nurse tried not to look at them. She did not want to know them, did not want to see the changes in their expressions when they received the results.

In one small room, Ruth pondered the fact of those remaining few minutes of uncertainty before she would know her fate. Her thoughts raced through the minutes, devouring the possibilities of her future. Should she pray to a neglected God, hoping to avoid the wages of her sins? Should she live a shortened life differently? Conservatively? Recklessly? Go to Brazil to live with people who knew how to make the passage out of life? Take the drugs that make you sick but keep you alive? Tell her mother? Tell the whole world? Swallow a shaman's poison to end the whole drama? She watched the clock on the wall.

In another small room Stefano closed his eyes while he sat in his chair, allowing himself to slide pleasurably into sleep. He knew what was coming. He had battled with himself for the two days before Ruth had come; had resisted his fate like an indignant child. But after she had been next to him again – he felt full, satisfied, sated. Maybe only temporarily. Maybe he fooled himself that he could accept a disease that would ravage his body; a disease that mocked the legions of scientists who studied it. A disease using nothing more than two ingenious strings of RNA to wage a global war, a bit of RNA destroying humanity more effectively than the century's accumulation of battles and bombs. For this moment, though, he felt only pleasure in the possibility of sleep.

Fifteen minutes passed. The nurse attached results to two anonymous numbers. Positive and negative.

When the man and the woman rejoined each other in the hospital waiting room, both were relieved. The woman was relieved that she still had time. The man was relieved that he had not stolen her time.

Chapter 35

Ruth demanded they have an extraordinary feast. She called the maids to the room to clear away the chaos. She ordered nearly everything on the room service menu: wine, Gulf shrimp, lamb curry, basmati rice, Italian bread, endive salad. At the last minute, she asked for a plate of French cheeses and Sturgeon caviar from the Caspian Sea. She knew her choices were ridiculous, maybe even obscene, but she felt compelled to make a celebration of the day. She wanted to start eating while the sun was still high; to cling to the brightness of the moment; to avert the tidal wave of fear and panic she felt sure would come crashing down on Stefano.

Just as the room service arrived, he emerged from the bathroom, clean-shaven and dressed in a miraculously unwrinkled white shirt. The air between them practically crackled with electricity. The Filipino butler who pushed the linen covered dinner cart into the room looked back and forth at them, noticing the way they looked so eagerly at each other. As he closed the door, he congratulated them, saying "Congratulations, enjoy your honeymoon."

"Congratulations, indeed," Stefano said after he closed the door. "I am now one of the planet's millions of walking dead." He moved toward her with an exaggerated stiff-legged gait.

"No, you should be congratulated because you will be spared." Ruth said, pulling him down to a chair in front of their feast.

"Spared – I'm sure, because of my unfailing faith in a merciful God. Just ask my mother."

"You don't need faith in a god to be spared, this disease is not about God or mercy." She opened the tin of caviar; spread its glistening black paste on a white cracker. "Here, the very stuff of life, stolen from the ovaries of an overhunted fish, just for your pleasure today." They both laughed, the darkness of another tragedy somehow lightening their own. They ate for a few minutes in silence, greedily tasting foods like it was the first time.

Finally, Stefano declared the meal "Fantastic!"

"I love to hear you say that. I've missed this word. I can't say it like you. Stefano?"

He looked up, a forkful of lamb in one hand, a prawn in the other.

"If not for this, would you have contacted me?"

He put down his fork, fed her the prawn. "I did not know what more to say. The time in Ethiopia with you, so extraordinary it was, I could not imagine how it would be possible again."

"Your imagination is so small?" she said with surprise.

"I have been a long time a bachelor, I have always had women when I wanted some company, a man does not give up the freedom of that life easily. I did not understand the longing I felt after I left Ethiopia." He looked directly into her eyes for a moment, before looking away. "Maybe I hoped it would disappear. But in Turkmenistan I saw two people, a husband and a wife, sharing both love and work."

"And you could imagine that life?"

"I couldn't imagine how I would have it, but for the first time I felt I wanted it..."

She reached for his open palm and placed her own over it. "So imagine this, you can come back with me. For now. It's no sacrifice for either of us. My work offers you the best chance to keep you working, to keep you alive."

"You have that much faith in your work?"

"Do you doubt me?"

"Never."

They finished the meal, every last morsel, without letting go of each others' hands.

Stefano pulled his chair back from the table, exhaling after the effort of such unabashed consumption. He looked at her hungrily. He looked away. "I am tainted now, but I can think only of touching you."

She stood in front of him, and for the first time since she had arrived in the Arabian desert, they kissed. Holding his gaze, she backed into the bathroom and made a noisy spectacle of rummaging through his things. "Aha!" She waved a plastic condom packet out of the bathroom doorway. "You came prepared, and I am accustomed to taking calculated risks."

They made love on the suede couch, next to the window in the searing late afternoon light. Neither of them spoke, they could only laugh as they merged their bodies playfully. The act itself required all their courage, to be in each others' bodies, to touch and live, to repeat a creative ritual that had become mortally destructive.

When they lay still, full with each other, he fell asleep, exhausted from the effort. She listened to his labored breathing drop into a regular pattern as she looked out over the expanse of desert, flat and pale beyond the thin line of skyscrapers. She followed the expanse of sand into the distance to the place where the line – the border between the land and the sky – disappeared.

"Let me take you to the airport," Stefano said as she gathered her few things back into her suitcase.

"No, don't waste your time with that, you have plenty to do today. You will have to let your institute know you will be taking a leave of absence, and you will have to apply for your U.S. visa at the embassy in Abu Dhabi, don't waste time with the consulate here in Dubai."

He nodded, amused to be taking orders from her.

"And get plenty of rest," she said wagging her index finger like his childhood schoolteachers.

"Of course, *mia cara*." He reached out to pull her onto his lap. "My life now is in your hands. Please take the best care of it."

She wrapped her arms around him and squeezed him to her, breathing in his smell, feeling his heart beat against her chest. "Of course, mio caro," she whispered into his ear. Then she stood up, picked up her handbag and her suitcase, opened the door and walked out, looking back only long enough to blow him a kiss.

Waiting at the gate for her flight, Ruth felt the same cold fingers of fear wrapping around her heart that she had felt in Ethiopia. Maybe he would not come as they had discussed, maybe this would really be the last time she would see him.

As the plane rose above the ocean and the land fell out of sight, her fears subsided, giving rise to a giddiness bubbling up from her center. She ordered red wine, feeling that she must celebrate some accomplishment. She caught a vague reflection of herself in the window, as if her image were projected over the ocean. And through this lens, her life suddenly appeared in sharp focus. Her work, her passion, her purpose, had all suddenly aligned with her love for this one man, every past action had somehow led directly to this point. She looked into her glass, the surface of the wine vibrating from the power of the jet engines. *Fate or chance?* she asked herself.

Perhaps it did not matter. She wrapped both hands around her wine glass attempting to steady herself, to prevent herself from descending into the abyss of uncertainty.

Chapter 36

Washington, D.C.

Robert signed an ethics declaration form – dotting the 'i' in *Kresovich* with a little flourish – and attached it to the document outlining the proposed design for the phase three clinical trial.

Although paperwork usually irritated him, and although he missed the feel of the lab instruments and the rhythm of working at the bench, he congratulated himself each time he completed some new round of documents. Each one served as a small marker demonstrating an incremental progress toward what he envisioned as the pinnacle of his ambitions, his aspirations.

The closer he felt to this goal – to the possibility that he might help slow a disease, might assuage an incomprehensible suffering – the more he worried about his own mortality. He worried about car accidents, about developing cancer, about anything that might compromise his role in the research. Instead of articulating these fears, he asked Sidney to pack more fruits and vegetables in his lunch, and developed little safety rituals; double checking the front door locks before they slept, looking both ways three times before crossing the street, walking with extra vigilance through the parking garage.

He patted the signed documents once more before taking his briefcase and lunch bag. He walked out into the corridor and locked the laboratory door, enjoying the click of the lock as it slid into place. His life was in order. He double checked the lock, and walked carefully to his car.

Ruth had called him to dinner at her apartment. She had not given him a reason, other than to tell him the purpose was not social – she would arrange another night when he and Sidney could both come – and his attendance would be essential.

He knocked on Ruth's door, surprised when she opened it, at the sound of Zahara's voice coming from down the hall. She sounded excited, ebullient, so different from her reserved manner at his dinner table a few months ago. Ruth's face was resplendent, as if he had just walked into a surprise party. "Bob, there's someone here, a friend you haven't seen in a while. Here, let me take your coat."

As they walked into the living room, Zahara jumped up from the couch with a wide smile. Robert said hello and looked past her to a tall, lanky man in a navy wool fisherman's sweater. The man smiled, reached out a hand. Robert looked at the man, unable to place him. And then the man spoke with an Italian accent, "Roberto, it has been a long time."

"Stefano! Stefano. Why didn't anyone tell me you were coming?" The two men shook hands warmly.

"This visit is also unexpected for me," Stefano said pulling Robert in for an embrace. Robert quickly released himself, looking again at Stefano.

"I hardly recognized you. You look thinner."

Stefano only smiled ruefully.

Robert awkwardly looked away, taking in the room, looking for something else to say. He noticed candles on all the window sashes, hors d'oeuvres on coarse hand carved wooden trays on the table, and a centrepiece of showy phalaenopsis orchids. He wondered if Ruth had set out decorations for Thanksgiving early.

Ruth effortlessly stepped into Robert's awkward pause, "Bob, I have some mulled wine, can I get you some?"

He nodded and sat in an overstuffed chair next to the sofa and finally thought of a neutral question. "Stefano from where have you arrived? What faraway corner of the world?"

"Turkmenistan, then through Dubai."

"Dubai? What's to collect in Dubai?"

"No collecting. Dubai has the biggest airport in the region, I was working in Turkmenistan."

Ruth returned with wine for Robert and went to the stereo to fiddle with the volume as Stefano launched into descriptions of Turkmenistan, his words seeming to fall into time with the upbeat Afro-Cuban music coming from the stereo. Stefano's voice led them vicariously through the remote valleys he had hiked in the mountains bordering Iran. He outlined the wild pomegranates with his hands, standing up to pick imaginary walnuts, apricots, grapes, and even wild salad greens carpeting the ground.

Robert listened politely, somewhat embarrassed at the excesses of Stefano's descriptions. "Sounds like you made a trip to the garden of Eden," Robert remarked with an edge of skepticism.

"Yes, very much like it," Stefano continued, "although, certainly I have been exiled like the first man."

The comment stirred within Robert a pang of remorse, maybe even envy, that he would never see the world as Stefano had seen it, never know the rootlessness on which Stefano somehow thrived.

As Stefano wound down his verbal hike, Ruth sat on the couch next to him, very close to him, Robert noticed. "Stefano, tell them about the wedding you went to." At her request he launched into another vivid tale about following the sound of music on the night air to its source at a village wedding. With Zahara sitting on Stefano's other side, the three of them struck Robert as an odd family tableau. The intimacy between them all caught him unawares. He felt Sidney's absence acutely.

The stories lasted through another round of wine. Robert, although pleasantly entertained, grew anxious wondering if Ruth had called him, without Sidney, simply to be an audience for Stefano. He inhaled and sighed, shifting his weight in his seat, when Ruth stood up, gracefully drawing the attention away from Stefano.

"I think we should move on to dinner. I have everything waiting in the oven."

They all stood up and moved toward the table, Robert following last. Stefano's thin frame moved slowly in front of him, seeming so much older than when they had last met. Robert slid a hand across his own waist, which had begun to bulge over his belt, feeling his own slide into middle age.

Robert reached for his second helping of lasagne and salad when Ruth sat up straighter in her chair. "I asked you all to come, because I wanted to discuss something." She looked at Stefano. "Something that is my idea."

They all looked at Ruth, and she opened her mouth, but no words could come.

Robert said, "I am only too happy to come and eat your meals, Ruth, but tell us what this is all about." He looked at the faces – suddenly solemn – around the table. "Or at least tell me."

"I'm not sure how to say this," Ruth started. "The drug we are working on, the cure that Zahara's father may have discovered, may be more important to us than we had imagined. It may have far more personal implications than we would have expected." She looked again at Stefano and he nodded before looking down at his plate. "We will all wish for it to be ready faster than may seem possible." Ruth reached out grasping for Stefano's hand. "But now I am asking you, Bob, to work with me and Zahara to help us use our work to save the life of our friend."

No one said anything. Robert looked from face to face searching for clues. "Ruth, I'm not understanding. Which friend?"

Stefano pulled his hands into his lap, "What she is saying..."

"What I am saying," she interrupted him, "is something that's difficult to talk about. Stefano is infected with HIV."

There was a silent drawing in of breaths around the table.

"But we have an opportunity here." She paused before plunging into an explanation. "We have the ability to treat Stefano, his disease doesn't have to be a death sentence." Robert watched her flounder, searching for more to say to combat his silence. "We can produce a small quantity of both the leaf extract and the fungus for Stefano. I know it is unorthodox. But this is an extraordinary situation. I think we have an opportunity, a responsibility to help him in this way..."

"Wait," Robert held up a hand to stop her. "It's not just unorthodox, it's illegal. Not to mention that it could completely jeopardize our work. My responsibility is to this research, to the science. No offense to Stefano, he's a great guy, but perhaps he should have thought a little more about his responsibility to protect himself." He turned to look at Stefano, "I don't know what kind of needles or brothels you have come across, but your mistakes are hardly my responsibility."

An expression of shock passed over Ruth's face. "Are you judging him? Who are you to judge a man..."

Robert did not wait for her to finish. "He is an educated man, there is no excuse for risky behavior..."

They both continued, raising their voices, their words overlapping in dissonance.

"HIV is not an act of God Stefano can't understand..."

"So you are developing drugs only for people who become infected because of ignorance..."

"...monogamy...around the world..."

"...compassion...ethical neutrality..."

From the far end of the table other words came, so quietly at first that neither Ruth nor Robert noticed. Stefano was the first to turn his head to focus on Zahara's words.

"...did not know how they got so sick. They thought it was the will of God. My father, he suffered so much to watch so many die. It is a big responsibility, so very big, to have people come to you. They think you will save them. But only they die. At least for me, they didn't think I could save them. I was only his daughter. It was for me only to care for them, not to save life. I got to know from the smell of their breath, the color of their lesions, the feel of bone directly under skin, when it was too late. Then they would die."

Ruth and Robert fell silent, staring at her. She did not notice, she looked into the open palms of her hands as if reading from a book. "We saw so much suffering. We lived it. I always cried when someone died. Even though I did not know them before, I cried because I knew them in my village. Their death was another death in my village. Chochotte has the trees and birds, but it came to be a sad place." She looked up at Robert, her eyes fiercely focused. "Do you know how it feels to return someone's life? Do you know how much joy will come to your heart when you cure a man from his sickness, a woman, a mother? That joy comes from God, that is God working in your hands." She spoke very quietly, he almost could not hear her. "If you are able to do that, you have no right to stop God's work."

Robert had no words for such a directive. He looked at Ruth to avoid Zahara's gaze. "But...it's not like our drugs are ready, and we can just pull out our secret stash of pills for...him." He gestured to Stefano, unable to look at him. "It's unethical to try experimental drugs on your *friends*." He spit out the final word derisively. "And this is not like taking an aspirin, if the dosage isn't right, these drugs are toxic, fatal."

"I understand the risks. So does Stefano." She moved her wine glass to the side of her plate, clearing the space between them. "Bob, you have known me for thirty years, you know my life and my work. Have you ever known me to do something that was too risky?"

"*Everything* you have done was too risky," Robert said, throwing up his hands.

"But they were calculated risks. I have always come back from my travels, I have always had something, something otherwise unattainable, to show for the risks I took."

Robert turned to Stefano, changing his direction. "There are other options for you. You can get the latest AIDS cocktails, I'm sure you have good insurance to cover the drugs."

Robert's direct stare forced Stefano to break the silence he had maintained as the argument had swirled around him. "You are right. But the side effects are serious, and the protection is temporary. You know the virus will mutate every few years, so the cocktails lose their power to suppress the virus. How can I travel into capital cities where there is cholera and typhoid? How will people trust me if they should know about my disease? There are countries that will even refuse me entry if they know my status." He spread his hands out on the table before him. "The world I have loved, the places I have been will become like a minefield. I will have to compromise my work."

"Compromise? You are asking me to compromise every ethical code and scientific safeguard to give you drugs that no one else in the world has access to. Most people in the world with HIV are dying because they can't afford AIDS drugs, and you would refuse them because they might make you nauseous? Or keep you from travelling to some god-forsaken backwater? What right do you have to think you should be cured?"

Stefano pulled back his chair, turned his whole body to face Robert. "What right do any of us have to the luxuries we enjoy? Let me please to remind you, Dr. Kresovich, that we would not be making this conversation if I had not been to Zahara's village, if I had not sent you that package from Ethiopia. You did not discover this medicine. I did not discover this medicine. A man who is now dead discovered this and this brave young woman shared it with me. I shared it with you. And for this gift, you would to sit there and judge me."

Robert recoiled for a moment, as if whiplashed. He recovered, turned his own body to face Stefano, "So what do you want from me?"

Robert said in a low voice, almost a hiss. "You want me to stop my work, to treat you? I spend most of my waking hours in my lab, devoting my life to this work, because I believe in it. I believe it will benefit millions of people. Millions. Not just one man, not just you."

"Oh Bob, please, no one is suggesting you stop your work," Ruth said with exasperation. "We are only asking you for access, for a supply."

Again Zahara spoke, her words soft but powerful, a wave far out at sea. "I will be the one to treat him. I learned from my father. If Stefano had come to us while my father was alive, we would have cared for him. There is not clinical trials in Chochotte. Only life and death. And hope."

There was only a table with a half full tray of lasagne between them, but a gulf separated Robert from this woman. She spoke from some other world. And he could not comprehend the arrogance with which she could claim such expertise. She had spent a few weeks in a tissue culture lab. He had spent a lifetime in the business of finding and developing drugs.

"Zahara, this is America," Robert said. "Stefano is an educated man, he is not a villager in Ethiopia that you can treat with potions."

"This is America. Yes," her eyes narrowed with anger, the candlelight glinting off her gold earrings. "America is a powerful country. America can change the world. America can make the drugs that will save lives. Then America can ask so much money for the drugs that people still die. America can send aid to feed the people in my country. Then America can decide to pay very little for our coffee beans, so we are forced to starve again. You think America is the only country in the world. You think your way the only way to live."

"Look, I'm not trying to argue about America versus the rest of the world. I'm a scientist, a damn good one, thank you. I'm trying to ask how you can think you can cure this man, with experimental drugs from my lab. What proof do you have that the villagers your father treated survived? Do you have records? Do you have lab tests? How do you know they didn't go off and die later?"

"Our lives are not small, Dr. Robert. We are not stupid. My father and I treated one of the most powerful men in our country. He survived. He no longer has HIV, I have seen papers that record his sickness and his cure. He was the one who make it possible for Ruth and Stefano to go back to Chochotte and get the fungus for your drug."

Ruth gasped. "You mean you treated your uncle, Zahara?"

Stefano reached out a hand to Zahara, who was stiff with rage. "Ato Worku is not your uncle, is he Zahara?"

She shook her head. "Ato Worku came back to Chochotte for to thank my father for his life. But my father was already dead. Killed by someone who hated him for helping Ato Worku. Ato Worku who will sell our coffee for nothing to the Americans. Ato Worku who grew fat while we had nothing to eat." Two big tears sprung from her eyes as she struggled to blink them back. "Maybe he is a bad man, greedy. But he gave me a different life, in exchange for the life I had with my father, the life that was stolen from me." She stood up at the end of the table, casting her shadow across the forgotten food, the empty wine bottle until it darkened Robert's face. "Ato Worku, he knew at least he owed my father something. You also owe him."

Robert grasped the sides of his chair seat, as if to stabilize himself. He looked at his wine glass, wishing he had not drunk it, wishing his thinking were clearer. He had to get out. He had to get back to the smoothness of his world, the clean lines of his lab, the right angles, the order. He looked around the table, feeling its jagged edges, resisting the air charged with blurry emotions, the memories of a dead man he had never met.

"This is not what I am working for. This is not my drama." He tossed his napkin on the table, immediately regretting what looked like a gesture of surrender. He stood up and walked toward the door, wanted to storm out and slam the door behind him, but remembered his coat. He burned with humiliation, forced to turn and ask Ruth where she had put his coat.

Ruth followed him down the hall, swung open the closet door until it provided them both a kind of protection from the dining room. She slid his coat off its hanger, but did not give it to him. Robert resented her pride, her insistence on a last word. She clutched his arm, he almost shook it off, but her grip was firm.

"Robert, you are going home to Sidney. You know how it feels to love someone like that. What would you do if she were sick? Wouldn't you do everything you could? Wouldn't you risk everything, call in every favor, try every option to help her? In all the years since you and I were together, I have never allowed myself to imagine how that love would feel. It would have gotten in the way of my work. Now I have that chance to feel it, to live it. I am asking you for a personal favor, Bob. Not just for Stefano, for me."

He snatched his coat from her and opened the door. "You were right. It has gotten in the way of your work."

Sidney sat up in bed listening dispassionately to Robert's retelling of the whole evening. When he finished, she brought her fingertips together, looking at the space between her hands while she thought. "Well," she looked up at him, "what have you got to lose if you give Ruth what she is asking for?"

"Sidney, it's not right. She is putting the good of this one man above the good of society, of science."

"Bob, is it really so grandiose? The whole scientific method would be threatened? It sounds like she just wants a small quantity of the compounds you are working with."

"What if it doesn't work? What if it's toxic and Stefano gets sicker, or what if he dies?" He paced back in forth in front of the grandfather clock she had insisted should rest with them in their bedroom.

"Well if he isn't willing to take conventional HIV drugs, he will die one way or another. If you need to, draw up a legal waiver that you all sign, so you are not liable if the compounds result in harm." She sighed, "Why are you always so afraid?" She pulled back the covers, clearing the space next to where she was sitting up in bed. "Enough. Sleep."

The clock struck once, with a familiar finality, announcing the hour had half past.

Wordlessly, he took off his watch and tossed it on the bedstand, then moved toward her, instinctively, like a child surrendering to authority.

Chapter 37

Zahara knocked at Ruth's apartment door, waited a moment and knocked again, impatiently.

"Minuto, minuto," came the muffled sound of Stefano's voice.

He swung the door wide open, laughing with pleasure at the sight of Zahara. "Welcome, come in, you are welcome." His encompassing embrace received her, quickly relieved her of the book-laden backpack she constantly carried. He brought her to the couch. "Coffee?" he offered, displaying the customary hospitality he had enjoyed in a thousand different homes.

"Yes. No," she said. "I mean, yes, but later." She could not sit still, anxiously began unzipping her backpack. "I have something for you, some things. Something you gave me and some thing like I gave you." She looked up. "Where is Ruth?"

"Ruth is still at the office. Would you like to wait for her to return?"

"No, impossible. All through my classes today, I felt to burst."

"What is it, my dear?" he asked, amused.

"First, something you gave me," she pulled out a heavy book and placed it in his hands.

"Aha, my field collection manual! I had forgotten I gave it to you. You have kept it all this time?"

"Of course. And I promised to you I will return it."

He stroked the cover before opening it and fanning through the pages. The tiny breeze they created carried back to him the memory of the girl to whom he had given the book, immeasurably younger, but not immature, a preface to the woman emerging before his eyes. "Yes, you promised. Grazie."

"And the other thing. I am wishing Ruth would be here, but I can not wait." Reverently, she pulled out a plastic bag, filled with a white powder, and placed it on top of the book, as if offering it on an altar.

He looked up at her, his eyebrows wrinkled in question.

"I gave this to you as leaves, in Chochotte. This is Robert's version."

Stefano inhaled, slowly, deeply, taking in the weight of the gift. "How?" he finally spoke.

"He brought it to me last night, only before I am finishing my work in the lab. He asked me about my progress with the *Katanii*, and then he gave me this in an envelope. He said only I am to give it to you and he will give me the *Katanii* when you are ready." She could not suppress a luminous smile.

Stefano turned away, saw the table, the scene of the previous week's confrontation, now innocuously covered with newspapers and magazines. Stefano had not dared to hope that Robert's anger would subside, had instead suspended all thoughts of the future, and simply filled his days with Ruth's presence, with the pleasures of her music and books, hoping to crowd out the world beyond her walls. Now he closed his eyes and offered a silent prayer of thanksgiving.

"When Ruth comes tonight, we can discuss," Zahara continued. "But I should like to begin tomorrow. I will come everyday for treating you, monitoring any symptoms and to give you the medicine."

"Tomorrow," Stefano savored each syllable, welcoming back the exiled idea. "You will come each day?"

"Every day," Zahara said decisively. "My father would not approve anything less." She looked down at the book and the powder, unable to imagine the perfect whiteness of the medicine in her father's hands. She looked up, saw again the confident explorer who had come to her village, and felt the awe of the young and naïve girl who had approached him in the forest. "And will you trust me…to take care of you every day?"

"I could hope for no one more qualified."

Chapter 38

Timothy pulled the handle to the extreme left allowing the bath water to thunder into the tub. He poured in Chinese medicinal oil until the steam in the bathroom filled his nostrils with the pungent scent of menthol. He walked into his closet, carefully removed his suit and hung it on a wooden hanger with an almost militant precision. He never let the housekeeper handle his suits, disliked the cavalier way she would hang them on the rack, looking away toward her next task before she had finished the one at hand.

He returned to the bathroom, turning off the water just before it reached the reserve drain. He lowered himself into the water, flinching momentarily at the heat. A high school football coach had taught him this ritual as a way to fortify himself the night before a big game. The menthol oil brought a pervasive coolness to his skin, so that he could withstand the heat of the water. Simultaneously hot and cold, he could relax his muscles, while focusing his mind. For almost thirty years, he had used the technique with unfailing success. His reputation as the "turnaround man" had as much to do with an adequate bathtub as his connections or his education.

He looked around the room, satisfied with the order, the spotless gleaming of the porcelain and chrome fixtures. Pastel towels in several complementary colors were the work of his interior designer, who had sought to compensate for his short-lived marriage with a few hints of feminine softness.

He focused his eyes on a single spot on the wall, just above the faucet, where a line of black tiles marched between white tiles. Without moving his eyes, he played out several different scenarios about Ruth's research, considering the possible actions of people he did not control, the way a chess player would try to anticipate an opponent's strategy.

He imagined actions and reactions, risks and responses, roughly calculated costs and profits, weighing the relative influence of multiple parties. The almost painful contrast between hot and cold allowed him to see the possibilities, make decisions without the clutter of emotion, the unnecessary static of personality. *'Keep your eye on the ball,'* his coach had drummed into him, *'as a receiver, you can never be sympathetic to the pain of the men who your teammates tackle. There is no need to apologize for pain you may cause indirectly. You are working for the greater good of the team.'* He also won much of the glory for himself, loved that a receiver could so effortlessly assume credit for the skills of those behind him, around him.

A bead of sweat dripped from the ridge of his brow, down his cheek and along his jaw line. He selected the course of action with the highest probability of ultimate success. *'Be firm about your decisions,'* his father had told him, *'but be charming enough to persuade other people that your decisions serve their interests.'* The old Senator from Massachusetts had strictly forbidden his son from entertaining hopes of a football career, consistently reminded Timothy that his young and powerful mind destined him for greater things than running around on fields distracting the American people so the politicians could get down to business unobserved.

Timothy stood up, felt his own sense of power stiffening his body as water ran off his skin. Once more he ran through the scenario in his mind, and then flipped the drain open with his toe. As the water whirled down the drain, he reached for himself, the pleasure of release would allow him to sleep soundly.

"What time is the meeting, Timothy?" Ruth asked into the telephone.

He spoke into his speaker phone, "Didn't you get my email? I've moved it up to noon. Robert is here in my office now. Can you come down?"

Irritated, she slipped her feet back into her high heels where she had kicked them off under her desk. She saved the file she was working on, a memo to the Federal Drug Administration, the latest in a string of delicate negotiations about the clinical trial designs, and walked down the hall to his office.

Timothy sat perched on the edge of his desk, practically towering over Robert who sat like a schoolboy in one of the stylish chrome and leather chairs in front of the desk. Timothy nodded to Ruth when she walked in, motioned for her to sit in the chair next to Robert.

She glanced from one man to the other, a middle-aged man, slightly doughy, who had once been her lover, clearly out of place here in the domain of the other man, a consummate executive, who could have easily been her current lover. Robert displayed no change of expression, no hint of the generosity he had shown Ruth and her actual lover three weeks earlier. He greeted her with a simple "Hello."

"Good, thanks for coming so quickly," Timothy said. "I wanted to talk to you both privately before we talk to the research committee about the *Katanii* research." A thinly drawn smile momentarily veiled the tension evident on his face.

Robert eagerly spoke first. "Things are going very well. We seem to have nailed down the chemical protocol to keep us in a ready supply of *Katanii*, and the toxicology results have been great so far."

"Wonderful," Timothy said disingenuously, fluttering his hand as if brushing away a fly. "However I'm not looking for progress reports at the moment. I want to talk with you about the long range research schedule."

"We're right on schedule so far," Ruth said. "FDA is reviewing our trial designs and they have some issues, but we figure that by next fall," she tapped an imaginary watch on her left wrist, "we can start screening volunteers for field trials in Kenya."

"And that's the issue." Timothy paused and took a deep breath, the faint smell of menthol lingering in his nostrils. "I have been talking with the finance department about the design of the trial, which looks like it will be incredibly complicated. First a two-year phase for the leaf extract drug and a second six-month phase for the *Katanii* drug. And depending on the mid-term results, ethics considerations may require we give the leaf extract instead of a placebo for the second phase. That would mean we would need a much bigger sampling to get statistically meaningful results. There is a real concern that the trial cohorts will have to be too large to manage, and the trial too expensive to administer."

"It's a combination therapy, so it has to be a sophisticated trial like that," Ruth said. "You know that clinical trials are always expensive, but this would hardly have to be bigger than most cancer drug trials."

"Cancer drug trials are in America, Ruth, where there are enough competent health care professionals and reliable tracking systems to ensure good data. Your trials will be in Africa." Timothy turned to Robert, "I don't think I need to explain to you the additional complications of trying to do clinical work in the third world where desperate people can compromise our dosage regimes with nostrums and witch doctors."

Timothy stepped down from the front of his desk. He walked around it, sliding his fingers along its glassy surface, before sitting authoritatively in his high-backed chair. He folded his hands in front of himself on the desk and began as if with a rehearsed speech. "The leaf extract seems to be promising so far, and we have a process for producing a good synthetic version that could be scaled up easily, right?"

"Exactly," Robert confirmed.

"But the *Katanii* is more problematic now, right?"

"Well, we still haven't isolated the active compounds, so we haven't been able to synthesize it." Robert looked to Ruth for reassurance. "But like I said, I think we have a good tissue culture protocol in place now."

"But even if we continue with that, maintaining commercial scale tissue culture labs and technicians will be cost prohibitive." The determination in Timothy's voice seemed designed to lead them to some specific conclusion.

Ruth jumped into the path of his words, trying to set up a roadblock, "But for now we're just getting research supplies. Bob has been successful at isolating dozens of compounds before. Once we can isolate this one and produce a synthetic version we can streamline the logistics and reduce costs."

"But we're not there yet," Timothy said heavily. "And if we produce a therapy with this cumbersome set of ingredients, it will be so expensive, nobody in America will be able to afford it, much less in Asia or Africa. It would be as good as useless."

Silence.

"So I've decided we should rethink the strategy." Timothy started with his prepared line of reasoning. "The leaf extract has the potential to be a good anti-retroviral, if I am understanding it correctly."

"Correct. Except," Robert countered, "with prolonged exposure it kills not only HIV infected cells, but healthy cells as well."

Timothy picked up a scientific journal from the credenza behind his desk and let it flop in front of Ruth and Robert with a crack. "There is some interesting reporting in Lancet this month. In one trial, patients took highly active anti-retroviral therapies in intervals, one week on, three weeks off. They got some intriguing results."

"But Timothy, that is a therapy," anxiety tightened Ruth's lips, clipping the ends of her words. "Even if the interval strategy works, the treatment goes on indefinitely. No one is cured. Our whole objective here is a cure. Of course this is risky, but no one else is doing this kind of research."

"Ruth, I don't think you understand the internal resistance. The lawyers – our general counsel, our intellectual property counsel, our litigation counsel – they all have major reservations. The finance department is worried we aren't going to have the cash flow we need to front this research." He glanced over at a mute television on the wall behind Ruth, the gains and losses of the day's trading perpetually scrolling across the bottom of the screen. "I have been trying to defend our position, I don't want to compromise, but I don't run Klaus Pharmaceuticals by myself. This is not my grandfather's company. Until we have some good concrete results, we are financing the research on faith, excuse my frankness, but faith in a dead village witch doctor. That's a tough sell around here."

Ruth sat unmoving, only her nostrils flaring. "What kind of results would you need? How many people would need to be cured to get the internal buy-in to continue with the original trial design? One man who is cured, one man whose life is saved?" Ruth held up her index finger as though pointing toward the river beyond the glass walls of Timothy's office. "Would one life be enough?"

"Even if we had that, the intellectual property issues are complicated. This supposed cure, this traditional medicine," Timothy spoke the words "traditional medicine" between quote symbols with his fingers, "was supposedly already known in a village in Ethiopia. That presents a whole new set of complications. What kind of patents can we hold? Do we have to negotiate with the community for rights? Who are the owners of the traditional knowledge? We would have to bring in a small army of bush-ready lawyers in hiking boots to go out and negotiate in huts." Timothy raised his hands, framing the apparent absurdity of the hypothetical scene he had created, the next stop in his line of reasoning.

"Timothy, Ruth's biggest accomplishment has been the benefit sharing agreement she helped negotiate with Brazil. You already have the expertise to negotiate those kinds of arrangements," Robert's voice cracked almost imperceptibly.

"That deal was for wild materials, plants and insects collected in plastic bags from a rainforest. Child's play compared to the legal issues, and emotions, that traditional knowledge and traditional medicine raise. It could take years of haggling." Timothy continued inexorably with his arguments. "Even if we negotiate a deal and escape litigation, the marketing people say the market might not bear our costs. You sell someone a cure once, you sell a therapy for a lifetime. A lifetime that we extend."

Ruth stood up, assumed a more aggressive position, holding onto her chairback, looking down on Timothy at his desk. "If it works, there will be a huge market. The cocktail market is almost exclusively Westerners with insurance coverage. You can market a cure worldwide, precisely because you only have to sell it once. Governments will be willing to purchase bulk supplies. The World Bank and USAID would lend for the purchases."

"Perhaps, if the global economy remains strong." He stood and walked to the window, turning his back to Ruth and Robert. "Our two biggest-selling drugs are coming off patent this year. Within six months we will be competing with a dozen low cost generic versions. Finance predicts it could cut our revenue by twenty percent. They argue we should only fund projects where the return on investment possibilities are realistic."

"So you would abandon research into a cure because finance is resisting?"

He did not turn to face her. "No. No, I'm not saying that at all. I believe in this just as much as you do. But this isn't a good time for Klaus Pharmaceuticals. My plan is to stagger the research. We redesign the trials to look at the leaf extract as an ongoing anti-retroviral therapy. Once that is commercialised, we can proceed with the combination therapy as a possible cure. That gives Robert and his team time to isolate the active compounds and develop a synthetic version. The revenue from the commercialized therapy can support the next phase of research."

"Timothy, listen to yourself. How long would you wait until you proceed with the *Katanii* trials? How many more people would you condemn to death?" Ruth looked imploringly at Bob, who sat rigidly, cradling one index finger in his other hand.

Timothy walked back to his desk, folded his arms and remained standing. "I am not running a social service. I am the CEO of a pharmaceutical company, a profitable pharmaceutical company. When I came to Klaus Pharmaceuticals two years ago, it was practically insolvent. I have a responsibility to the company, to our shareholders and to the people who use our drugs. If I push too hard, the board can easily push me out, and you along with me. If we go, the *Katanii* research may never happen. I am proposing later, not never." He had arrived at his destination. He sat down. "I have not come to this decision easily. I wanted to have this meeting with both of you now, because I am meeting with the research committee tomorrow. I will give them instructions – the same instructions I am giving you – to redesign the trials."

Chapter 39

R uth opened the door to her apartment and shuddered in the cold. She had expected to see Stefano, with his characteristic open arms, but saw only the weak light of the late afternoon settling through the sitting room window. She checked the table, the telephone desk, the counter to see if he had left a note. Nothing. She changed into jeans and a bulky wool sweater, and sat in an oversized wicker chair in front of the window. She looked at the bricks and pavement, the dirty edges of snow in the gutter, a man on the sidewalk who walked by and threw his cigarette on the ground. Cars drove by, steam and grey exhaust billowed from tailpipes. She could think of nothing, except the hardness, the ugliness of the world.

She had grown accustomed to the company of Stefano and Zahara, so that now she felt their absence keenly. She felt inconsequential amongst the rooms, amidst the things they had animated these weeks, hearing only the dry creaking of the chair's woven fibers as she shifted her weight. She did not want to be here. She closed her eyes to imagine Brazil, Colombia, Nicaragua; anywhere warm, anywhere she would be surrounded by green. She wanted to escape, at least temporarily, the hardness of the city and the hard people who inhabited it.

She heard a key in the door and Stefano came into the hall. "*Ciao bella*! Ruth?" She turned in her chair to see him enter the room. "What are you doing in the dark?" He switched on a lamp and she could see the redness of his cheeks from the cold.

"I got bad news today," she said flatly.

"Well, I have good news today. So you must to listen to mine first." He took off his coat and threw it over the back of a chair.

"What is it?" she asked half-heartedly.

He stood in front of her with his back to the window. "You must guess. No…first I have a clue for you." He pointed toward his hip.

"What?" she asked.

"In my pocket." He pointed again toward his hip pocket and nodded his head.

She looked up at him, reaching her hand into his pocket. She could feel the lingering coldness in the cloth and the warmth of his thigh under her hand. Her fingers wrapped around a small box. She pulled it out and examined the silver letters inscribed on top. Her eyebrows wrinkled into a question.

"Yes, open it." He stifled a laugh.

She opened the box, closed it again, a smile spreading slowly across her face.

"Does it fit?" He reached out for the box, pulled out a ring with a single diamond and held it out for her.

She slid it onto a finger on her left hand. "Yes, it fits." She held his hand, and looked up with a mischievous smile. "So what was the news?"

"A little bird came to the window, told me that I must to tell you I want to spend the rest of my life with you, *amore mio.*" He reached for her other hand, lifting her to her feet. "However long that will be."

She fixed her gaze on his eyes and he bent down to kiss her ear. "But Stefano," she whispered, "it's winter, the birds are gone to warmer places."

"Yes. So it's winter…maybe I only imagined the little bird."

A man with silver sunglasses hanging from his breast pocket stood on the sidewalk across the street and lit a cigarette. He looked up and saw through an apartment window a man and a woman embracing and laughing. He opened his phone and dialled, asked for Timothy. "She went straight home," he said, "and a man…he looks like a lover…is here with her now."

Chapter 40

"Mr. Crosby? Excuse me for calling so late on your cell phone, but your secretary gave me the number when I asked her to take a message. This is Josiah Klaus."

The beer he had shared with Robert emboldened him to make a call on behalf of his mentor before he even left the pub parking lot. Unsure what difference he could make, he only knew he had to act. Robert's voice had trembled in the pub, as he described the decision, the implications for their work.

"Yes Josiah, I am happy to take your call. It has been some months since we spoke at the company holiday party. How are you?"

"I'm fine thanks. Well, yes, I'm fine. And you?"

"Fine, thank you."

Josiah continued past the obligatory pleasantries. "But I just left Robert Kresovich, he seems pretty shaken up…"

"Hmmmm. Yes, I was concerned about him when he left my office today."

"So I was wondering, um, if you might have some time so we could discuss the research schedule. I could give you some of the details of my work with *Katanii*."

"Very good, yes. We could arrange some time tomorrow, please call my assistant in the morning to get on my calendar. I have a pretty good sense of what is happening with the research, but it is always helpful to have another set of eyes and ears, especially right there in the lab with Robert."

"Thank you Mr. Crosby. I will call your assistant in the morning. Good night." Josiah ended the call and gave the phone a puzzled look. *"Eyes and ears…"* he said to himself in the silence of his empty car.

Chapter 41

Zahara sat down with her lab tools, occupying the same space two full-time technicians had to share during the day, when hoodspace was tight. Phil had left instructions. She was to mix up the solution for the growth medium by herself, and prepare a dozen new petri dishes with the tiny *Katanii* samples she could now cut expertly. She read his instructions aloud to herself, and when she finished she heard her own breathing and the whisper of air sucked up by the ventilation hood. She copied the proportions of chemicals into her notebook: nitrogen, phosphorus, potassium, trace minerals. She thought of Stefano taking notes in his field notebook, both of them recording details in foreign lands. Soon he would be well enough to take her preparation of the *Katanii* fungus and an extra strong dose of the white powder, the synthetic leaf extract Robert had given her. And then...

She inhaled. Her father had waved so happily every time people walked out of the clinic gojo and away with their families; children jumping with delight at their mother's hands, wives immeasurably relieved at their husbands' renewed strength. Would Stefano walk away, out of her life, out of Ruth's life once he was free from the disease? Would he continue his own private worship in the remotest corners of the world? Would he resume his work with gratitude that she had continued her father's work? Would she wish him to do otherwise?

Twelve new dishes – all impregnated with small cuttings of the fungus – would foster the growth of *Katanii*, a substance that would be more precious than gold to those with the sickness in their veins. Just as Robert had said, this work could benefit millions of people. And one man. She reached her arms up, expressing praise for the alchemy. Then she prepared a thirteenth dish – just for herself. She would take the dish with the growth solution to her own room, to possess a symbol of her father, a kind of living relic. She thought she heard a whistling, could make out a melody, could almost remember the tones her father strung together on his walks. As she put away her tools and turned off the ventilation in the hood, the melody faded, perhaps nothing more than the random patterns of moving air.

Chapter 42

Josiah glanced at his watch. 7 am, the glass doors to Klaus Pharmaceuticals corporate offices had yet to open for the day. He knocked on his reflection in the door, caught the attention of the security guard just inside. Josiah flashed his NIH identity badge, spoke his name with exaggerated precision. The security guard opened the door.

"Mr. Klaus, welcome. Can I help you?"

"I have an appointment with Timothy Crosby." The guard stood aside, motioned him toward the elevator bank.

Josiah had not bothered to schedule a time with Timothy's assistant. He had arrived early, expecting to catch Timothy when he arrived. Timothy, though, was already sitting at his desk, talking into his mobile phone. "...yes, I want to know all his whereabouts. And let me know immediately about any deviations...good." He closed the phone.

Josiah knocked on Timothy's open door. "Mr. Crosby, excuse me for coming so early. I was hoping to catch you before you were busy with your day's schedule."

Timothy looked up, startled. "Josiah? Ah, yes, please, come in. Good morning. Unfortunately my schedule is a little hectic these days."

"I understand. I think we are all feeling some, you know, urgency about our work."

Timothy gestured towards the leather chair and Josiah sat where Robert had sat just a day earlier. Rather than remaining in his desk, Timothy sat down in the other chair, next to Josiah, giving the appearance of deference to the younger man.

"Robert told me a bit about your, you know, your decision to redesign the trials, I wanted to explain...I mean...I think...well the work we are doing is unpredictable, of course." Josiah's hands hovered at his sides, then found a safe resting spot on the chair's arms, bolstering his confidence. "But we are making good progress toward isolating the active compounds in the *Katanii*. I am working with different precipitating agents, and..."

Timothy abruptly cut him off. "I have no doubt about the quality of your work Josiah. My concerns are more global than the details of your lab work."

"Well, isn't working on a cure for AIDS a pretty global concern?" he said, his fingers tightening around the armrests.

"Of course, and I intend that Klaus Pharmaceuticals will be the global developer, rights holder and distributor of that future cure." He leaned forward with his shoulders, a holdover from his years of competitive football. "My issue with the original trial design is the matter of timing and roll out. As of this year our sales indicators and share price have turned around, so we are competitive again. But we don't have the reserves or good new products far enough down the pipeline to buffer us against the risks and the R&D costs for this drug."

"OK, but what about the future sales of a drug that cures?" Josiah asked. "Can't you raise investor funds against those to pay for front end costs?"

"The market projections we have developed are not as profitable as you might expect. Most of the market will be international, governments in developing countries, with non-existent public health budgets," his lip curled in the hint of a sneer.

"But..." Josiah grasped for some effective counterpoint, "what about, like, USAID grants or World Bank funds?"

Timothy rested his elbows on his knees, lowering his shoulders like a battering ram. "Look," he said in a low voice, "let's be frank. You and I have a common interest here, to keep this company profitable. With no disrespect to your uncle, who preceded me, Klaus Pharmaceuticals was tanking when I got here. You might have been lucky to work in R&D with one of our competitors, or fight your way to some mid-level management position if we had been bought out."

Josiah did not speak, looked down at his hands.

"I know the firm's financials, I know your trust fund is tied to the company's profitability, your grandfather was extremely prudent to structure his grandchildren's' inheritance so you would all have a vested interest in the business."

Josiah felt the blood rising in his cheeks, shifted his weight uncomfortably in the chair.

Timothy shifted to a more avuncular tone, "You have obviously distinguished yourself among your generation in the Klaus family, you are not the typical spoiled trust fund kid. It is not a stretch to imagine you at this desk in another decade."

Josiah looked up, seeing no hint of irony in Timothy's expression.

"Right?"

Josiah nodded slightly, acknowledging the possibility.

"So the best possible scenario for you would be to come to the helm of Klaus Pharmaceuticals with the support of a profitable therapeutic AIDS drug to finance the development of a cure. Imagine what you could do with the company in that kind of position. Imagine what it would mean for you, not only your trust fund, but your career, your legacy."

Josiah pressed his lips together, silent at the tantalizing proximity of the chair on the other side of the desk.

"For that all to happen, for that incredible future, Robert and his team will have to redirect their work in line with the new clinical trial designs." Timothy looked directly into Josiah's eyes. "I know you are close to him, your sympathies understandably lie with your mentor. But remember where your *loyalties* lie. Think about what is really at stake for you."

Josiah attempted to flex his toes, encountered the resistance from his shoes. He let his hands fall to his lap, a silent capitulation.

Timothy sat back in his chair, his shoulders pressing his suit coat back into its perfectly constructed angles. "You will need to be supportive of this direction, and more importantly, you will need to keep me informed. Visitors to the lab, media inquiries, solicitations from our competitors, changes in Robert's schedule, anything that might compromise the integrity of our position, I want to know about."

"And Robert?"

"There is no problem for Robert, as long as he continues to be a scientist. He should not try to interfere with the business. He is not trained for that, he doesn't understand the big picture. But you, young man," a smile cracked through Timothy's sternness, "you will go far if you understand both the science and the business."

Chapter 43

Buds sprouted prematurely from the cherry trees along the Washington Mall. Robert had detoured from his daily route to the institute specifically to see the trees, craving distraction from the conflicting emotions he had battled all week. The week's unexpectedly warm weather had fooled Washington's signature trees by mimicking spring. Robert hoped and worried in turns, both for the trees and for himself. An early spring would be lovely, marking an end to the long cold days. But winter could easily return, shutting down the buds' delicate cellular machinery, obliterating beauty's scheduled return to the Capitol.

Timothy's unilateral decision to redesign the trials affected Robert like a blow to the head, cruelly and powerfully. He had spent the week, unbalanced, dazed by the pain. The research committee had rubber-stamped Timothy's decision. Robert, unable to adjust mid-step to the new course, had simply suspended his efforts.

Behind his office door, Robert had spent the week reading books: biographies and memoirs of the great scientists he admired: Darwin, E.O. Wilson, Schultes, Vavilov. He searched for some advice, some scrap of insight from the pages of the past to direct him. He took some comfort from Darwin, who had required a quarter century to produce his opus *On the Origin of Species*. And E.O. Wilson, whose great advocacy for biodiversity developed almost as a by product of decades of studying ants. Schultes' tragic story – the US Department of Agriculture had abandoned his wild rubber tree research after he had invested years – ended happily with the subsequent development of synthetic rubber. Robert had comforted himself with these famous setbacks and scientific cul de sacs.

His eyes concentrated on the bright yellow line on the pavement before him, marking the shoulder boundary. Science is not linear, he reminded himself, not a simple progression of discoveries leading to success. Unable to refute Timothy's icy logic, or the realities of the pharmaceutical business model, he tried to take comfort in the idea that the research would ultimately lead to a cure.

Vavilov's stories, though, undermined his nascent patience. Yesterday he had read Vavilov waited for nothing, never wasted a moment, even using the time hurrying to or from his institute in Leningrad to read scientific journals. *"We must hurry,"* Vavilov had said with eerie prescience, *"there is much work to do and not much time."*

Robert looked in his rearview mirror, seeing only cars where he had expected to see the cherry trees. The conflicting messages from his heroes' lives so preoccupied his thoughts, that he had driven directly onto the freeway, missing the opportunity to pull over and inspect the cherry trees. The mirror reflected only the endless stream of morning commuters, starting with the Chevy Impala directly behind him. His own car reflected back to him in the mirrored sunglasses of the Impala's driver. Instinctively, Robert merged onto the Beltway, and flowed off at the Bethesda exit. Some minutes later – he had no sense of time this morning – he pulled into the security gate at the institute. The Impala, still behind him, slowed and then sped away.

The telephone, jangling for attention, greeted Robert before he could even unlock the outer lab door.

"Hello?"

"Robert do you have any samples of the *Katanii* in your lab?" Robert struggled to place the gruff voice. "Because I have been directed to turn over all the samples to Klaus Pharmaceuticals, for *security* reasons. Whose security, I would like to know." Robert recognized Phil Krueger's particular sarcastic tone. "They say everything has to be removed from NIH labs, anything living, anything in process, anything in liquid nitrogen. They're sending over a van this afternoon to collect all the *Katanii* material."

Flustered, Robert attempted to comprehend the words streaming through the phone. "Who? What van? I don't know what you are talking about, no one is in my lab yet to get the call."

"No one called, Timothy emailed. Check your messages. I'm none too happy about this," Phil groused. "They disrupt my whole lab, then pull this service agreement budget out from under me. Damn Klaus company directives. At least I got my shelving out of the deal." Phil hung up without saying goodbye.

Robert checked his email messages, thinking of the *Katanii*, nearly two hundred grams, stored in liquid nitrogen in the lab. Two messages from Timothy Crosby had been sent just after 6 am. The first one, the same one Phil had received, ordered the *Katanii* tissue culture program suspended and samples transferred to Klaus Pharmaceuticals. The second message, addressed to Ruth and Robert, outlined a new inventory procedure for the synthetic leaf extract. All acquisitions and uses of the compound had to be accounted for, to a thousandth of a gram, twice daily. Timothy expected morning and evening quantity reports, with a full description of any experimental use.

"I expect you will adhere to these new procedures as a prudent safeguard against competitors, ensuring both the confidentiality of our work, and the viability of our long-term research program. Any discrepancies or deviations in the protocol will be investigated swiftly and seriously.

Thank you for your cooperation, Timothy Crosby"

Robert closed the messages, sat back with a sigh, and looked at the calendar. Today's date, March 21, heralded the spring equinox, equal parts light and dark, promise and peril. With a sudden clarity he recognized a window of opportunity, briefer than this day of solar balance.

Quickly, assuredly, he moved to lock the lab door from the inside, then unclipped the keys from his belt and opened the biohazard refrigerator at the far end of the lab. He removed a large plastic bottle, unscrewed the cap, pulled out the stopper and measured one hundred grams of white powder onto an electronic gram scale. He funnelled this one hundred grams – ten thousand milligrams – into a sealed plastic bag. He turned off the scale, replaced the bottle, and closed the refrigerator. Then he unsealed the liquid nitrogen tank, removed a single glass tube, moisture condensing on its surface like lemonade on a hot day. He resealed the tank, a dozen glass tubes like the one in his hand still safely resting within its confines, and returned to his office.

The insulated lunch pouch Sidney prepared for him everyday sat on his desk. He unzipped the pouch and pulled out his coffee thermos. Typically, he took his coffee break at eleven o'clock. But this morning he consumed the entire contents of the thermos in a few minutes, while contemplating the map above his desk. Even an ordinary life, he mused, even a life like mine – a single dot on this map, defined by routines and familiar people – even this life includes dangers and risks and promise. He shook the last drops of coffee into his wastebasket and slid the narrow glass tube, wrapped with the sealed plastic bag of white powder, into the empty steel thermos. He screwed the cap and cup back into place and returned the thermos to the pouch before zipping it shut.

From beyond his office door, music suddenly blared. Josiah must have arrived, using his own keys. Robert's heart beat faster, jolted by the abrupt sound and the caffeine. He opened the door, watching Josiah adjust the dial to tune in the rock and roll station's morning shock jockeys.

"Morning Josiah," he said with a forced nonchalance.

"G'morning Robert."

"Can you do me a favor before you start your work? Can you take a measurement of all the leaf extract powder we have in the lab?" he did not look directly at Josiah, afraid his eyes would reflect his duplicity rather than his authority. "From now on, we will need morning and evening inventories to provide reports to Timothy."

"No problem," Josiah said, moving from the stereo to the sink.

"And this afternoon we will need to transfer all the *Katanii* we have in our lab to the Klaus labs."

"I know," Josiah said rinsing his hands under a steady stream of water.

"You do?" Robert looked up, surprised.

"I mean...I...I understand," Josiah stammered. "Makes sense given Timothy's decision."

"I guess you understand the business better than I do," Robert said, hesitating before returning to his office.

The Klaus Pharmaceuticals van arrived in the afternoon. The *Katanii* samples were transferred from the Robert's lab's storage tanks to the Klaus storage tanks, liquid nitrogen vapors spilling seductively over steel edges before disappearing along the floor. A tamperproof wire and plastic seal fastened to the tank's release lever confirmed the finality of the transfer.

The evening measurement of the synthetic leaf extract indicated no change from the morning measurement.

Robert picked up his coat and his insulated lunch pouch, with the thermos inside, locked his office and the lab door on his way out. He drove carefully, deliberately, to the Irish pub, where he had asked Ruth to meet him, for a reason he would not give over the phone. They hardly spoke, quickly drank their thick dark beers and said goodbye. He returned to his car with his lunch pouch, lighter without the thermos. She returned to her car, her travel-ready bag heavy with the weight of a thermos, a gift – a potentially life-saving gift – from an old lover for her new lover.

Neither of them noticed the Chevy Impala in the parking lot, as it pulled out behind them, following Ruth's right turn after Robert's left turn.

The next morning Robert chiselled a thin coating of ice off his windshield with a plastic scraper, cringing at the thought of the buds on the cherry trees. The unexpected return of freezing temperatures this spring would have frozen the water in each of the tender buds' cells. Water, expanding into ice, would have ruptured the cells' walls. Ice, thawing again into water would produce only mushy, impotent clusters of cells.

Robert's fleeting grief for this fruitless attempt at growth, gave way to the profound contentment, the visceral sense of rightness that had settled in his body as soon as he had left Ruth the night before.

He drove this icy morning with self-assuredness, handling the steering wheel with an almost athletic grace. The car rose over a bridge, countless Washington commuters passing at right angles beneath him. He marvelled at the enormity of life flowing along the freeway. Each car, each person inside, journeying through their own relationships, their own complexities. Who could predict what decisions they would make, what consequences they would suffer, what successes they would achieve?

Suddenly he heard brakes shrieking and steel thudding against steel. His sureness at the steering wheel evaporated as the car, heavy but frictionless, slid over the icy surface of the bridge. The world spun around him...the Maryland license plate in front of him...the freeway guard rail...the line of cars inching along on the highway below...the big green exit sign...sunglasses and a black Chevy Impala. His head jerked forward and back as he came to a clumsy stop on the narrow shoulder. Blood ran down the back of his hand, where he had cut himself with his own teeth on impact. He looked through all the car's windows for the car that had rear-ended him. No one had stopped. Cars passed in endless succession, offering no explanation.

Ruth answered her phone. "Robert? What's wrong?"

His voice trembled and words tumbled through the phone. She understood there had been a car accident, he was not hurt seriously, but he needed to see her.

He instructed her to meet him at a park just near the Georgetown metro stop. "I will be on a bench near the central pavilion." She thought she heard his teeth chatter.

With her long black wool coat and leather boots, Ruth cut an elegant figure walking the path toward him. Robert looked around. A few Puerto Rican nannies gossiped as they pushed fair-skinned children in strollers. A dishevelled man with a bottle in a brown paper bag sat on another bench, lost in his own suffering. Robert's hand throbbed dully. The air hung tight and cold around him.

She kissed him on the cheek before she sat down. "Thanks for the beer yesterday. Thanks especially for the coffee thermos."

"Were you followed?"

"What?"

"Were you followed? I'm serious. I have noticed a black Chevy Impala several times." Bob glanced anxiously over Ruth's shoulder. "I drove to a mall then walked to the metro so I wouldn't be followed."

"Bob, what are you talking about? Who would be following you?"

"I was run off the road this morning, I don't think it was an accident. When I got to my office, the doors were still locked, but everything was slightly out of place. The bottles were turned, my papers were adjusted. I'm sure someone was going through my things."

"Someone like who?"

"I'm not sure. Someone who is very interested in our research.

Maybe someone who knows I had access to the *Katanii*. I think Stefano should get out of town. I really think he should leave the country."

"Bob, you're sounding just a bit paranoid. Stefano is not going anywhere right now, we are almost finished with his treatment. This week I took him for some bloodwork. The TB treatment was successful. His HIV viral load is low, and his t-cell count is really high. Zahara thinks by next weekend she should be able to give him the *Katanii* with an extra dose of the synthetic extract."

"Can he at least stay somewhere else? I don't like him at your apartment."

"Are you jealous?" she said, disdain creeping into her words.

"My God, Ruth! Listen to what I'm saying! This has nothing to do with our ancient history. I'm talking about a man's life. If your experiment works, if...*our*...experiment works, Stefano could be the only documented case of a cure. He would be the most compelling evidence we have to persuade Timothy to return to our research design."

"I know. Don't think I haven't thought about that. If Timothy hasn't changed his mind about the trials by the time Stefano finishes these treatments, I am thinking to go to the media, to let them see a cured man. If that doesn't persuade Klaus," she inhaled deeply, "maybe it will persuade competitors."

"You would risk your career by going to the media?"

"My career? You mean my job with Klaus?" her upper lip turned in a sneer. "I would gladly wave good bye to Timothy and the whole lot of them if someone else were willing to back the research into a cure."

Robert pressed the bandage on his hand. "And what about me, where is my role if you go with a competitor?"

"Wouldn't you follow the research, whoever sponsors it?"

He pressed his fingers to his temples and briefly covered his face with his hands. "Probably. But if you go to the media, what will you tell them about where Stefano's drugs came from? Klaus will know I am the breach." He thrust his hands into his coat pockets. "I'm worried about Stefano's safety. Mine too."

"Understood."

"Promise me you will let me know before you go to the media?" his voice was almost childlike.

She nodded reassuringly.

"I think it is safest if I don't see you again, unless Timothy summons us again. And I will not see Stefano again, it's nothing personal." He noticed the diamond on her left hand. "I am happy if you have found someone to love, but God, you do take your risks, don't you?"

A fleeting smile crossed her face.

"For the time being, I have to be completely committed to Timothy's research schedule. I am not willing to compromise what we have already accomplished."

He could hear the fear in his own voice. "At least not anymore than I already have."

"All right Bob. I'll see you when the time is right." She kissed his cheek again and left him sitting alone on the bench.

Chapter 44

Z ahara closed and curtained Ruth's bedroom – the place where Ruth and Stefano had dreamed their separate dreams together – as if in preparation for mourning. She welcomed the darkness, her American version of Chochotte's dark gojo, in preparation for the hallucinations Stefano would experience once she gave him the *Katanii* medicine.

She had arrived this Friday morning, skipping a molecular biology lecture, because she wanted a full three days at Ruth's to watch over Stefano.

With the bedroom ready, she went to kitchen, mashed the thawed *Katanii* in a white marble mortar and pestle, then mixed it with soft bananas to help buffer his stomach. Stefano sat on the counter next to where she was working, recounting a story about Afghanistan at this time of year.

"In the spring, in the countryside, all the trees are in bloom. I thought the whole country is white and pink with the blooms of apricot trees. Most of the men had rifles across their backs. They look as if to kill you if you make a bad joke." He pantomimed aiming a firearm at an imaginary offender. "But they are so gentle with their apricot trees, they prune them, they admire them, like little boys. I even heard some men sing to their apricot trees. Beauty can to inspire even hard hearts."

He avoided looking at the bowl and spoon Zahara had set next to him. "But that was before the drought, before the last war with the Americans."

"Stefano. We should to start."

"What do you think Zahara?" he asked pointing at the bowl. "Are you sure about this? I remember the screams I heard that night when I came to the gojo where you were – the one next to the forest in Chochotte. Will it be very much painful?"

"The medicine will pass through you after some time. I will be here and Ruth will come after lunch. You shouldn't fear for the pain." She feigned confidence, inwardly second-guessing her dosage. "This is what

I did with my father for many people. And it has worked. You saw Ato Worku with your own eyes, yes?"

"Yes I saw him." He raised the spoon in toast. "OK, here's to life." He delivered it to his mouth. "Mmmm," he grimaced, "tastes awful, no wonder Ato Worku screamed."

Zahara forced a smile and turned her back to him to rinse out the mortar in the sink, her heart thumping. What if something goes wrong, she thought. What if this man should die? Will I have poisoned him? She looked out the window over the sink. Will it work without Papa, without the trees, without the faith, or the prayers of the village? Her hand rested on the small plastic bag of white powder. Yes, here was the proof. Real American scientists thought it would work. Big companies and millions of dollars would prove it. She need not worry. She forced her fears into silence by singing a song from her childhood, her lips forming words that linked her to her distant home.

She spooned powder onto a gram scale, measured out a thousand milligrams, double the dose she had been giving him these last weeks. She remembered her father saying "*he is a big man*" as he had increased the amount of medicine for Ato Worku. She measured out another two hundred milligrams and stirred the powder into a glass of orange juice. She said a quick prayer and handed it to Stefano.

He looked at the surface of the juice, still spinning in a tiny whirlpool. He inhaled, paused, and exhaled. Two gulps and the juice was gone.

They looked at each other, both recognizing the anxiety on the other's face, as they waited for something to happen. She blinked. He laughed, "I'm not dead yet! What now?"

Gratefully, she laughed. "Now you should rest, your body will be working hard."

She led him into the darkened bedroom. "I can just imagine the clinical trials," Stefano joked, "thousands of hand holders to a bunch of raving HIV zombies in tiny dark cells." He sat down on the bed.

She bristled at his joke, at the impossibility he described. The hallucinations her village took for spirits, Americans would declare an unacceptable side effect. She closed the door to complete the darkness, only to be overwhelmed by homesickness. She could not reconcile her healing work with these actions in Ruth's home. In Chochotte, she had

had complete faith in her father; in his methods, in the tools he used and the knowledge he embodied. But this country – with its precision and its demand for reason – challenged her faith. Maybe Robert was right, she thought. *Who am I to think I can cure this man? What credentials do I have? What kind of dangerous game am I playing?*

She felt the darkness in her bones, but appreciated how it masked her doubtful expression. "Please, Stefano, tell me more about Afghanistan."

"Yes. When I was in Afghanistan, I kept thinking how little the countryside must have changed from the time Vavilov was there. 1924, I think, he was there. Europe was busy becoming modern and he was to collecting plants from primitive farms. He was in Afghanistan for months, travelling everywhere on horseback. He suffered much there. It is a very hard country. But with secret wonders too. I thought of him sleeping beneath the gaze of the giant Buddhas at Bamian. I got to see them also. They don't exist now. Imagine the Taliban taking a rocket launcher to something so sublime. I felt the same way about Chochotte."

She suddenly shot upright in her chair. "What? What about Chochotte?"

He winced. "Is this how it starts? You start to feel it in the lymph glands? Armpits, throat?" He let out a little moan, "I'm not good with pain. I have no endurance for it."

"Concentrate on your breathing. Here, take some water." She held a glass out for him, guided his hand through the darkness. "Stefano? You were talking about Chochotte."

"Chochotte, yes. We collected so many samples. Did we get them all packed? It's almost sunrise. I want to get back to Addis, I want some pasta, there is a wonderful Italian restaurant in Addis."

It had started – the timelessness, the disorientation. She knew this process, felt reassured to observe it proceeding as she remembered. She felt his forehead – the fever had not started yet – and covered him with a blanket. She sat back next to him and began to sing, the same song her father had told her pilgrims sang when they went to the sacred churches in Lalibela. A joyful song, with a brief melody line, that she repeated over and over, providing Stefano a focus, a distraction from the pain that would shortly make him wish he had chosen death over this.

By the time Ruth arrived – a blinding crack of light exploded into the darkness as she opened the door and entered the bedroom – the fever and visions had begun. Stefano cried out at the light, raising hands as if to shield himself from blows. Ruth closed the door, restoring the darkness. Zahara reached out for Ruth, her night vision destroyed.

"What's happening, what is he doing?" Ruth said.

"I gave him the *Katanii*, he is going through the process. Don't worry."

"How long has he been like this?"

"Couple of hours. This is just the beginning."

Ruth and Zahara sat on either side of him, listening to him whimper, watching him turn from one side to the other, occasionally wiping the sweat off his brow. Zahara continued to sing until his breath became deep and regular.

"He will sleep a little now, maybe an hour."

"OK, good. Zahara, go ahead and take a break, there's food in the bag on the counter. I'll stay here."

A second crack of light cut the darkness as Zahara left the room. Confronted again with the rigid, dustless world of Ruth's American apartment, she shielded her eyes until they grew accustomed to the orange light coming through her lids. Only then could she open her eyes and find the bag on the counter – Chinese food. She carried a paper carton of fried rice to the couch, left the chopsticks in the bag. Ruth had tried to show her how to use chopsticks once, but they had felt stiff and awkward, so she just scooped up food with the tips of her fingers.

She listened with one ear, and ate with one hand. She could relax a bit until he woke again.

Looking over the stack of books Stefano had left on the table, she chose Vavilov's *Five Continents*, open where he had left off reading this afternoon. She pulled it closer with her clean hand. Stefano's handwritten notes filled the margins, he had underlined and marked specific passages, one with an exclamation point.

A moonlit night around the giant Buddhas and among the snow-covered peaks of Hindu Kush created an especially solemn mood. It could be said that one looks into the depth of thousands of years.

Zahara remembered Stefano's own flowery language from just a few hours ago evoking this same place, Bamian.

She found another passage Stefano had marked; a nonchalant description of danger:

We were considered suspicious in the eyes of the fanatical and moody mullahs and from the roofs stones were presently flying at the peacefully resting caravan. There was no time for explanations and persuasions came to nothing; it became necessary to continue on immediately.

He had marked stories: horses falling off treacherous mountain paths in Afghanistan; outdrinking drunken government officials in China; even Vavilov's meeting with Haile Selassie before he became the emperor of Abyssinia. Zahara lost herself in the book, choosing passages at random, coming again to the photos from Abyssinia. Regardless of country or climate, Vavilov consistently appeared in all the photos as a dashing figure dressed in a suit with a hat and a leather shoulder satchel. She observed in his eyes and straight nose something of Stefano, as if they shared a common ancestor.

A crashing sound from the bedroom interrupted her reading. Zahara rush backed into the darkness. "What happened?"

"He just knocked over a glass of water, he's kicking and flailing. Careful, don't cut yourself." Ruth switched on a small flashlight to quickly sweep up the glass with a wet washcloth. Stefano's labored breath came quickly.

"I think he's hyperventilating," Ruth said apprehensively. "What should we do?"

"He's all right, this will pass. I have seen this many times, always only a few minutes." Zahara took Stefano's hand and talked to him in soothing tones. She breathed deeply and deliberately until his breathing eventually mimicked hers, and Ruth exhaled her anxiety.

Chapter 45

R uth and Zahara spent the next two days in an orbit around Stefano's
bedside, taking shifts, following him through his incoherent
dreams, his terrifying visions, his periods of painful lucidity.

For moments Zahara would escape from the darkness and travel
with Vavilov across the globe, to Syria, Japan, Mexico. His humor,
obvious even through the translation, made her smile. Always
serious about his science, he somehow managed to find the whole
world amusing. She longed to be so nimble in the world, to travel
without trauma.

The hours of their vigil telescoped and collapsed with a strange
elasticity. While Zahara travelled on brief vicarious journeys with
Vavilov, Ruth remained almost constantly in seclusion with Stefano.
When she stepped into the kitchen after two full days of darkness
sunlight seemed to dazzle off her white porcelain sink. The contrast
made her nauseous. She slid to the floor, exhausted as much from the
emotional strain as the physical strain. She could barely comprehend
how she had arrived at this juncture, where everything she valued
seemed to hinge on the surreal events taking place in the stifling
darkness of her bedroom.

She had no sense of how long she had been on the floor when
Zahara called out for help. Ruth braced herself for the darkness and
tried to decipher the meaning of Stefano's groaning and grunting.

"Grab his arms," Zahara said, sotto voce, trying to keep Stefano
from hearing.

Ruth reached blindly for where she expected his arms to be, finding
nothing of the movement she heard. Eventually she could discern the
outlines of the sweat-drenched sheets wrapped around his waist. He
pulled the ends in opposite directions with all his remaining strength,
as if he meant to sever himself in two within the tightening knot of
the sheets. Ruth and Zahara struggled to pry the sheets from his hands
as he screamed at them, "It's dirty, it's dirty, I have to be rid of it!
Bitches, don't touch me. You will go to hell with me!"

He spat at Ruth, and then proceeded to vomit into his lap. He heaved again and again, doubling over with the involuntary convulsions of his stomach. But nothing came. There was only the hollow roaring of his body trying to turn itself inside out.

Something in Ruth's consciousness snapped, the darkness became intolerable. Angrily she flipped on the lights. "Oh my God, what are we doing here in the dark! He's going to die, it's poisoning him. Call an ambulance."

The two women blinked, unseeing.

"God damn it, Zahara, I'm calling an ambulance." Ruth lurched toward the door, opened it, closed it, opened it again in a panic. "Jesus, Stefano, hang on. I'm going to do something." Ruth bolted into the kitchen and fumbled for the telephone.

Zahara pulled Stefano, still heaving, over on his side. She pushed his head in line with his spine so he wouldn't cut off the flow of air in his windpipe and rushed to Ruth. Zahara struck the phone out of her hands mid-dial. "What are you doing?"

"You're killing him, I'm not going to let him die!"

"No, this is how my father cured the sickness. This is what happens every time! He's not dying. If you call the ambulance, what will you tell them? We have give him experimental drugs, stolen drugs?" Her eyes blazed. "And what will they do with me? Some mad village girl? And with Robert?" Zahara pushed Ruth to the floor with surprising force. Ruth crumpled against the refrigerator, sobbing. Zahara picked up the telephone from the floor and carried it into the bedroom, slamming the door behind her.

Stefano had stopped his heaving. She gently unwrapped the sheets from around his waist. She mopped the sweat from his body, and he drifted into unconsciousness.

Zahara must have closed her eyelids on verge of sleep, oblivious to Ruth's return. She heard only a disembodied whisper. "I just can't bear the thought of losing him now. He can't go now. Don't go now. You know what this feels like? As if each fiber of your heart is being torn apart?"

"Yes," Zahara whispered, "I do know."

Chapter 46

Moonlight shone in through the kitchen window as Zahara poured coffee into three cups on a wooden tray, methodically measuring out spoonfuls of sugar. She brought the tray to the coffee table, setting it down next to Vavilov's book with a pleasing thump.

She walked back toward the bedroom, feeling an incredible lightness as she passed the windows, casting moon shadows on the floor. After nearly eighteen hours, Stefano had finally woken and immediately asked for coffee.

In the bedroom, now bathed in the welcome warmth of the lamp on the bedstand, Stefano sat upright in bed, holding Ruth's hand, wearing the grin of a child who has accomplished some mischief without punishment.

Zahara giggled in the almost unreasonable air of giddiness in the room.

"How are you feeling?" she asked.

"I'm still alive," he smiled "and ravenous."

"Good. Then the medicine is gone from your stomach."

Ruth and Zahara each held one of Stefano's arms, led him slowly across the silver stripes of moonlight on the floor to the couch.

Ruth lit a candle, then another and another until the room glowed and their shadows bounced in the flickering light like children at a playground.

"We did it," Zahara finally declared. "It happened just like when my father used the medicine."

"Every time your father treated someone it was like this?" Ruth asked.

"Yes, except no Chinese food for me in my village." She grinned at Ruth. "He should eat only something small now, some toast maybe, and honey."

"Yes, toast and honey for all of us," Ruth said, heading into the kitchen.

Stefano took both of Zahara's hands in his. "Can I ever tell you enough thanks?"

"Your thanks should go to my father, and to God, I only did their work."

He leaned in toward her, kissed her forehead, closed his eyes and gave silent thanks.

Ruth opened the curtains in the bedroom, watched Zahara step out onto the sidewalk below, heading back to her dorm for some hours of sleep before returning to her morning classes.

She returned to the bed, lay next to Stefano between fresh sheets. With infinite slowness she touched every inch of his body, confirming to herself his wholeness. They did not speak, but both sensed some profound difference in his veins. The assault Zahara waged within his body had succeeded.

Instinctively he responded to her touch, closed his eyes, and relaxed in the pleasure of her hands on him. She raised her body over his, moved back and forth over him, the way the ocean caresses the shore. Then a cry, saltwater tears, a release of gratitude.

He framed her face in his hands, kissing the tears off her cheeks.

"We have time now," he said. "There is time."

He stroked her hair until her breath slowed with sleep. He drifted off. They slept together in the same dream.

Chapter 47

Timothy closed the phone, softly uttered a curse under his breath as he restrained the impulse to throw the phone against his night table – the messenger of betrayal.

"How could she?" he asked, as if expecting a response from his empty bedroom. "Did she really think I wouldn't find out?"

He sat upright in bed, a coiled spring, his body unable to release its tension. Throwing off the covers, he strode into the bathroom.

He pulled the handle to the extreme left allowing the bath water to thunder into the tub. He poured in Chinese medicinal oil, the pungent scent of menthol rising into his flared nostrils.

"Does she think I don't know what I am doing?" He looked into the mirror, seeing only the outline of his body in the darkness. He made a fist and struck the air before him. Misjudging the distance, his knuckles hit the mirror, the glass cracked with a strangely beautiful ringing.

He recoiled in surprise, his hand numb. He closed his eyes, forced himself to notice only to the sound of three carefully measured exhalations.

Then he lowered himself into the water, flinching at the heat, and focused his eyes on the row of black tiles. Aside from the rhythmic rise and fall of his lungs, he did not appear to move. He sat for a long time, envisioning all of his possible options. He eliminated one potential course of action after another, finding some flaw, some unacceptable associated risk. Finally, only the most impossible course remained as possible.

As the first shards of the dull morning light began to infiltrate into the bathroom, he closed his eyes. He repeated to himself the words of a superior he had worked with at the Central Intelligence Agency, *"We balance the lives of the many over the lives of the few, it is an unassailable ethic."*

He played out his action in his mind long enough to feel that it had already happened, he had only to wait for the clock to catch up with events that had already transpired.

As he finally opened his eyes, daylight had claimed its victory over the night. The water surrounding his body had cooled, so he shivered with the menthol and the temperature. As he returned to the present, he perceived the ache in his knuckles and a red tinge in the water. Blood. His own. He stood up, lifted the drain with his toe, then opened again the faucet, allowing the water to wash the blood from his hands.

Chapter 48

Stefano stepped outside and stood still, simply experiencing life. He felt the air moving in and out of his lungs. He smelled the gentle perfume of spring. He watched a businessman on the sidewalk – how wonderful to see a man scowling, hurrying somewhere along the sidewalk. He knew a week after Zahara had left the apartment that she had been right. He wasn't going to die. His viral load tests showed undetectable levels of the virus in his blood, though it would take another year to confirm that his body had stopped producing antibodies to the virus. He could not have hoped for more. He did not know he would have much less.

He walked down the sidewalk, away from the scowling man, seeing a yellow fire hydrant, a fat black American car – *Impala* – he noticed, a weed growing audaciously through a crack in the pavement. *Fantastic.*

Today was Wednesday. He had decided Wednesday would be a good day for a wedding, had arranged for Ruth to meet him at the courthouse at lunchtime. Zahara would be their witness. Tomorrow he would send photos to his mother.

But first the flowers.

Zahara handed her blue book to the proctor at the front of the hall. Drained, but satisfied with the final exam she had written for her molecular biology course, she stood next to the door and watched as the students filed out. Where would they go now? How would they spend their summers? She would return to Ethiopia in a few days, to stay again with Ato Worku and she wanted to remember how the hall looked: the chairs with their hinged desktops, the girls in tennis shoes, the book bags, the paper coffee cups, the big black and white clock ticking away the minutes above the projection screen.

In a long skirt with an Ethiopian sash, she looked overdressed, but she planned to head directly to a wedding.

In the metro she opened her bag and pulled out Vavilov's book. She would start at the beginning now. She would read the preface to the

English edition. She read about his academic career, his early professor-ship at an agronomy institute. She read about his steady rise in the Soviet system. She read about his arrest. His arrest? She read of Stalin's trumped up charges that Vavliov's theories of genetics threatened the party. She read of Vavilov's imprisonment. Imprisonment? The story continued: this man – this scientist who had scoured the world in search of plants to improve Soviet agriculture, this man whom Stefano called the father of his science – this man died of starvation in a small prison cell. She looked at the cover; at Vavilov's eyes and long nose, so similar to Stefano's. She shuddered.

Robert peered into the microscope. He observed very few viral copies in the blood sample. The therapy might work in humans, as it was working in vitro. Staggered doses of the synthetic extract wiped out most of the virus. When the drug was withheld the viral load bounced back almost to initial levels, but slowly. When they got too high, the drug could be re-administered to suppress replication.

The drug did not have to be administered constantly. The therapy, just as Timothy had envisioned it, would be cheaper than conventional therapy regimes. Robert pushed back his stool and looked across the lab. This was a success, a limited success.

He would call Sidney and tell her. He would tell her how much he loved her.

Ruth picked up the phone, dialled the number of the Washington Journal, asked for the reporter who had called her a half dozen times before for comments or background on his stories. She said she had a breakthrough to discuss, she would give the story to him exclusively if he would meet her the following day. He agreed.

It was a long shot, risky, but she reminded herself that she specialized in risks.

She picked up the phone again and dialled Robert's number. "Bob? It's me. I am giving you warning. The experiment was successful and tomorrow I am meeting with a reporter." She hung up, didn't wait for an answer, didn't want to hear his apprehension, his list of possible catastrophes.

She looked at a clock on her desk. It was almost time. Almost time to be married. She picked up her bag and walked out of her office.

Timothy Crosby heard the jingle of Ruth's bag disappear as she walked down the hall. He walked directly into her office and closed the door. He pressed a few buttons on her office phone, bringing up the call log. He dialled the last two numbers, hanging up as soon as the parties on the other end greeted him.

He pressed the receiver button again until he heard a dial tone, slowly dialling a number he knew from memory. He did not say hello, did not force any pleasantries. "It's time...yes, it must be before tomorrow. It must be outside not in the apartment...yes...all right." He hung up the phone, deleted the number from the call log and walked out her door, closing it quietly behind him.

Flowers. Stefano stepped inside the flower shop. He would buy her the flashiest, sexiest members of the plant kingdom; evolution's advertising, the exquisite colors and smells and designs that attracted pollinators and seduced humans.

He chose gardenias, for their heavenly smell, white lilies, for their sexy shape, pink chrysanthemums, for their amazing design, red roses, for their deep color, and finally, orchids to remind her of how exotic the world can seem. The shopkeeper chuckled a little at his choices. Stefano proudly acknowledged his excess. The flowers' plastic wrapping crinkled as it brushed against the door on his way out.

There can be no greater sweetness than this, he thought. Life cannot possibly offer more than this fullness. To be alive, to be in love, to smell gardenias on the way to my wedding.

Stefano stepped off the sidewalk, his face nose deep in flowers, so he did not notice the fat black American car. He heard a car accelerate. He looked up just in time to see a driver with silver sunglasses. He held up his hand, to be sure the driver saw him. The driver nodded, close enough that Stefano could see his own reflection in the mirrored lenses before his world went black.

The shopkeeper ran out of the store at that horrible sound. She saw a tall man lying still on the pavement, his bouquet of flowers just beyond his reach.

Chapter 49

Few people attended Stefano's memorial. Robert sat a short distance from Zahara and Ruth, next to a couple of colleagues who knew Stefano's work. Ruth, shocked into numbness, had nevertheless arranged for the memorial and for the body to be shipped to Italy, to the woman who had nearly been her mother-in-law.

Three days after the memorial, the day before Zahara was to fly to Ethiopia, Ruth asked her to come to the apartment to go through some of Stefano's things together. She gave Zahara his field collection manual, his fountain pen, his camera and his copy of Vavilov's book. They sat before his things for a long time in silence, holding onto each others' hands.

Finally Ruth closed her eyes and spoke. "My future is shattered. It was all there for me, everything I had wanted was within my reach. And now..." her voice trailed off, wandering down paths she could not speak.

Zahara waited, looked over each of the items of her sudden inheritance.

"Does it get easier?" Ruth's voice finally returned, "do you miss your father any less?"

Inhalation. "I will never forget him, never stop to wish that he was still with me. But this is my life now, and thanks to God, he is still in my heart. And we continued his work. At least for a while."

Ruth winced at Zahara's words.

At the airport Ruth gave Zahara a letter, asked her to read it on the plane. The embraced and wept, both unable to say goodbye.

Zahara could see more and more of Washington as the plane gained altitude. Her now familiar world, once again dropped away from her, shrinking until her life there seemed utterly inconsequential. Would she matter again, somewhere else? She looked around at the other passengers. Did they all experience this physical separation, this painful change in perspective? Were they leaving their lives behind as well? Were they similarly caught up in the pain of their fates, in the anticipation of returning to their homes?

The flight attendant asked Zahara what she would like to drink.

"Nothing now, thank you. No, wait. Coffee. Please bring me coffee." She turned over the letter. She could not read it yet, did not want to acknowledge Ruth was already so distant from her. She put the letter into her bag, next to the field manual she had inherited. She pulled out a cosmetics case, reached past compacts and round containers of powder packed only for the purpose of camouflaging a single round plastic petri dish. She pulled out the dish, with its miniaturized versions of the orange scalloped fungi growing inside. She held it in her lap so that it caught the sunlight from the window, closed her eyes and waited for her coffee.

She recognized Ato Worku, immediately, his arms out, leaning back with a wide grin. She sank into his embrace, her gold earrings pressed between them. "And so, my brilliant scholar is back with me." He shooed away the thin men with baggage carts vying to take her luggage to the car. "I am planning a party for you, a great big party. All my friends will come." She smiled, her life no longer inconsequential.

"Yes, Ato Worku. Thank you."

Mohammed joined them, quietly took charge of the luggage, and opened the car door for her. She climbed inside, imaging that Stefano or Ruth may have sat in the same spot.

She reached out to touch Ato Worku's hand on the seat next to her. "I have an important package to deliver. Do you mind if we stop somewhere before we go to your house?"

"Anywhere, my dear. We have all the time in the world."

"Maybe, maybe not," she said.

From the driver's seat Mohammed greeted her in Oromo, asked her where she would like to go.

Inhalation. How sweet it sounded to hear her language again. She told Mohammed where she wished to go. The National Institute for Biodiversity and Conservation, saying the name in English and translating it loosely into Oromo. She had looked up the address while she was still in Washington and knew it was near the Mobil roundabout on the Palace Road.

Addis Ababa appeared to her so shabby and slow compared to Washington. Gradually, with each road they passed, each sign she read, each horn honk she heard, she absorbed the fact that she was back in her country. Back where the signs were hand painted in the jazzy lines of Amharic, where the other women on the street looked like her, where she was not an outsider, where things reflected the imprint of humans not machines. Here – a fruit stand, a white butcher shop with two goat carcasses hanging inside, further on – a grove of eucalyptus trees, a stretch of brilliant green grass along the road.

They arrived at a complex of buildings at the edge of town. The guard waved Ato Worku's car through without asking their names. Zahara and Ato Worku walked into the main building. She stopped and inhaled; surprise, recognition. A display case held the grainheads of some of the country's diverse sorghum varieties. Above the case, as if presiding over it, as if welcoming her to the institute, as if knowing that she would come, a portrait of Vavilov gazed down on her. The same portrait she knew so well from the cover of his book.

She put a hand to her chest. She stepped closer and laughed, certain about where she was – as she had been certain when she first saw the photograph of the leaf in Robert's lecture. Certain she had arrived at the right place. Perhaps Stefano had stood here and thought the same thing. She would never know.

A young woman walked by in a lab coat, smiled, revealing a broken tooth. "Hello? May I help you?"

"I was hoping to talk to someone in your tissue culture lab. I have a specimen from Chochotte that should be maintained here in the collections."

"Well, that's my lab. You can come with me and then we can talk to the director, is he expecting you?"

"No." Zahara looked up at Vavilov. "At least I don't think so."

Ato Worku, disappointed that Zahara wanted to postpone the party until after she returned from Chochotte, did not protest. He even masked his hurt when she told him she would make the trip to see her father's grave without him.

The next day, as she sat in the car next to Mohammed, she finally opened the letter from Ruth.

My dearest Zahara,

How can I tell you everything in my heart? For the possibilities you have brought into my life, I will always be grateful to you – and your father. For the ways you have shared my losses with me, I am grateful to the universe for your companionship. I hope we may continue that companionship under happier circumstances someday.

I don't know if you will return to the university in the fall or not. But please don't abandon your work, what was our work. You have something very valuable, a knowledge the world desperately needs. For now, it is still yours. Klaus Pharmaceuticals has not patented the combination of natural substances. Remember this. If you can document your father's cure, in English, before Klaus resumes its combination research, they cannot claim it exclusively. Publish an article about it in Ethiopia, Ato Worku can help you. Then send it to Robert, to me, to Stefano's institute. Then Klaus will have to negotiate rights with you, with Chochotte as a community. In exchange for the rights to commercialize your knowledge, you could press for funding for conservation programs, AIDS prevention, things that could benefit Chochotte and your country.

Or you could turn to the non-governmental organizations, try to collaborate with the international traditional knowledge networks. Of course they have very little money, so couldn't commercialize your cure on a large scale, but perhaps the knowledge of how to use the natural substances could be promoted throughout East Africa.

There is no guarantee of a happy ending either way. Perhaps the pharmaceutical industry is not really interested in a cure, perhaps they fear it. Stefano's death – I am sure it was no accident – tells me that even the possibility of a cure is threatening. I have no proof of who killed him. But surely it was engineered, if not carried out, by someone close to me or Bob. The power of money and markets can be intoxicating. Even good people can rationalize reprehensible decisions in the name of good business principles.

Josiah, from Bob's lab, has accepted an offer from Klaus, a research fellow position working on cholesterol drugs. It would take Bob at least a year to bring a new researcher up to speed, even if the Katanii work were allowed to continue. Timothy has pulled me off the HIV research. I am devastated to think about how close we were, how close we could be to a cure. I am thinking of leaving the company to work with some colleagues at the International AIDS Vaccine Initiative. But I must make my moves very carefully, my life may be in danger as well.

I am sure you will try to return to Chochotte. I am sorry to tell you about Chochotte in this way. I wish I could have told you this in person, but I couldn't bear to hurt you. Please remember Chochotte with its trees and the birds and coffee plants the way it was. I never saw what you saw. By the time Stefano and I arrived in Chochotte, those things were gone. The trees had been cut to make way for chat farms. Your Chochotte still exists, but only in your heart.

Think carefully about how you can stay true to your values and what you father would have wished for you. And then have faith in your decisions. You have already made so many good ones.

Be well, my dear friend. Know that I love you, as did Stefano. I will miss you. But who knows what the future will hold?

Always,

Ruth

Zahara looked out at the brilliant landscape through a kaleidoscope of tears.

Mohammed looked over at her. "Is it difficult to come home?"

"I'm not sure where my home is."

"Well, Ethiopia will always be your country." He slowed down to swerve around a man on muleback.

"But what is a country when it is just the place where you have lost the most?"

"Hmm," he nodded with a little smile. "Then it is the place that best reminds you of all you had. That I know for sure."

The villages rolled past, the ridges rose and the gorges fell. She breathed in the colors, the air, the world she had left: pink dresses, blue cans, a red door on a roadside shop, a golden bird, yellow flowers, a green leaf with red veins.

"Stop!"

"Here?"

"Yes, Mohammed, please stop here."

The car was still moving as she opened the door and sprinted back into the forest along the road. Green leaves with red veins. She crashed through the underbrush to a big tree, as if she were running to greet an old friend. Green leaves with red veins. It was the same. She looked up at the light fluttering through the branches. She looked down and parted the underbrush over and over, as if looking for something she had dropped. Twenty feet from the base of the tree she found it, a sapling with three new green leaves. One leaf had red veins. She dug it up with her bare hands, dirt crumbling off the root ball as she ran back to the car.

"All right, good. We're nearly there, right?"

"Almost there, Zahara."

She knew exactly where Nataniel's grave lay, even robbed of the nearby trees that had shaded it. Her stomach clenched as she walked past a few empty gojos, past the bare ground where the clinic gojo had stood. She heard the silence in the village where once had been the sound of children and cooking. She walked to what had been the edge of the forest, now blanketed in chat. She pushed back the plants that tumbled over the edge of the grave.

"Papa. Papa, look what has happened to us. It's all gone Papa." She dropped to her knees, touched the earth with her hand. She grasped at blades of green grass, the only markers of her father's grave. And she pulled them up, ripped them out of the earth, tore away at the earth itself. "I miss you. I miss you so much. What am I supposed to do? What am I supposed to do with this life?" She looked at the hole she had made, breathed the smell of soil on her skin.

Then, gently, as if she were praying, she set her sapling in the ground. Three green leaves – one with red veins – nodded in the breeze as she pressed the earth in around the roots. She put her head down, her ear against the earth to listen for an answer. She was still for a long time. Until she could hear the individual blades of grass rubbing against each other. Until she could hear the roots pressing their way into the tiny spaces in the soil. Until she could hear the insects burrowing in the darkness beneath her. And she heard.

Glossary:

Al-hamd'Allah – (Arabic) 'thanks to God'

Amharic – the national language of Ethiopian, also referring to the dominant ethnic group in Ethiopia

asmari – from northern Ethiopia

Ato – an honorific, the Ethiopian equivalent of Mr.

betel nut – the astringent kernel of the seed of the betel palm, chewed in many tropical regions in combination with slaked lime and the leaves of the betel plant. Persistent chewing stains the teeth blood red

birr – the Ethiopian currency, one birr equals approximately 12 U.S. cents

chat – (spelled qat in Arabic) a tropical evergreen plant with leaves chewed as a stimulant

ciao bella – (Italian) 'hello beautiful'

ELISA – *Enzyme-linked immunosorbent assay (ELISA)*, a biochemical technique used mainly in immunology to detect the presence of an antibody or an antigen in a sample

eruca sativa – the Latin name for arugula or rocket

faranji – a bastardization of the word Francais, used in Ethiopia to describe foreigners, particularly Europeans, or those of European descent

Five Continents – a volume of Nikolai Vavilov's field notes published posthumously

gabbi – a light, woven cotton shawl traditionally worn in Ethiopia, wrapped around the upper body in cool weather or wrapped loosely around the head as a turban

gojo – a typical rural Ethiopian dwelling, with a circular base constructed of straw, wood, or stone with a conical thatched roof

grazie – (Italian) 'thank you'

injeera – a traditional Ethiopian sour pancake made from the flour of the native teff grain mixed with water to make a batter and then allowed to ferment before it is poured onto a hot griddle to cook

Insha'Allah – (Arabic) 'God-willing' a phrase commonly spoken by Muslims, indicating their belief that their fate is already written by God

Isaan – the Northeast region of Thailand

ishy – (Amharic) 'thank you'

Kazanchis – a popular area of Addis Ababa known for its abundant bars and night clubs

Khorat – the capital city of Nakhon Ratchasima Province in the Northeast of Thailand, a region commonly referred to as Isaan

Lalibela – a town in northern Ethiopia, one of the country's holiest cities, home to a dozen monolithic churches carved out of the ground, Lalibela is visited by many Ethiopian Orthodox Christian pilgrims

mamasan – a woman who supervises the prostitutes in Southeast Asian bars, roughly equivalent to a madam in Western prostitution

mia cara – (Italian) 'my dear'

mi amore – (Italian) 'my love'

On the Origin of Species – Charles Darwin's seminal work on evolutionary theory, published in 1859

Oromo – an Ethnic group in Ethiopia and Northern Kenya, also refers to the language of the group

oud – agarwood, which is burned for its fragrant oil in Africa, the Middle East and South Asia

Patpong – Bangkok's red light district, and busy night market known for catering to foreign tourists

punica granatum – the Latin name for pomegranat

shamma – a native Ethiopian robe-like dress of white cotton

spasiba – (Russian) 'thank you'

taej – a fermented honey wine

teff – an important food grain native to Ethiopia, the seed of the teff grass is used to make injeera

Vavilov, Nikolai – a prominent Russian and Soviet botanist and geneticist best known for having identified the centres of origin of cultivated plants

wanniye – a bird native to Ethiopia

wat – Ethiopian stew made of chicken or lamb, usually eaten with injeera

Acknowledgements:

I owe a debt of gratitude to a small army of people around the world who have helped me with this book in myriad ways. Whatever this story may inspire in others is to their credit. Whatever errors or short-comings it contains are my responsibility alone.

Stefano Padulosi's charisma and stories inspired a sleepless night in May of 2000 that served as the genesis for this story. He has subsequently allowed me to tag along on his travels, and he has enthusiastically read of his fictionalized doppelganger.

Thanks to Ruth Raymond, formerly of Bioversity, who tirelessly promoted the organization's work and introduced me to Stefano.

Dr. Ashir, Dr. Gregory Levin, and Emma Levin hosted Stefano Padulosi's pomegranate expedition in Turkmenistan, which I was lucky enough to join in the fall of 2000.

John Kirsch connected me to T.J. Semanchin, of Peace Coffee, who provided background on the Ethiopian coffee trade. T.J. in turn connected me with Oxfam America, which allowed me to travel with the group to Choche and Jimma, Ethiopia in 2002.

Sheikh Taja Nuru proudly showed me his coffee plants and dozens of his neighbors in the highlands welcomed me into their homes and shared their stories with me.

Workshet Bekele generously hosted me in Addis Ababa and provided further insight on the coffee trade.

In Thailand, the remarkable Dr. Krisana Kraisintu of the Government Pharmaceutical Organization taught me much about HIV drugs, generics, natural compound research, and the politics of the international pharmaceutical industry. The late Dr. Abraham Benenson of the Walter Reed Institute Army Institute of Research in Bangkok provided background on research into an AIDS vaccine, and VaxGen gave me a window into the world of start up biotech companies, financing research and clinical trials.

The engaging and compassionate Dr. Aldar Bourinbaiar allowed me a first-hand look at the controversial V-1 Immunitor HIV treatment at a clinic in Bangkok.

Anu Bhardwaj and Tameer Barnslee joined me in visiting several hill tribes in Northern Thailand to talk with traditional healers.

Nina Wimuttikosol and Julian Spindler, my wise adoptive mother and father in Thailand, provided me with research books, tales of their travels, and encouragement at a critical juncture in the book's development.

Celeste Wesson of American Public Media Group and Suzanne Marmion of Public Radio International helped make my research trips possible by broadcasting my stories from countries that don't usually make the news.

Calestous Juma has been an inspiration and hero through his work with the UN Convention on Biological Diversity, the Center for African Technology and Science at Harvard University and his book *The Gene Hunters: Biotechnology and the Scramble for Seeds*. He has given of his time and expertise at many points along the way.

Henry Shands from the USDA's National Plant Germplasm System, and Deborah Strauss, the former publisher of Diversity magazine introduced me to Nikolai Vavilov's incredible story, and allowed me to develop an understanding of the imperative to conserve biodiversity.

Michael Wall of the Rancho Santa Ana Botanical Garden taught me about field collection and conservation while I volunteered in their pioneering seed bank program.

Robert Kruger of the USDA's Citrus and Date Germplasm Repository, gave me the opportunity to see plant screening and DNA analysis in action after hiring me despite my lack of qualifications.

My husband, Isvinder (Lali) Grewal, provided the gift of three months to write the first draft while we lived in Abu Dhabi in the United Arab Emirates. He has never doubted this project, encouraged me and supported me in at every turn.

Linda Bastian, Sarah Munster, Zak Cook, Sidney Higgins, Sarah Jane Lapp, Kris Ruff, Dureen Ruff and her book club, Anita Barnes and her book group all provided helpful feedback on early drafts. The Los Angeles Public Library has unknowingly provided me with free office space for my writing over the course of a decade. Erika Williams, Valerie Perrott, Bart Ramsey, Sally Barry, Cynthia Goldstein, Madeline Baugh and Michael Wall all read later drafts.

Wondwossen Mezlekia provided feedback on the Ethiopian characters and much moral support.

Jon Cohen of Science Magazine, and author of *Shots in the Dark: The Wayward Search for An AIDS Vaccine*; read an early draft and provided technical comments on HIV and AIDS related details.

Holly Prado edited the manuscript with a keen eye for structure and gaps, reminding me at many points that I wasn't really done, despite my declarations to the contrary.

Kate Steffens copyedited, made key suggestions late in the editing process, and has given me a window into Skylight Books and the world of independent bookstores.

Barbara Baer has been a tremendous resource from the minute I heard about her expedition following in my footsteps in Turkmenistan. She has read multiple drafts, provided moral support, published Dr. Gregory Levin's memoir, *Pomegranate Roads*, and served as an inspiring and generous mentor.

Stona Fitch of the Concord Free Press has magnanimously taken me and this project under his wing, sharing valuable insights on publishing from the micro to the macro.

Ann Ursu, Vicky Curry and Gary Nabhan all assisted me in navigating the road to publication.

Emily Birnmaum has been my coach, holding me accountable in the final stretch of this project.

My sister, Kris Ruff, has hurried up and waited several times with her spot on design work for the cover, according to my stop and start internal deadlines.

Many people I have not yet had the good fortune to meet have contributed to this book through their research and books. Specifically, Edward O. Wilson on biodiversity in general, and the value of evolutionary variety; Peter Pringle, author of *The Murder of Nikolai Vavilov*; Wilfred Thesiger, author of *The Life of My Choice*; Mark Plotkin, author of *Tales of a Shaman's Apprentice: An Ethnobotanist Searches for New Medicines in the Amazon Rainforest*; Cary Fowler and Pat Mooney, authors of *Shattering: Food, Politics, and the Loss of Biodiversity*.

Val Zavala of KCET TV, Dr. Ahmad Jamil of the Emirates Center For Strategic Studies and Research, Jennifer Hamm and Martin Berg of the Daily Journal, Kelly Pepper and Geoff Yarema of Nossaman LLP, and Todd Tukey and Nancy Abell of Paul Hastings LLP all hired me over the years, allowing me to make a living while this project nearly took over my life.

My little sons, both born between fits of revising, have never questioned my slavish devotion to my laptop at odd hours. May the world they grow up in still shimmer with the extravagant beauty of biodiversity, and may the current fiction of a cure for AIDS become a reality in their lifetime.

About the Author:

A nne Marie Ruff Grewal has reported on AIDS research, drug development, biodiversity conservation, and agriculture from Southeast Asia, the Middle East and East Africa. Her work has been broadcast by National Public Radio, Public Radio International, the British Broadcasting Corporation and PBS TV. Her articles have appeared in Time, Christian Science Monitor and Saveur among other publications. A Minnesota native, Ms. Ruff lives in Los Angeles with her husband and their two sons. Through These Veins is her first novel.

8653672R0

Made in the USA
Charleston, SC
01 July 2011